"McGhee uses thoughtful language and rich, meditative imagery to paint a picture of one young woman facing a difficult new path ahead."

—*Booklist*

"*The Opposite of Fate* dives deep into one of the more terrifying—and yet hopeful—questions of life. How do we choose when we don't know the right answer? Alison McGhee is a fearless writer, full of love for humanity and a tender touch with words. You'll love this book."

—Rene Denfeld, best-selling author of *The Child Finder*

"This is, at its heart, a novel about family—including chosen family—autonomy, and identity . . . Thoughtful and moving."

—*Kirkus Reviews*

"Alison McGhee's *The Opposite of Fate* is, like everything she writes, as close to poetry as prose gets, full of metaphor and imagery and lyrical repetition. I was driven to turn page after page to find out what would happen—Would Mallie reassemble her life? What would 'the whole truth' look like when it was pieced back together?—but I also wanted to slow down and savor each beautiful sentence, each image. *The Opposite of Fate* is a story about stories: the ones we tell ourselves in order to bear the unbearable, solve the unsolvable and live."

—Maggie Smith, author of *Good Bones*

The Opposite *of* Fate

ALSO BY ALISON McGHEE

Never Coming Back

What I Leave Behind

All Rivers Flow to the Sea

Was It Beautiful?

Rainlight

Falling Boy

Shadow Baby

The
Opposite
of Fate

ALISON McGHEE

Mariner Books
Houghton Mifflin Harcourt
Boston   New York
2020

For John Zdrazil

First Mariner Books edition 2020

hmhbooks.com

Library of Congress Cataloging-in-Publication Data
Names: McGhee, Alison, 1960– author.
Title: The opposite of fate / Alison McGhee.
Description: Boston ; New York : Houghton Mifflin Harcourt, 2020. |
Identifiers: LCCN 2018051343 (print) | LCCN 2018057190 (ebook) |
ISBN 9781328518316 (ebook) | ISBN 9780358172475 (pbk) |
ISBN 9781328518439 (hardcover) |
Classification: LCC PS3563.C36378 (ebook) | LCC PS3563.C36378 O66 2020
(print) | DDC 813/.54—dc23
LC record available at https://lccn.loc.gov/2018051343

Book design by Kelly Dubeau Smydra

Printed in the United States of America
DOC 10 9 8 7 6 5 4 3 2 1

PART ONE

In the beginning, a girl lay in a hospital bed in a room with white walls and a single window. Her name was Mallie Williams. She was twenty-one years old. She lay there for many months, months in which people came and went from the white room. Had she been conscious, she would have recognized some of them, the ones she had known most of her life. William T. Jones, her neighbor up the road. Crystal Zielinski, his girlfriend and the owner of Crystal's Diner. Charlie, her younger brother. Lucia, her mother. And Zach, her boyfriend.

Others, Mallie would not have known. The doctors and nurses in their scrubs and white coats, stethoscopes slung around their necks, noiseless shoes on their feet. The lawyers. The guardian ad litem. The members of Lucia's church, who gathered around her bedside to pray. The young orderly with the yellow cap, gold earring dangling from his ear, who once a day entered the white room and pushed his mop around the tile floor until it gleamed.

Months went by. Most things remained the same in the white room. The doctors and nurses settled into routine and resignation and finally into the kind of watchful resentment that sometimes happens in the face of hope turned hopeless. Until they were banned from the room, William T. and Crystal and Charlie gathered daily around Mallie's bed. So did her boyfriend, Zach. They tried hard, but in the end even Zach's face changed from worry to anger and finally to resignation.

Outside the hospital, others also kept watch, protesters carrying signs, trying to sway the decisions of the people within the hospital's doors.

In the quiet white room with the double-glazed window, Mallie lay silent and asleep and unaware of the debate and protests and media coverage swirling around her. By all appearances, she was also unaware of the complicated emotions that anguished the people who loved her, the ones who came and went from her bedside. Her dark hair grew long and silky. Her skin softened, its freckles and few lines smoothing and disappearing over time. These changes were small and subtle, noticeable only to the people close to her.

It was Mallie's stomach that everyone noticed. Flat and muscled on the night she was admitted, her belly over time mounded itself and became the first thing anyone looked at when they walked into the white room. Such a small thing in the great scheme of the world: new life. But this particular new life was complicated. For a while, it was all anyone who knew her talked about.

Sixteen Months Later

William T. Jones

D ARK BIRDS.

That was the second thing Mallie said, when she began to talk again. Her eyes were open and looking toward the window of her room at St. John's.

"Dark birds," she whispered, and he quickly followed her gaze. Did her words mean her vision was unharmed, along with her ability to talk? Crows? Grackles? Starlings, maybe. But he saw nothing. Nothing but sky.

"I don't see any birds, Mallie."

Back and forth she turned her head on the pillow, trying to shake it, maybe. He was holding her hand. Her fingers were so smooth. She was young, only twenty-three, but still. This was what happened when you didn't use your hands; all the roughness went away. Her hands were the hands of a baby, and he remembered her as a baby. He had been in his forties then, a neighbor helping out her widowed mother, Lucia. Over time, he had grown to be a father of sorts to Mallie and her younger brother, Charlie.

"Dark birds," she whispered again.

Her soft fingers twitched in his. She was trying to tell him something, but what, he didn't know. That was all right. She would find a way. All the long months of waiting, of watching, of hoping that her body would finally recover, had taught him something about time and the nature thereof.

What had she said first?

"William T."

All his life he'd heard his name spoken, yelled, called out by familiar and unfamiliar voices, people who loved him and people who didn't. But had he ever *thought* about his name until now? Had he ever felt his name as a physical thing, whispering into his body in the voice of someone he'd known since she was a child, someone he'd helped raise, someone he thought of as almost a daughter?

"William T."

She knew who he was. She was saying his name. Welcome back to the world, Mallie.

————

When he got home that afternoon he waited on the porch for Crystal. It took her an hour after the diner closed to put it in order for the next day. When her headlights swept across the driveway he stood up. The look on his face must have told her what she wanted to hear, because she flung open the car door, broke into a run and threw her arms around him.

They stood there on the porch, swaying from side to side, while he told her how Mallie had looked at him, right in the eye, and said his name. How she had gone back to sleep within a few minutes but still, she had spoken. *William T.* She had recognized him.

"What should we tell her at this point? That she was just unlucky?" he said later. "That she was unconscious for a long time with an undiagnosed brain infection?"

The initial excitement had passed and the reality of the situation —everything that Mallie didn't know—was already weighing on them. Crystal stood at the kitchen counter, measuring coffee into the coffeemaker for the next morning.

"I mean, there was the initial brain injury," he said. "But still, it's the truth."

"It's *part* of the truth," she said. "It leaves out the most important truth."

"I just want to buy her some time."

"Would you rather she found out the whole story from us, or from the rest of the world?" She clicked down the lid on the coffeemaker and turned to face him. "Because as of today we're out of time, William T. If we, or maybe Charlie, don't tell her, then someone else will. Better the news comes from us. We're the ones who love her."

———

He punched in Charlie's name on his phone. The 315 area code gave him an obscure sense of relief every time he saw it, as if the boy were still an upstate New Yorker, still physically *in* upstate New York, even though it had been nearly half a year since he moved himself into that fancy prep school in Pennsylvania.

"What's up, William T.?" Charlie's voice was deeper every time William T. heard it, a young man's voice. He was seventeen now.

"It's your sister. She's awake. She spoke."

"*Mallie? What?* Wait. How awake? Does she know what happened? Is she, is she . . ." and the young man was gone, replaced by a boy, his words tumbling over themselves.

"She's okay," William T. said, and then backtracked, because was she? It was too early to know. "I mean, she spoke."

"What did she say?"

"My name. And something about birds."

"*Your* name? Why?"

"Because I was the one in the room."

"Does she know what went down? Does she know . . . any of it?"

"I don't think so. I'm not sure where to start."

"She needs to know the whole story, William T. We can't keep anything from her."

"Agreed. But let's let her lead the way, Charlie. Okay?"

He closed his eyes and waited for the boy to speak.

"Okay," Charlie said, finally.

"You want to come home and see her?"

"I don't know if I can face her, William T. The whole thing was my fault in the first place. And I should've done more."

"You couldn't have kept your mother and the church people away from her. None of us could."

"There must have been *something* I could have done," Charlie railed, and William T. held the phone away from his ear. It was useless to try to convince Charlie he had done everything he could. The last sixteen months of hell had turned him fierce, which made sense, given everything that he had gone through with the sister he adored, but what a way to grow up. Trial by fire.

"And what are you talking about, Charlie? She'll want to see you. You're her brother. Get on up here. Please."

There was a touch on his arm and he turned to see Crystal looking at him, warning in her eyes. She raised both hands in the air and brought them down slowly, a gesture that meant, *Slow down, calm down, back off.* She was right. Everything from now on was new. They would have to figure it out together, with Mallie leading the way. Badgering her little brother wouldn't help anything.

Mallie Williams

WILLIAM T. WAS SAYING SOMETHING ABOUT BIRDS, HOW HE
didn't see any and where were they, but she hadn't said
anything about birds. She closed her eyes and her fingers
pressed against his — *Please be quiet*, they were trying to tell him —
and he must have gotten the message, because he shut up. The blanket on her was soft and William T.'s hand was big and warm, and
maybe this was a dream, the kind that felt real. She opened her eyes
again and looked toward the window, toward the blue green foothills
of the Adirondacks. But the window was a blurry gray rectangle. She
tried to focus her eyes but it was too much effort.

If she was home, though, then why was William T. there, sitting
next to her bed?

There was something in his eyes, something he must not have
wanted her to see because he blinked, but too late, she saw it anyway.
He began to nod. Nod and smile and cry, all at the same time.

"I don't know what you're talking about, Mallie, with the birds.
But we'll figure it out."

Tired. Sleep.

When she opened her eyes again she turned her head and saw a
sink with a mirror above it. *Look in the mirror*, was the thought that
came into her head. But when she tried to sit up, swing her legs over
the side of the bed, they hardly moved. It felt as if they were buried
in sand.

"Legs," she tried to say.

"What is it, Mallie?"

Again she tried to move her legs—kick off the invisible sand—but it took enormous effort. Tried to talk, but nothing. Tried to move her arms, but they too were leaden. *Move*, she commanded her body, *MOVE*. William T. was looking at her, and he knew, she could tell that somehow, he knew what was going on inside her.

"Don't be scared," he said. "It's your muscles. They have to build back up. But now that you're back, now that you're on the mend, it won't take long. A few months."

For the first time, he sounded like the real William T., even though his voice was ten times quieter than usual. He smiled at her. His eyes and his smile and his whole big body were so full of hope and so full of something else, something she didn't understand. She looked at the sink again, the mirror. The linoleum floor and the few steps it would take to cross it, steps she couldn't take. *Now that you're on the mend. Now that you're back.*

Back from where?

———

"What happened to me?" she said.

She was awake again. It was the next day. Or the next week. Time had passed, that was all she knew, and William T. was back. She was tired.

"Do you remember anything?" he said.

"No."

As soon as she said that, something did come to her, though: Rain. Less rain and more mist, mist that felt like petals of water. William T. picked up her hand and closed both his hands around it. Those big paws.

"Rain, maybe," she said. "Maybe it was raining that night."

"That night?"

"Yeah, that night."

She didn't know what she meant by *that night* but yes, that night. That night was dark, and she was walking. The sidewalk—or was it the street—shone under the street lamp. The street lamp was at the end of the block, a shining block with an old stone church set back on a lawn. William T. held her hand and waited.

"Dark," she said. "I was walking. It was pretty."

Pretty because the street, or was it the sidewalk, or both, glimmered under the light from the street lamp. The sensation of falling came to her.

"Pretty?"

There was something in his voice. He didn't like that word. He hated that she had said the word *pretty*. She could feel his tension.

"Yeah. The sidewalk was pretty. It was shining."

"Shining."

She pulled her hand out of his and laced her fingers together. "Am I right? About the rain? And that it was dark and it was pretty and I was walking down a street?"

"I don't know for sure. I wasn't with you."

"Where were you?"

She was a robot who could talk only in sentences that ended with question marks. A dark night? Rain? Pretty? She tried to follow her memory to the end of the street, past the church. A church? Where had she been, and where had she been going? But that was where memory stopped.

"Did a car hit me? It was wet—did I slip? Was I drunk? Did I wobble into the street?"

The sensation of falling was a clear, soft memory. So she couldn't have been too drunk. She didn't even like being drunk. Buzzed, yes, but not drunk. William T. was shaking his head.

"It's been a long time, Mallie."

He kept saying that. Like it would explain everything. *It's been a long time.* Which would explain why her hair was so long. And she had bangs now, tickling her forehead. Bangs? She had always hated bangs.

"How long?"

He looked past her, at the door that led to the hallway and its smooth cinderblock walls and Beanie, the orderly with the yellow cap. The murmurings behind the ajar doors of other rooms. It was the rehab wing of St. John's—that much she had learned. Hospital-like, fluorescent-lit. Not like the places where she worked as a massage therapist. Those places—the Massage Center and the massage room at the women's shelter—were quiet and serene, lit with soft lamps.

"More than a year, Mallo Cup. You were unconscious for sixteen months."

Not "Mallie," but "Mallo Cup," the nickname he alone called her. His favorite candy bar. It brought her childhood rushing back over her, but the way he was saying it—in that hushed voice—was new. Where was the William T. she had known all her life, the William T. who used to sit on his old green tractor and roar her name across the cornfield?

"What?"

He said it again: "Sixteen months."

She couldn't take it in. What was sixteen months? Not possible, that's what. Fog clouded her head. Was this a dream, one of the weird, wandering kind? *More than a year, Mallo Cup.*

She backtracked to a memory that she knew was real: First there was touch. Then someone saying her name. Then she woke into the world, and William T. was holding her hand. But what world? She waited for William T. to start talking again, to make sense of the whole thing. But his eyes had that same look in them and they kept sliding away from her.

"Where am I, William T., and what day is it?"

"Utica. Tuesday."

"Winter? Fall? Summer?"

Robot Mallie, with her robot questions.

"March," he said, and his voice meant *Slow down. Stop shooting out questions.* "A Tuesday in early spring. Two weeks now since you talked about the dark birds."

She looked around the room. Bed. Sink. Mirror. White walls. Blue blanket. Dark birds. On a Tuesday in early spring.

"How old am I?"

"You are"—he stopped to figure it out; William T. had always been bad with ages and birthdays—"twenty-three years old, Mallie."

She shut her eyes.

William T.

THE THREE OF THEM — CRYSTAL AND WILLIAM T. AND CHARLIE, on the phone — agreed to keep quiet and volunteer nothing unless Mallie specifically asked. The hospital and all the employees who worked with Mallie had been told to keep her recovery confidential, to tell no one. They all wanted to avoid another media circus. It would be a long recovery, the doctors had warned them, and it was best to let her lead the way. She slept most of the time, at first. Her brain was fogged and there was no treatment for it but time, according to the specialists. *If and when she begins to talk and make sense, when she begins to move on her own volition, that'll be the turning point,* the doctors had said.

It might take many months, they had said.

But it didn't. Full range of motion was back within a few weeks, and she was walking without assistance two months after that. The doctors and the physical therapists and the occupational therapists were surprised. She was young and healthy, and her immune system hadn't been compromised by the coma and subsequent brain infection, so her body rebounded. Damage to the lymphatic system, edema, loss of bone density from so much time not moving, drifting in and out of consciousness: none of those were issues the way they'd be in someone older, someone with less mobility.

Memory, though. What about memory?

Be prepared, they had warned them. *Be watchful.* She might always have memory issues surrounding this particular period of her life.

The initial trauma could cause it, the long period of unconsciousness could cause it, and any and all potential recovery was unpredictable. She might sleep and sleep and sleep, they had said.

She did, at first. But not for long.

The human body wanted to live. That was the thought that came to William T. throughout the weeks he watched Mallie shuffle a few feet out from the bed, and then back, with assistance. He was the one who watched over her all that time from his chair by her bed. Crystal had to keep the diner running. Charlie had still not made the trek from Pennsylvania, had still not spoken with his sister directly. It was all William T. could do to stay calm when Charlie called him, instead of her, to check on her progress. Yes, the boy's guilt and sorrow were overwhelming. But he was her brother. She was his sister. Mallie had asked no questions about Charlie. And consequently, William T. volunteered no information.

Resist the urge to do things for her, they had cautioned. *Let her figure it out.* He was watching the first time she made her way to the mirror. She had avoided it thus far. He didn't know why and didn't ask. William T. watched as she leaned on the sink and studied herself. She didn't smile. She bent her forehead to the metal and stared into her own eyes. One second, two, three, maybe fifteen, ticked by without sound or movement.

Then she turned sideways, inclining her neck and head, taking in her body's profile. He had once watched Crystal look at herself that way, smileless and appraising, when she thought she was alone. Crystal, in her T-shirt and jeans. He had wanted to tell her she was beautiful, that the thought she might not think so hurt his heart. But he had said nothing. Then, as now, it had seemed a private communion between a woman and her reflection. Mallie turned from the mirror.

"Okay, William T. What happened to me?"

She had not asked since that first time. But he was ready. He had practiced. Let her lead the way.

"You had a brain injury which was followed by a brain infection," he said. "You were unconscious for a long time."

She looked at him and waited for more. She had always been good at silence. It was one of the things that made her so good at her work as a massage therapist. She was intuitive to an unnerving degree. Her brother called it her "witchy stuff." *Tell her only the truth,* the therapists had instructed him, *and only when she specifically asks.* Eventually she spoke.

"A brain injury? How did I get it?"

"Do you remember anything else, besides the rain and the street?"

"No. There's a gap. A big gap. I don't know where I left off and then . . . picked up again." She shook her head, as if she were looking for the right words. Which was something that she'd had to do throughout the recovery—look for the right words. "I keep trying to go back and fill things in, but everything's cloudy. Blurry."

He stood there by the window, his mind sifting and turning.

"Why hasn't my mother called?" she said then. "Is Lucia still in the cult?"

The "cult" was her and Charlie's term for the church that their mother had joined while Mallie was still in high school. She had gone deep into it and not returned. And now she would never return, William T. thought, because pancreatic cancer had claimed her, seven months ago now—but was Mallie ready for that news?

"We've all been focused on your health," he said. "Getting the use of your muscles back. Mobility. Standing. Walking."

He was stalling and she knew it. Her eyes darkened.

"You're hiding something," she said. "I can feel it."

She had always been able to feel invisible things, sense when secrets were being held in the mind or body. *She was born for this kind of work,* the director of the massage therapy program had told him after Mallie had completed her advanced certification. *She's a magician.* Now her hands were moving in front of him, as if she were pulling in invisible information from his body, his thoughts. It was hard to hide from Mallie Williams.

She had been the one to nickname him "William T." when she was a child. Until then he had been William Jones. *Your first name is my last name,* he remembered her saying. *We don't want to confuse people.*

So you're going to be William T. now. T *for* Thaddeus, *because that's your middle name.* As if anyone could confuse a skinny little girl with big, loud William T. Jones.

His strongest memory of her from that time was the memorial service for her father, struck by a truck when she was nine and Charlie barely three. The two of them had hidden beneath the long table while mourners gathered with their plates of food. William T. had watched as she silently fed bites of cake to her little brother.

Should he tell her everything that had happened? She was asking, wasn't she?

He was not a man who had ever lied to her. His head filled with the photo that had been used and reused in the newspapers and on the television and online: Mallie Williams in a blue sundress. The photo that had turned him, a computerless man, into a demon, who, for over a year until Crystal told him he had to stop, had typed MALLIE WILLIAMS into search bars and then sat scrolling. Scrolling. Scrolling. It sickened him to realize that even though his Mallie was two yards away from him in the living and breathing and standing flesh, that photo of her felt more real than the real her.

A girl in a blue sundress, hair floating over her shoulders, arms held out to her sides, a girl captured halfway through a turn to music that no one could hear.

The photo had been taken at her high school graduation party. All the details were there in his memory: friends milling about the cooler of soda and beer on the porch, the grill smoking to one side of the rhubarb patch, the long, spindly folding table that William T.'s friend Burl had lent them, covered with hamburgers and grilled chicken, salads and chips and the big sheet cake that Burl himself had made and iced and decorated with lilies from his garden. Burl, no family of his own. Burl, man on the sidelines. William T. must have been inside —fetching more ice? more beer? more hamburger patties?—when the photo was taken. Her eyes almost closed and one slender strap of the blue sundress fallen off her shoulder. She was smiling, a slow kind of smile.

Pretty girl. Dancing, pretty girl. That photo held something secret, something that should have stayed hidden and private but had been thrown open for the world to tear into.

"Wait a minute," came her voice. "It's not Charlie, is it? Nothing's happened to him, has it?"

This was the first time she'd asked about him. Had she just now remembered she had a brother? Or had she not asked before out of some kind of self-protection? Because any other time Charlie would've been right beside her. They had always been close, even with the six-year age difference. Playing their endless Once Upon a Time game with their thumbs on their phones, sometimes while they were right in the same room. *What the hell is that game you're always playing?* he had asked them once, and without looking up, Charlie had answered. *You start out with "Once upon a time" and then you go back and forth until the story's finished.* Their preferred method of communication, which had always struck William T. as strange. But he tried not to judge. *Remain neutral,* he told himself. *Be Switzerland.*

"Charlie's fine," he said now. "He's fine."

"Then just tell me what you're not telling me. Please, William T."

But he couldn't. Not yet.

Mallie

———

S HE OPENED HER EYES TO SEE CHARLIE THERE IN THE ROOM, sitting in the chair that William T. usually sat in. He wasn't looking at her. It was him, wasn't it? Charlie. Her brother.

"Charlie," she said, but he didn't move.

Was she not speaking out loud? That happened sometimes. Her brother's head was bent, as if he were listening to a song with a sharp beat through earbuds, or as if he were praying. Then he raised his head and looked at her. No song, no earbuds, no prayer.

"Mal."

He was different. She saw this immediately. He wasn't the brother she had last seen a year and a half ago. He had been through something terrible and it had recast him. She could feel it. She reached out to touch him, to put her hand on his shoulder and feel what he was feeling and how he had changed, but he flinched away.

"No. Don't do your witchy stuff on me."

Witchy stuff was his name for her knowing what his mood was like and why, just by his walking into a room where she was. For when she woke in the night, knowing he couldn't sleep, and she would get up and walk down the dark hall and stand by his bed and send calm into him until his breathing slowed and softened and he relaxed into sleep. *Your witchy stuff.* Her witchy stuff was why she was so good at her work. She could feel the stories behind the tightness in muscles, behind the knots in shoulders and backs. She could pull the stress out through her hands.

"What's going on, Charlie?"

He got up from the chair and began pacing. She waited. Charlie had never been someone who caved when pushed. Push him too hard and off he'd stomp.

"I know there's more than anyone's told me," she said.

"So much more," he said, his voice low and rapid. "There's so much more. But I'm not the one to tell you, Mal."

"You're my brother, Charlie."

"Charles. It's Charles now. I was there the night it happened. I *saw* you, Mallie. In a way the whole thing is my fault."

His fault? He paced to the door and back to the window, to the door and back to the window. She watched his body—bigger than she remembered, heavy with muscle—and then he wheeled about to stand at the foot of the bed. Those eyes, dark and shadowed. He looked so much older.

"If I start talking, I'll say too much," he said. "I won't be able to stop."

"Don't stop, then."

He shook his head.

"Charlie, talk to me."

"I go to school in Pennsylvania now, Mal. I drove up this morning. William T. called me and told me you were awake. I wanted to talk to you but—"

"Talk, then. Just talk."

"I can't."

Desperation rose in her. He was her brother. Her little brother. They had always been closer than close, the two of them against the storms of their father's death and their mother's loneliness. He was pacing again, nearing the door. She could tell he was on the verge of disappearing, of yanking the door open and leaving. How could she stop him from going? His hand was on the door. Her mind seized on something.

"Charlie! *Once upon a time there was a sister.*"

"No, Mal. I outgrew that game a long time ago."

"You couldn't have. We've played it all our lives."

"I outgrew it exactly eighteen months ago," he said. "When I realized that no story could ever make this easier."

"Since when did we play Once Upon a Time to make something easier?"

"Since forever. Which you know. And what happened can't be spun. Nothing can make it easier. I'm sorry. I don't know how to talk about this."

Then he was gone, had disappeared through the door. She folded her hands together and cradled them against her stomach. *It'll be okay*, she chanted silently, *it'll be okay, it'll be okay, it'll be okay.* She waited for him to come back through the door. She waited a long time, but there was no Charlie. All right. She would play the game herself. Eight words per sentence.

Once upon a time there was a sister.

And the sister had a brother named Charlie.

And Charlie was alive and in the world.

This was her mantra now. William T. was alive and in the world, and Crystal was alive and in the world, and Charlie was alive and in the world. One by one, the people she loved were appearing, were walking through the door. Each time another appeared, she added them to the Alive and in the World list. Charlie was alive and in the world. He would come back. Wouldn't he? It would be okay. Wouldn't it?

The door pushed open again, slowly this time. Charlie? No. It was Beanie, the young orderly with the tiny yellow pom-pom cap. He stood in the doorway, a mop and bucket in his hands and a question on his face, as if he needed permission to start mopping.

"Did someone knit that hat for you?"

Beanie shivered when she spoke, as if she had sparked a kind of electric current in him. A tiny stud in his ear glinted gold in the overhead fluorescence. He leaned on the mop, an old-fashioned one with hundreds of whitish cotton worms swirling along the tile floor, and studied her. A ray of late-afternoon sun slanted through the far window and he stood in an oblong of golden light, a thousand dust motes floating around him. He said nothing.

"It's cute," she said. "I like the color."

Hearing herself talk was like listening to someone she used to know. Someone she used to be, someone who knew how to talk to people. Her voice was slower than she intended it. But it was her voice, and she didn't have to think each sentence through anymore. Her words were back. *Charlie and Crystal and William T. are alive and in this world.* The lullaby sang inside her, like background music. The orderly was looking at her as if she were an alien being.

"Is that why everyone calls you Beanie? Because of your cap?"

He laughed. White teeth and a soft but big laugh that reminded her for a second of William T.'s until it broke into a gravelly cough full of phlegm.

"You sound like an old man who's been smoking a pack a day since he was twelve."

"I *have* been smoking a pack a day since I was twelve. Not anymore, though."

"When'd you quit?"

"Three days ago. On my twenty-fifth birthday."

He laugh-coughed again. She started laughing too. It felt good. It felt like something she used to do a lot of.

"Congratulations. I'm proud of you."

"You don't know me enough to be proud of me."

"Well, I know that nicotine is supposed to be harder to quit than opioids. Did you ever hear that?"

"Did not, nope."

"So what are you doing with all your free time, now that you quit smoking?"

"Stand-up comedy."

"For real?"

"For real in front of my daughter, yeah."

He laughed again, that smoker's chuckle, and the tiny yellow pom-pom wiggled.

"So tell me a joke," she said.

"Knock, knock."

"Who's there?"

"Orange."

"Orange who?"

"Orange you glad to see me?"

"You got to work on your material, Beanie. Everybody knows that one."

"My daughter didn't."

"How old is she?"

"Four."

"Well, no wonder. That's how old I was when William T. started telling me knock-knock jokes. Including that one."

He touched the pom-pom on his yellow hat, as if making sure it was still there.

"It's something, watching you walk down the hall," he said suddenly. "And hearing you talk."

And with that, she was back to being the strangeness in the room, the girl who had lost time. Beanie pushed the mop back and forth without moving his feet. He studied her, guarded fascination on his face.

"Go ahead," she said. "Stare at me."

How many people besides the ones who loved her had seen her, debilitated and out of it, all the months she'd been there? The way he looked down and started moving the mop in little ovals made her feel bad.

"I guess I can't blame you. It must be weird to see me talking."

His mouth opened as if he were going to say something, then he shut it.

"Not weird," he said finally. "Good. It's good to see you talking for yourself instead of the way it was, with them all thinking they could talk for you."

Them. Who was *them?*

"I mean the others," he said. "Not Mr. Jones. Or your brother. Or Zach. Zach more than anyone."

Zach.

William T.

BEANIE WAS LEAVING MALLIE'S ROOM AS WILLIAM T. TURNED the corner from the nurses' station. The orderly pushed the mop before him, making a swirly pattern on the shining floor. William T. quickened his pace and pushed open the door. Mallie lifted half off the bed at the sight of him, her eyes burning.

"Where's Zach?"

Goddammit.

The air in the room vibrated with aliveness. He forced himself to meet her eyes. There must have been something awful in them because she went rigid. His mind whisked through possibilities. What could he tell her to make it easier? Jesus H. Christ, Zach Miller was just the beginning.

"William T., you tell me that Zach Miller is alive and in the world."

"Zach's alive."

"Then where is he?"

Her voice was quiet now, as if she knew something bad was coming.

"Montana. He works in a restaurant there."

"But" — her fingers fumbled the blanket again — "where in Montana? Which town? What restaurant?"

Wonder. Confusion. Bewilderment. Which town, which restaurant: the answers didn't matter because the real question wasn't a question but a want, a longing. A girl come back to life, wanting the boy she loved.

"He's Zach, William T.," she said patiently, as if there were an answer in there that he had missed. "He's *Zach*."

"He is," William T. agreed, because he knew what she meant. Zach Miller had been there every day. Day after day. Until they had all — Zach Miller and Crystal and Charlie and himself — been barred from the room because he, William T. Jones, had raised a ruckus one too many times. And then came the day when Zach took off.

"He's in Montana," he said again. "In a town called Coburn."

A shadow passed over her face as she absorbed the information. Another piece of the much bigger puzzle she didn't yet know or understand. Her eyes went flat for a minute. Maybe she was relegating this knowledge to the same place she seemed to have relegated Charlie and Lucia.

"Charlie was here," she said.

He didn't know that. He tried to hide his surprise, but she was watching him. Little escaped her.

"He was here, and then he left. He wouldn't talk to me. He wouldn't play the, you know, the . . ."

Words sometimes failed her still. "The Once Upon a Time game?" he said, and she brightened.

"Yeah. He wouldn't play it. And he left before I could ask him about Lucia. Where is she? Will the cult not let her out to visit me?"

Mallie had begun calling their mother by her first name when she and Charlie moved in with Zach Miller during her senior year of high school, when Lucia had disappeared into the arms of the church, down in Utica.

"Does she even know I woke up?" Mallie said. "I mean, did you even tell her about what happened to me?"

William T. cleared his throat.

"She's gone, Mallie."

"Gone where?"

"She died. Seven months ago now."

"What do you mean *died?*" She pronounced the word as if it were foreign. "Died how?"

"She had pancreatic" — he sounded it out carefully; it was a difficult word—"cancer, and there wasn't anything that could be done. It happened very fast."

There was a long silence while she absorbed this information as well. The look on her face was guarded and calm, and William T. could feel her decide to put it behind the same invisible wall that barred off the knowledge that Zach Miller was living in Montana. She would leave them both there until she could turn to them again. In his view, Lucia had slipped away by increments, first years ago to the church, then forever.

"So you're saying that my mother is no longer alive and in the world," she said, finally, and he nodded. "But Charlie and Crystal and you are. And so is"—she shook her head once, abruptly, and he guessed that Zach had been next on the list. "And Johnny?"

"Johnny's still here. Still in his group home, still coming home most weekends."

"What about his red crayons?"

"Of course. Where would Johnny be without his red crayons?"

He watched as her face softened. She had always loved Crystal's nephew Johnny, born with the cord twisted too tight around his neck. Who didn't love Johnny, though? Thirty-two years old now—hard to believe. Zach Miller and William T. and Charlie and Crystal and Johnny, alive and in this world. All the people closest to Mallie, all returning to her mind and heart. *Let her lead the way,* the team had told him over and over. *Take your cues from her. Offer no information unless she asks for it. Trauma, no matter the source of it, lingers in the body and in the psyche. It manifests in unpredictable ways. And she has experienced overwhelming trauma.*

———

After he left her, after he nodded to the nurses and Beanie, who was cleaning and mopping and smiling his silent smile, William T. drove to Foothills Park, the city park with the playground, and backed the truck into his usual spot under the sugar maple. *Clank.* He needed to do something about the rusted door.

The ball field at the far end was empty save for a man raking it clear of the last of winter's debris. The outfield grass was green-ing. At the playground, a few toddlers careened around the grav-elly sand while their parents stood chatting. William T. looked at each one in turn, studying their faces, their hair. Beyond the obvi-ous of skin and hair color, it was hard to tell most of them apart still, at this age. Too young. Too unformed. The child he was look-ing for would be ten months old now. Every step of the way, he had mentally charted the child's progress, from infancy to now. At ten months he would probably be a little small—he had been born at thirty-six weeks, after all—but certainly crawling. Maybe even be-ginning to walk?

A couple and their baby approached from the ball field, closing in on the playground. They were young, both of them, and the child stumbled along between them, holding one hand of each. The hood of his red sweatshirt was tied in a bow underneath his chin. William T. studied his face: pale, red-cheeked, strands of brown hair plastered to his forehead and visible under the hood, the way Mallie's had been as a child. This child looked too old, though. Didn't he?

"Sarah, do you want to swing?" the father said.

Girl, not boy. William T. pushed himself up off the bench, mission unaccomplished. On the way back north, he stopped at Hassan's Su-perette a couple of blocks from the park. Hassan's had not changed since Mallie and Charlie were little. He used to bring them here some-times in the summer, when they were out of school and Lucia had to work and whatever babysitting arrangement she'd pieced together had fallen through. The mural on the side of the red-brick building was faded but still visible: the flying toaster, the slice of bread run-ning away on its little legs, the winged candy bar.

Inside, the wooden floorboards creaked. They were swept bare but dull and streaked, the look of wood that had never been sealed or pol-ished, that had borne the weight of snow and rain and mops over a lifetime. William T. scanned the candy aisle. Hassan's was the only place he knew of that still carried the candies he loved: Mallo Cups and Sky Bars, a glass jar full of Mary Janes and Bit-O-Honeys and Atomic FireBalls. He fished out a handful of Mary Janes and a single Atomic FireBall.

"You love those things, don't you?" the girl at the cash register said, poking at the cellophane-wrapped FireBall. "Every time you're in here, you buy one."

He smiled and handed her a five.

"Hey, remember that girl who was attacked over on Hawthorne?" she said. "You know, a while back? It was big news?"

William T.'s stomach turned to ice and he felt the color drain from his face. She didn't notice, too busy clanging open the register and stepping out of the way as the drawer shot out. "So my cousin works at the rehab unit," she said. "And she told me they thought she was just going to be kind of a zombie forever, but"—she spread her fingers wide, as if she were mimicking a firework explosion—"she woke up. She can, like, walk and talk and everything now."

She counted out his change into the palm of his hand.

"That's confidential, though," she said. "No one knows yet."

"Thank you," William T. heard himself say.

Then he was back on the sidewalk, yanking open the rusty truck door, heading north to the foothills and Crystal's Diner. The CLOSED sign was turned outward and the front door locked when he got there. He went around back to the kitchen door and peeked through the little window. Crystal would be finishing cleanup, and that was something he could help her with—wipe down the grill, scrub the bigger pots and pans. But he stopped short before turning the door handle, because had he ever seen Crystal dance before?

Look at her. There in a corner of the kitchen by the grill, late-afternoon sun filtering in through the grease-spattered window, her face half in shadow and her eyes closed. He held his breath for fear she'd turn around and see him. She swayed, her head dipping and turning, into the sun, into the shadow. Now her body curved and tilted as if an invisible someone was turning her. Now she twirled in a slow circle. She was humming—he could hear through the cranked-open window—and the words *Vienna waltz* came into his mind. Crystal was waltzing, and from the smile on her face and the grace in her movement, it was clear that she loved to waltz.

How did he not know that Crystal was a dancer? How many times had she danced like this, alone, when she thought no one could see her? He and Crystal had come together in middle age. What else did he not know about her?

William T. eased himself away from the window and walked around to the front of the diner. He waited until she appeared through the big front picture window, scrubbing the length of the counter with a red sponge, then tapped on the glass. She opened the door for him, the sponge dripping suds down her arm. The fund-raiser jar still sat on the counter next to the cash register.

HELP BRING MALLIE BACK!
EVERY LITTLE BIT COUNTS!

A washed plastic container that had begun life as a takeout soup container from the Golden Dragon in Utica, with Mallie's high school yearbook photo, blown up so that the outlines of her face and hair were fuzzy, glued to its side. Surrounded by smiley faces and bunches of hearts. The first time he saw it, only weeks after Mallie had been attacked, William T. had stood staring at the thing—Jesus H. Christ, who the hell had come up with this monstrosity—but Crystal had given him a warning look: *Don't say a word.* Burl had come up next to him then.

"I wanted to do something," Burl said.

Crystal's eyes had beamed a message at him: *He's your oldest friend, William T,—don't yell at him.*

"It's probably stupid," Burl had said, reaching for the jar, his fingers covered in Band-Aids, like always. Curse of the postman. "But it's something, you know? A tiny little thing."

A couple of tens in the jar, some fives, many ones, and, visible near the bottom, a lone fifty.

"That was me," Burl had said, stubbing his finger at the fifty.

"What do you plan to do with the money from this jar, Burl?"

"Every little bit helps, William T."

Burl was mild-mannered but stubborn to the core. It was people like him who would eventually rule the earth someday, millennia from now, when everyone else less obstinate had just given up.

At that time Mallie was in a coma and they were starting to think it was permanent. The battle over her future had begun. The hospital staff, with the exception of Beanie and that one nurse, had taken to averting their eyes when William T. and Crystal walked in the door. This was the beginning of the siege, the time that, when William T. looked back on it, would appear in his mind as a combination of television reporters, telephone calls and trips to the lawyer and judge.

They had paraded her across the news as if she were a freak at the freak show. Night after night, the photos. The high school graduation photo, the blue sundress photo. And the other one. That other one, the one the onlooker had put on his Facebook page, the one William T. couldn't stand to think about. Where in the world could you go to get away? In the beginning the thick black headlines repeated themselves ad infinitum. On the a.m. talk-radio shows the callers were as sure of themselves as the host. Turn the TV on, turn it off. Open the computer and shut it down. News, news, it was everywhere in this world, and so was Mallie's face. William T. was convinced that it was the sight of his big sister everywhere and nowhere, argued over by strangers, along with the loss of his mother, that had driven Charlie to apply to Braxton Preparatory Academy in Pennsylvania.

Now, all this time later, the plastic container was still there. St. John's, both hospital and rehab unit, along with all the medical professionals, had at some point decided to donate their services, maybe to look good in the public eye, maybe to offset accusations on the part of protesters on either side, so there was no real point to the money in the container, was there? But by now it was part of the scenery of the diner. People dropped their change in sometimes, occasionally a bill or two, but only as a reflex. The girl in the photo was long gone. A hole had opened up around her and sucked her in. She was still living in the land of the lost, or so everyone thought. They had managed to keep the fact of her long, slow recovery under wraps. Let her get her life back in peace, had been the thinking, and everyone at St. John's had been a willing participant in the secrecy. At least until now.

Crystal ducked through the gate and came around to the front of the counter. He put his arms around her and kissed the top of her head. Crystal, the secret dancer.

"The news is out," he said. "Tomorrow morning I'll get her out of there."

Mallie

HE KNOCK-KNOCK CONVERSATION WITH BEANIE WAS THE FIRST time she had talked with someone new, and when she pictured him in her mind, she smiled. Smiling felt like a strange new thing. So did laughing. But she had smiled and laughed with Beanie and it felt easy. Because he was someone who didn't know her? Who wasn't hiding something from her? Who wasn't walking around with invisible dark birds on his shoulders?

"You will need to figure out how to let go of the emotions that come at you during a session," her teacher had told them in massage therapy school, "because otherwise you will absorb them and become burdened with the pain of others."

The specific means by which a massage therapist kept herself whole and contained varied for each person, the teacher said, and it might require time and experimentation to figure out what worked for you. It had taken Mallie a long time to figure out how to disperse pain from her clients. What had eventually worked was to envision sorrow and grief as silent, heavy birds, hovering in the room. Most of the time she could mentally shake them off. But sometimes she had to physically windmill her arms, shout at them to go away, dislodge themselves from inside a human being. To go back where they belonged, riding the wind, high in the sky.

It was always hardest when working with women at the shelter. All that sadness and pain and fear stored up inside them. To release it from their tense and guarded bodies was work of skill and intuition. She had once been able to do it, and without risk to herself. But that was in the before world, the world before this one. During the months she had lain unconscious, dark birds had settled inside both William T. and Charlie. She could sense them.

No dark birds were trapped inside Beanie, though. He was lightness. He had come by again this morning, poked his head around the door, which was ajar. Both hands behind his back, his eyes bright.

"Pick a hand," he said.

"What is this, kindergarten?"

"Pick a hand. And quick, before it melts any more. Aw, crap, now I gave it away."

She pointed at his right hand and he brought it forth, an ice cream cone dripping down his fingers, and she clapped her hands like a child and laughed.

"When's the last time you had a cone?" he said. "I mean a real cone with real ice cream, not that cheap shit they bring by on the cart."

She shook her head. A long time. Probably since the last time she and Zach had driven down from Forestport to the Kayuta drive-in on Route 28. She turned the cone, licking the drips. Vanilla with mashed-up chunks of strawberries. It was delicious.

"Good, isn't it?" he said. "Homemade."

"By whom?"

"Me myself and I. And my daughter. She decides on the flavor, and we take turns turning the crank."

"Tell her she did a good job, will you?"

He nodded, watching her turn and turn the cone in her hand. Cold, creamy sweetness slid down her throat and the Kayuta appeared in her mind, sun glinting off its tin roof. She and Zach sitting on one of the picnic tables, laughing and eating ice cream on a summer night. Mosquitoes. Cars swishing by. Tires crunching on the gravel parking lot. Tears filled her eyes.

"Aw, M.W.," he said. "It's just ice cream. Don't cry."

She shook her head. "It's not the ice cream," she said. "It's . . . everything."

He came over to the bed then and sat beside her and put his arm around her. He smelled like the mop and laundry detergent and sweat. She tried to picture his little girl, turning the crank of the old-fashioned ice cream maker, but no little girl swam into her mind.

"I know it is," he said. "I know."

Later, when the door opened softly, she looked up, hoping it would be Beanie again, but it was William T., with his familiar worried face. She was tired of his worry. Of the hushed tone of his voice.

"What's going on, William T.?"

"We're going to get you packed."

"Packed."

"Then we'll walk out of the room like normal. Like we're going for a normal stroll, like usual, up and down the hall. Then we're going to head down the stairs, one flight, then out the side door to the back parking lot. If anyone stops us, say that you just want a little fresh air. You're of sound mind and body, after all."

"Fresh air."

"Right. Then we'll get in the truck and head up to Sterns."

"Sterns."

She listened to herself, repeating his words like a parrot. He squeezed her hands as if he were glad she understood, but she understood only that he was trying to act calm when he wasn't. She did as he asked. Jeans and T-shirt and toothbrush and hairbrush, he put them all into a little Hassan's Superette paper bag. He pushed the door open and she followed. Beanie was down the hall next to a utility cart, unscrewing a thermostat cover.

"Beanie," she said, and raised her hand. He nodded, then shifted his gaze to William T. She felt William T.'s fear, even though she didn't know what he was afraid of.

"M.W.," he said. "That's what I'm going to call you from now on."

"I'm going for a walk," she said. Her voice was wobbly. "Out back" —she pointed at the side door—"to get some fresh air."

Beanie tossed the screwdriver from hand to hand, lightly, without looking, his eyes moving from William T. to her and back again.

"Keep working on your stand-up, Beanie," she said. "I mean, it can only get better."

William T. took her hand and they started walking. They were almost past Beanie when he reached out and touched her shoulder.

"M.W.," he said. He held up one finger and reached for a pen from the utility cart. He scratched something onto the back of a scrap of sandpaper—a phone number— and handed it to her. "Text me. I'll practice my material on you, okay?"

William T. was urging her toward the stairwell. He pushed open the stairway door and she took the steps one at a time down to the first-floor landing, and then through the door beneath the big red EXIT sign. Outside. The air was sweet, it was sweet, it was sweet. Spring air, crisp and blue and full of promise.

Yank. "*Mallie*. Keep walking."

"Oh. Sorry. It just smells good, is all."

He pointed in the direction of a blue truck with OWEN DRYWALL stenciled on the side in uneven white cursive. The R and Y and W in DRYWALL were smaller than the other letters.

"You got a new truck?"

"Burl had a friend who retired. I bought it off him."

"Burl!"

She stopped right there in the gravel, halfway to the truck. Another person she loved, alive and in the world. Burl, William T.'s oldest friend. William T. gave her a little push. A keep-walking, act-natural, don't-attract-any-attention push. They climbed into the truck and William T. turned the key in the ignition. The gearshift numbers had worn off, but she watched his hand moving on the knob and recited the gears to herself, the way he had taught her to do back when she was fifteen and learning to drive stick. Something in the rearview mirror flashed and she squinted to see what looked like a TV news truck.

"What's going on, William T.?"

William T. glanced in the rearview mirror. "Don't know."

She twisted around to see, but they were already too far away. "Looks like a news crew."

At that, William T. shuddered. It was the tiniest motion—a shiver that lifted his shoulders and rippled through him instantaneously—

and she wouldn't have caught it had all her senses not been on high alert.

"I think you do know what's going on, William T."

He kept his head straight ahead and his eyes on the road, driving like the perfect, conscientious driver he had never been. As if any minute he could be pulled over and have to explain himself, so best follow every rule. He was not going to say anything. She gave up and leaned back into the ripped seat of the cab and turned her head to the window. The sights of Route 12: the Utica floodplain, Denny's, gas stations and auto repair shops, AmericInn on the left, La Quinta on the right, and then they began the slow climb out of the tattered city. William T. clenched the steering wheel and hunched forward. His Jim Beam cap was set perfectly straight on his head. She didn't speak again until they were heading down the biggest hill on Glass Factory Road.

"You're driving like an old man, William T. An old man wearing a hipster cap."

"I *am* an old man. Too old to know what the hell a hipster cap is."

"You're sixty-three. That's not old."

He opened his mouth as if he were about to correct her, then closed it again. *He's sixty-five*, she thought. This was something she would have to keep remembering: a year and a half had passed. She was twenty-three now, and William T. was sixty-five.

They were passing the diner, not slowing, when she saw where they were. Her whole body jolted, the way it had when she remembered Zach Miller. "Hey!" she said. "It's Crystal's," and he braked.

"Just for a minute," he said. "One minute only, okay?"

He glanced up and down the street with the wariness that had become familiar to her. She reached over and put her hand in his jacket pocket, the way she had done when she was small, and he pushed his own hand into the pocket and held hers. Then he shouldered open the door of Crystal's, eyes darting back and forth, and stood aside to let her in.

Specials were chalked onto the dusty blackboard behind the counter: tuna melt, New England clam chowder, cheese omelet with

American fries and toast. Red twirly stools in front of the counter, red booths lining the walls. The coatrack where the farmers hung their jackets and once in a while their caps. The coffeemaker with its four burners, full pot of decaf and nearly empty pots of regular. An old couple in the far booth, murmuring over coffee and pie. A coloring book with a Batman page half-colored in red lay open in the booth that Crystal's nephew Johnny always sat in when he was home for the weekend. Everything was the same as always.

Except for one thing.

HELP BRING MALLIE BACK!
EVERY LITTLE BIT COUNTS!

Her high school graduation photo was photocopied and pasted to the side of a lidded plastic container by the cash register that held crumpled dollar bills and change. William T. followed her gaze.

"Ignore that," he said.

He tugged her away, back toward the door, but she broke loose and picked up the jar and stared at her photo. There she was, the way she used to be, her hair French-braided and a serious look on her face.

"Ignore it, Mallie."

"But that's me," she said, "it's me," as if she were trying to explain something to him. The former Mallie kept revolving as she turned the big plastic jar around. Now she was there, now she wasn't, gazing up at them both with no smile on her face. Then the door to the restroom opened and Johnny emerged. He closed the door carefully, the way he had been taught, and then turned and caught sight of them. His whole face lit up and his good arm reached out. Johnny. He was wearing a T-shirt with a red owl on it. Red, the color he had loved his whole life. He started toward them in his slow, lopsided way, but Mallie was there before he had taken three steps, her arms around him. He laughed his stuttery laugh into her hair. He smelled the way he always did, like cotton and pancakes and the almond oil Crystal rubbed into his arms and hands.

The storeroom door opened and Crystal eased through, an industrial-size can of baked beans in her arms.

"Mallie," she said.

Her arms moved, as if she were going to set the big can of beans down on the prep counter, but she missed and the can fell to the floor with a big, hollow-sounding *thunk*. She shoved the little divider door between the counter and the grill up and ducked beneath and then wrapped her arms around both Mallie and Johnny. Her grip was gravity, holding them to her until William T. interrupted.

"Time to go, Mallo Cup," he said.

———

William T. had saved some things from Lucia's house for her, like the cow creamer and the pig salt and pepper shakers.

"I knew you always liked them," he said when he saw her pick them up from the shelf in their dining room. "When Charlie went off to Pennsylvania and they sold the house, I got to them before the vultures descended."

Then he grimaced, as if he'd said something wrong. "The vultures," maybe. There was a dark sound around the word, dark-bird word that it was, and she pulled a mental wall down around it. The little porcelain cow creamer was light and cool in her hand, and she focused on it instead. Lucia had given it to her when she was little. They had been at the Back of the Barn antique store off Route 12 and she had seen it in a locked glass case and wanted it. And when her birthday came around a couple months later, there it was: wrapped up in a puff of white tissue paper.

"Charlie took some things too. That green cap of your dad's and one of your mom's sweaters."

"So Charlie goes to school in Pennsylvania now?"

"It's a prep school." William T. pronounced the word carefully: p-r-e-p. "Braxton Prep. You know, a boarding school. With dorms and a cafeteria. That kind of thing."

"I know what a prep school is, William T."

She pushed aside the image of Charlie the way he naturally came to mind, living with her and Zach in the cabin in Forestport, where Charlie's room was a loft above the kitchen with a space heater next to his blow-up mattress. She looked around the familiar living room of William T.'s house. He and Crystal had lived here ever since she could remember, half a mile up the road from the house where she and Charlie and their mother lived. Used to live.

"Of course you do," William T. said. "He's got one more year of *prep* school to go."

Zach had built the cabin himself before his parents struck out for Alaska. He was eighteen the year he built it, two years older than Mallie. A senior in high school, he had worked on it evenings and weekends. *I'm not leaving Sterns,* he had told his parents. *I'm not leaving Mallie.* And they had not put up a fuss. Their dream of homesteading it in Alaska was not their son's dream. Besides, no one put up much of a fuss when it came to Zach. Zach, who was no longer in the little cabin. Zach, who was now in Montana.

William T. had saved a few things from their cabin in Forestport too. Some of her clothes and books. And the box of possible futures. He must have searched for it, because the box of possible futures wasn't easy to find, stuck as it had been on a shelf in the cabin mudroom. Look at all the fortune cookies, tumbled together in the same white liquor store box that Zach had picked up from the alley the night of their first date. They had wandered out of the Golden Dragon, dazed from being in the presence of each other so long without interruption, away from school, away from other people, except the waiter, who had kept refilling the teapot next to the soy sauce. Dazed by all the secrets that had tumbled out as they talked—his parents and their plan to leave Sterns and homestead in Alaska; her mother, who had joined the Faith Love Congregation a few years back; his secret plan to build a cabin in Forestport on a woodlot his family owned; her brother, Charlie, and the Once Upon a Time game she had made up when he was little. Dazed by something they hadn't talked about at all because they hadn't needed to, which was the intensity of their attraction. He had insisted on paying for dinner, and when she protested, told her she could pay next time. Which made her go silent with happiness, because *next time.* He wanted a next time. Maybe a whole bunch of next times. She had picked up one of the fortune cookies and was about to tear open the cellophane wrapper when he put his hand over hers—the first time he'd touched her—to stop her.

"No," he said. "Don't open it."

"Why not?"

"Because it might say something about your destiny. And don't you want to be the master of your own fate? Or mistress, I mean?"

She had smiled and tilted her head, not sure what he was saying. He had taken the wrapped cookie from her hand and picked up his own.

"Tell you what—we'll start a collection," he said. "We'll put these in a box, and from now on, every time we eat at a Chinese restaurant, we'll take the cookies and add them to the box. We'll call it the box of possible futures."

All Mallie heard was *from now on, every time we eat at a Chinese restaurant.* She had felt the future unspooling before them, like a secret only the two of them would share. That moment came back to her now in a sharp pang of recognition, like a rock thrown. The box of possible futures, *clunk.* Her high-school-senior face on the side of that jar, *clunk.* Other fragments were like feathers landing: The oval shape of the ceramic space heater by Charlie's mattress in the sleeping loft. The parrot-print pillows on the couch in their cabin. Charlie sitting on that couch hunched over his phone late at night, calling up song after song, reggae and blues and funk and rock, playing DJ for her and Zach as they danced around the living room.

She shut them all down, the images, and turned to William T. She needed to know about her mother.

"William T., was it awful for Lucia, the way she died?"

"Pancreatic cancer is bad, Mallie. It was fast."

So it had not taken long. There were things he wasn't saying about her mother—she could tell—but what were they? She was beginning to see that William T. would tell her nothing unless in response to a specific question, but what were the specific questions? This reminded her of another game she used to play with Charlie, the one in which you tried to figure out who the other person was by asking an ever-narrowing series of yes or no questions. *Was it awful*

*for my mother? Yes. Did she die fast? Yes. Did she think of me at the end?
___?___.*

She hadn't lived with her mother since her senior year in high school, when Lucia had chosen the church over her children. It had felt that way, anyway, to both her and Charlie. Lucia had moved to Utica, where both job and church were, and Mallie and Charlie had moved in with Zach.

"Mallie, you must be so tired."

That was Crystal. She led the way upstairs to the spare room, straightened and cleaned for her. Quilts and towels, a pair of old cotton pajamas on the bed. Crystal kissed the top of her head, as if she were a child.

"Sleep tight," Crystal said, and, "You too," Mallie said, like a normal person, even though nothing was normal. The conversation between her and William T. downstairs just now hadn't been normal. The way they had left the hospital hadn't been normal. Nothing was normal. *A year and a half, a year and a half, a year and a half:* the words danced and jabbed the corners of her brain like hummingbirds dipping in and out of flowers. And every day was another day gained, or lost, to the equation. She pulled the mental walls down around the thought.

The pajamas smelled like sun and wind, and the smell of sun and wind brought Zach Miller sweeping back over her. She had to keep him closed off too. No to all the disappeared time, no to Zach, no to thoughts that she didn't have the strength to think about. For now.

William T.

D OWNSTAIRS, WILLIAM T. AND CRYSTAL TURNED THE TELE-
vision on low. He was sure the news would have broken the
story, and he was right. There it was, the same canned loop
they'd used a year and a half ago, back when the story was a mainstay:
hospital entrance, parking lot, separate raggedy circles of marchers
with their same old signs, that same hefty fellow in the parka stum-
bling over the sidewalk curb, hoisting his homemade sign back into
the air. A few seconds of this, the narrator intoning, "We return to
the ongoing story of Mallie Williams, who for more than a year lay
sleeping," and then, suddenly, everything was new.

"We are pleased to report that Miss Williams has, contrary to
initial predictions, made a full recovery," hospital spokesperson
W. Albert Froehler read from a piece of paper.

Shouted questions from invisible reporters: *Does she remember anything? Has a lawsuit been filed? Has the perpetrator been caught? Have the
parents been informed?*

W. Albert Froehler did not respond to any of the questions. He
kept reading.

"Miss Williams's recovery was made possible by her own immune
system, aided by a team of skilled health-care professionals, including doctors, nurses, physical and occupational therapists"—*What
about psychologists? She'll need a whole team of them, won't she?* shouted
one of the more aggressive reporters, but she was ignored—"and
she has now left the hospital."

Left? Where'd she go? Are you saying she can walk on her own? Talk on her own?

W. Albert nodded. "She is fully cognizant, in full possession of mental and physical capacities. St. John's is humbled to have played a part in her recovery, and we wish Miss Williams the best as she returns to the joys of ordinary life."

He lowered the paper, turned and walked away from the reporters, back into the hospital. William T. flicked the television off and turned to Crystal. "'The joys of ordinary life'? What kind of horseshit is that?"

If he had been granted guardianship from the beginning, most or all of this could have been avoided. Not that there was a chance of that, given that Lucia was her only living relative besides underage Charlie. They had all watched Lucia get sucked into that church and its harsh rules and doctrines, watched as the members tightened their grip on her, watched as she pledged her allegiance to it even in the face of Mallie and Charlie's resistance. It had felt like duty to William T. to try for guardianship, but what a mess the whole thing had turned out to be. All the money he'd spent on that attorney, and in the end there was no chance. The judge had awarded guardianship to Lucia on the recommendation of Mallie's attorney and the independent court evaluator, without, it seemed, even a second thought, even though William T. and Charlie and Burl and Lucia's non-church colleagues from Forever Home and Crystal — even Crystal, who hated talking to strangers — had filed up to the judge one after another:

He's been as good as a father to her ever since her own father died.

Blood or not, William T. is the closest thing to a father that the girl's got. He didn't give up. He has never given up on that girl.

But no. Guardianship had stayed with Lucia. Which, in effect, meant the Faith Love Congregation, given Lucia's devotion to it. They were all in cahoots, it seemed to William T. at the time, and it still seemed that way to him.

"Jesus H. Christ," he had thundered finally, right there in court, with his attorney trying to shush him. "Who's speaking up for Mallie here? You think she'd want this thing to continue? You think she wouldn't terminate it the second she knew? Of course she would!"

Then came the months when he and Crystal and Charlie weren't allowed back in Mallie's room. Zach could've visited her but he hadn't, at least to William T.'s knowledge. It was only Lucia and her henchmen, which was how he thought of her fellow Faith Love congregants. William T. had tried to train himself out of thinking about the whole mess, tried to learn how to redirect his thinking, distract himself, but he was no good at that kind of thing.

It was only after Lucia died and he was finally appointed guardian in Family Court—according to the terms of her will, the judge said—that things had changed. He had watched over Mallie every day, helped move her limbs, kept her muscles in motion. Willed her to wake up, willed her strength to return. All the while talking to her, talking and talking, because he had heard that hearing was the last to go. And if Mallie had to go, then she would leave this world accompanied by the voice of someone who loved her.

But she hadn't left the world. She had returned to it. Deep inside his pocket his cell phone buzzed.

"Hello?"

"William T."

His heart jolted. He knew that voice. Zach Miller.

"William T., is it true that she's awake? That she left the hospital?"

Crystal watched him, eyes alert, waiting to see who was calling this late. William T. cleared his throat. *Stay calm,* he ordered himself. *Be Switzerland.*

"Yes, Zach. How did you know?"

Zach ignored the question. "Is she with you now? Is she there? Does she remember anything? How is she?"

William T. got up from the couch, Crystal's eyes on him, and began wandering around the living room. Something to do instead of sitting in an inert mass on the couch. He and Crystal had vowed not to be angry if and when Zach called.

"She's asleep right now," William T. said. "I don't know how much she remembers. Everything up until that night, I think. But nothing since then."

"What about me? Does she remember me?"

"She remembers you."

He let it stand at that. He didn't tell Zach how Mallie had risen halfway off the bed at the thought of him. Or how she was shutting down the thought of him now, out of . . . confusion? Hurt? Bewilderment that he wasn't there?

"Does she know anything about, you know, about—"

"She doesn't know about everything. She's been working full-time on getting the use of her muscles back. It's been a full-time job. Look, Zach . . ." and he could hear his voice beginning to rise.

Crystal's eyes snapped at him: *Don't get angry with him, William T.*

"I know you're pissed off, but it's complicated, William T. There's a lot to explain."

"To whom?"

"Her. You. Charlie. Everyone. A lot has happened."

Crystal was still on high alert, her eyes boring into him. She didn't want him to scare Zach away. He took in a deep breath and let it out twice as slowly. Something Mallie's physical therapist had taught him.

"She's here, Zach," he said. "That's all I can tell you."

After he hung up he hauled the box of clippings and photos—the box of Mallie—out of the back of the living room closet and began sifting through it again, even though he had long since memorized the contents.

"William T., why do you keep that stuff?" Crystal said. She hated the box, hated his sorting ritual. "It's just a box of pain."

"It's a record of what happened. For Mallie, if the time comes."

That had been his original intention, so that if and when she recovered, everything that had transpired in the absence of her mental capacity would be there in black and white. He wasn't sure anymore, though. There were things in there that he himself couldn't stand to look at, like the photo that accursed onlooker had taken of her and posted on his Facebook page for all the world to see. Her broken body, downloaded, copied, reposted hundreds of times. Burl had tried to hide that photo from William T., the day it came out. He had stood in front of the newspaper display at Queen of the Frosties, something awkward about his stance.

"Move aside, Burl."

Burl had hesitated, then stepped aside. There it was, right there on the counter, her body splayed out on the pavement in the dark rain. Black stars had swarmed in front of William T.'s eyes and he gripped the counter to steady himself. Everything was public and everything was forever on the goddamn internet. If only he had been the one to pick up Charlie that night.

"You didn't know Charlie needed a ride," Crystal had told him, over and over. "It was happenstance. It was bad luck."

But if William T. had been there, none of this would've happened. He should have been there instead of Mallie, good big sister driving all the way down to Utica to pick up her drunk little brother from a party. He should have been the one to park the truck on that dark night, but he hadn't been. Dark nights everywhere, dark things happening, and where was the God that so many claimed existed?

Mallie

OUTSIDE, THE WIND HAD PICKED UP. LEAVES AND BRANCHES of the maple tree brushed against the window in tiny scrapes and whispers. *Wake up, wake up, we have something to tell you.* The wind was westerly, steady and strong. In migration season, birds and insects would be high above the house right now, swept up on the invisible currents, themselves invisible to the human eye. Night birds, dark in the dark night. William T. was the one who had taught her about birds, back when she was a little girl. He had taught her about chickens, because he had a flock. He had taught her to say "gull" instead of "seagull" when she was a little girl.

"You can find gulls anywhere there's a body of water, Mallo Cup," he had said. "Lakes, for example. The Finger Lakes have their own gulls and they're nowhere near the sea. It's insulting to an inland lakes gull to be referred to as a seagull. Prejudicial. A pro-ocean, anti-lakes bias."

Their mother had taken her and Charlie to the Jersey shore once, the summer after their father died. They spread their blankets and snacks on the beach and smeared on sunscreen and ran into the waves. Then they returned to the blanket to find an enormous gull taking off into the air with their package of cheese. Mallie jumped up, flailing her arms, trying to get the gull to drop the cheese, but it had paid her no attention. It flapped its way up and up and up into the air, lugging its heavy burden, and then it was gone. Their entire block of cheese! It had still been wrapped! She had told William T. about it when they returned from their trip.

"Sweet Jesus," he had said, shaking his head. "And they wonder why people call them air rats. Gulls mate for life, they're good parents, they're smart as hell, but then they go and steal a poor defenseless kid's entire block of wrapped cheese. Gulls, it's hard to defend you when you do shit like that."

Defenseless? Mallie hadn't felt defenseless. It had been strange to hear that William T. thought of her that way. But he always looked out for her. When she was ten years old, her mother had refused to let her go on the school field trip to New York City. Lucia had glanced at the permission slip and frowned, as if it annoyed her. Shaken her head and brushed the air with both hands.

"But I'm in fifth grade," Mallie had said. "The whole entire fifth grade is going. It's the fifth grade field trip, Mom. To *New York City.*"

"No," their mother had said, and that had been her only statement on the subject. "Too far away."

Looking back, Mallie thought that maybe that was when Lucia's strangeness had begun. Mallie's father had been gone a year at that point, and Lucia had begun to harden in odd and unpredictable ways, ways that later would result in her adherence to the beliefs of her church and the flat rightness and wrongness of things. Mallie had not brought the field trip up again. The only person she had told was William T., and only because he had asked her why was she standing in the barn doorway when wasn't it the big day? The day of the fifth grade field trip?

"But why?" William T. said when she told him she wasn't allowed to go.

She shrugged. "Mom said no."

The words of the school principal sounded in her head as William T. stood there frowning, his hands full of chicken feed. *For some of you students, this will be the only time in your lives that you will visit New York City, the greatest city in the world. Make the most of it. And behave.*

"It's the fifth grade field trip, though," he repeated, as if he weren't sure she understood the implications. "Don't you *want* to go?"

It was the sound of his voice, the bewilderment and the concern, that opened a door to a room inside her. This was the legendary field trip, the one that every Sterns Elementary student looked forward to, from kindergarten on. She was suddenly as bewildered as William T., the force of her longing washing through her.

"Mallie," she remembered him saying, "aw, Mallo Cup." The clatter of chicken feed hitting the heaved-up cement of the barn floor came to her ears and then he was picking her up in his arms, as big as she was, and hugging her.

"Tell you what," he said. "I'll take you to New York City. We'll go on our own field trip."

"Mom, though," she had choked out, "my mom," because if her mother hadn't let her go on the huge chartered bus, the bus with the cushiony seats and the armrests and the bathroom in the way back that she had been looking forward to using, if only to wash her hands in the sink that the older students said was so tiny, so unimaginably tiny, then there was no way she would let her go with William T.

Her mother *had* let her go with him, though. Mallie didn't know how William T. managed it, but the day came when he picked her up before dawn, a glazed doughnut wrapped in wax paper for her breakfast sitting on the passenger seat, and down to Manhattan they drove. They parked at Yankee Stadium and took the subway into the city. They ate lunch in Chinatown in a restaurant that had Chinese writing on the menu. They touched each of the giant lion heads outside the public library. They rode the ferry to Staten Island and back. They saw the Empire State Building.

"Look up at the skyscraper and tell me what you see, Mallo Cup," William T. had said.

"Clouds. Blue sky."

"How about stars? You see any stars?"

She shook her head. Of course not. It was midafternoon; why would there be any stars? He crouched next to her and pointed up at the blue sky.

"You want to know a true fact, Mallie? The stars are up there right now. We just can't see them because it's not dark. But birds are waiting, all over this city, and when it's dark—as dark as New York City gets, anyway— they'll rise up all around these skyscrapers on currents of wind. The higher they go, the stronger the wind. There will be thousands of them, so far above our heads that no one will see them. And off they'll go, navigating by the stars."

She had never heard William T. talk like that. He was not a man of poetry, the way her fifth grade teacher was. But he stood there on the street looking up, up, up at the Empire State Building, and she looked up with him, at the invisible stars and the invisible wind that would carry the birds away.

Later, in an anthropology class at Mohawk Valley Community College, she had learned that in some cultures, dark birds were said to appear when someone died. They gathered in trees or on rooftops. They were messengers. When the dark birds settled on the tree, it was too late.

How many nights had she slept away in St. John's before she woke up to William T.'s hand on her arm? 365 = one year + 120 = another four months = almost 500. It was too hard to think about. Was her mind, William T.'s mind, this very house filled with dark and silent and ravenous birds? If so, they would have to be fought off. You couldn't let them take what they wanted—whether a block of cheese or your sanity or your peace of mind—and just fly away with it the way that ravenous gull had flown away that long-ago day on the beach. You had to fight. That much she knew.

William T. and Crystal were talking in low voices below, and she got out of bed and went downstairs. An old cardboard box, wearing out at the corners, sat on the table in front of William T. He and Crystal looked up, surprised at the sight of her, and William T.'s arm shot out and lay flat on the box, as if he wanted to keep it safe. She sat down opposite them and put her hands on the table. They were the suspects and she was the cop.

"Listen," she said. "Something happened to me before I was in a coma. And it wasn't like a stroke or a heart attack or something. Someone hurt me. Didn't they?"

William T. nodded. Reluctant. On guard. The two of them glanced from her to each other, cautionary looks, trying to talk without words. Mallie could feel it.

"A man?"

William T. nodded again.

"Who?"

"We don't know. Nobody does."

"The police?" A squad car appeared in her head, light turning and flashing, turning and flashing. A cop with a gun and a uniform.

"They don't know either. The evidence never linked up to anyone specific. No one in the known database."

"So it was a robbery? He mugged me?"

"Yes," Crystal said. "He grabbed your handbag."

But neither she nor William T. said anything else. Their silence was anguished. Silent birds massed in the heavens, waiting and watching. Mallie could feel them. She felt in that moment the way she sometimes had when working with one of the women from the shelter, that a dark story was hidden inside the body. Only this time it was her body. She tried to picture a man coming down a sidewalk after her.

"Did he beat me up too?"

"Yes," Crystal said.

"Anything else?"

Crystal nodded. Yes. Something else.

"He raped me," Mallie said. It wasn't a question. Crystal nodded again and William T.'s jaw clenched, but they both stayed silent. The man on the sidewalk morphed into arms and legs, a battering ram of a man.

"Did he try to kill me?"

"That's what the police figure, yes."

Then came a shadow, looming at the porch door.

Knock, knock, knock.

Crystal took Mallie's arm, urging her to the couch while William T. menaced his way to the door. It was far too late for visitors. Mallie could feel William T.'s tension, feel his thoughts: No one should be out, no one should have driven into the driveway without him noticing, no one should be on the porch. Damn the wind that drowned out the sound of car tires. Damn the branches clattering on the roof. He glanced back at her.

"Don't worry," he said. But it was him she was afraid of, the grimness on his face. A hand on the shadowy other side of the door pane knocked again. Then the hand came up and waved, and a face loomed in the shadows. Burl. Burl!

William T. unlocked the door — something else that was new since she had last been here, both a deadbolt and a chain — and the waiting wind blew the screen door open. Burl pushed his way in.

"Mallie," he said. He hastened past William T. to kneel by the couch and grab her hands. "Welcome home."

He looked so happy. Burl was a lone man, long divorced, no children, no brother or sister, parents dead a decade ago. Beneath his Agway cap, his face was shiny, as if he'd just come back from a jog, which was something Mallie couldn't imagine him doing. She barely had time to register this new Burl, because he stood up and waved something in front of them all. A thirty-two-ounce plastic cottage-cheese container with a smiling cow on the lid.

"The hell's that?" William T. said.

"Open it." A smile spread across Burl's face and suddenly Mallie could imagine Burl as a young man. "It's not cottage cheese," he added.

William T. pried open the lid and dumped the contents on the table. Two stacks of twenties, folded and rubber-banded. Another stack of fifties, rolled up and rubber-banded. And more: three rolls of hundred-dollar bills.

"Money!" Burl said. "It's money. For Mallie."

Money? For her? Burl looked at her and grinned. But William T. strode forward, frowning, and it came to her in a flash: the plastic container next to Crystal's cash register. There must be other plastic jars next to other diner cash registers all over upstate New York. Uneven slots in their lids, each one probably sawed by Burl with the Swiss Army knife he always kept in his pocket.

HELP BRING MALLIE BACK!
EVERY LITTLE BIT COUNTS!

"The jars," Burl said, beaming. "I collected the money from them all. Drove around and emptied every single jar. Then I went to the bank to get bigger bills."

Mallie closed her eyes and pictured them, **HELP BRING MALLIE BACK** jars on counters for a hundred miles in any direction. For all she knew, there might be jars as far north as Massena, as far south as Yonkers. Burl, a mailman, must have driven around after work and on Sundays, plotting and mapping the best routes. He would have factored in the opening and closing times of each location. His car appeared in her mind as if she were looking down at it from a helicopter, crawling around the byroads of upstate New York, a shoebox filled with bills and coins on the passenger seat.

"What did you say to them?" William T. said. "Why would they believe some random person who wandered in, claiming a jar of cash?"

"The truth. That I was there on behalf of Mallie Williams. The minute I said her name, they all started asking about her."

"How much is in here, anyway?"

"Thirty-seven thousand, six hundred and ninety-two dollars."

"Jesus H. Christ! That's a lot of money."

"It is," Burl said, and his laugh transported Mallie to a wedding in Sterns, years ago, where he had sung the bride and groom down the aisle. Burl's tenor, his famous Welsh tenor, was sustained inside that laugh. Sometimes she and Zach had driven past his house after supper and heard him singing, his voice drifting down the lawn from the garden, where he must have been weeding. Zach had turned to— *No. No Zach.*

"With the medical bills all pro bono and now this, she'll be able to get quite a ways away," Burl said now, and at that William T. glanced up sharply.

"What are you talking about?"

"I just figured she'd be going somewhere. To get away from all"— he waved an arm in back of him, as if to encompass the entirety of the Mohawk Valley—"this. Wouldn't you? What shape's the truck in?"

"Good. But—"

William T. and Burl stood there, talking back and forth over the cottage-cheese container. Crystal had disappeared into the bathroom.

"Tires? Engine? You had the transmission checked? What about the brakes?"

"Slow down now, Burl. Yes, the truck's in good shape."

"Good. She's got a getaway vehicle and now she's got money in her pocket."

"She can't ever get away, Burl."

But Burl shook his head. "Sure she can, William T." He was suddenly a Burl thinner and sterner than Mallie had ever known he could be. "She can get away from here. From them. From us. From the ghosts. You think you'd be helping her by keeping her here? Not so."

"Burl," Crystal said now, coming back into the room, "it's late."

Mallie stood up and put her hand out to stop them. All of them talking over her. William T.'s words about her in relation to the cheese-stealing gull of her childhood—*poor defenseless kid*—came back to her, and she was suddenly angry. She looked from one to another, needing to say something, but what? What did she have to say?

"Wait a minute, all of you. Where's Sir?"

That was what came out of her mouth. Burl and William T. and Crystal looked at one another, then back at her.

"Sir?" Burl said, and the studied way he said it made her angrier.

"*Yes*. Sir, our dog. Where is he?"

"What brought Sir into your head?" William T. said.

By the way he said it, Mallie could tell he was trying to buy time. Where her dog had gone must be another question he wasn't ready to answer. Was Sir dead? He couldn't be. Sir was young. Look at the way they were all staring at her. Burl was still standing at the door, turning his cap over and over in his hands.

"Tomorrow then," he said finally, and then he was gone.

She waited until the silence was unbearable and William T. and Crystal were forced to look directly at her.

"Sir," she said. "Where is he? And what was Burl talking about, that I could get away from 'them'?"

Nothing. They just stood there. Anger flushed bright through her. Enough of this.

"And why did Charlie say it was his fault? *What's* his fault?"

William T.

THERE WOULD NEVER BE A GOOD WAY TO TELL HER EVERY-thing, or anything. But there had to be a better way than this, every question and every answer a struggle. Burl appearing at the door so late, the shock of it. William T.'s first thought had been that it was far too late for Burl and Crystal to start one of the endless games of Bananagrams that they had been playing ever since Mallie had been taken to the hospital. But of course he hadn't shown up to play Bananagrams. Like everyone, he had come for Mallie.

The things she was asking about were still unbearable to him. Charlie, for instance. He hated thinking about it, how when William T. had finally gotten to the scene of the assault, driving like a madman from Sterns to Utica, he had found the boy screaming, still drunk, and unhinged by the sight of his sister before the ambulance had taken her away.

And Sir. On an already wretched day nearly a year ago, Trish the dog sitter had called, talking so fast and wildly that William T. hadn't recognized the garbled voice on the other end of the line.

"Is this about Mallie?" he said. "Whoever you are, are you calling about Mallie?"

He managed to make out a "No" from the choked voice. He looked at the clock on the nightstand: 1:45 a.m. "Look," he said. "Whoever you are, I can't understand you. I don't know if you reached the number you meant to call."

Crystal flicked on the lamp and bent her head to his so she could hear too.

"Sir's gone," said the voice, and then he knew it was Trish. Crystal took the phone from him. He tried to follow the conversation.

"Trish? . . . Where did he go? . . . When did you realize he was gone? . . . Is there any way he could possibly jump over that fence?"

But she was shaking her head, answering herself even as she asked the question, because Trish's dog fence was eight feet high. William T. knew this because he had helped Trish's husband sink the posts. No dog could jump over that fence. He reached out and took the phone back.

"Someone must have taken him," he said into the receiver. Next to him Crystal had pulled her knees up to her chest and wrapped her arms around them. She was a held-together ball of worry.

"I'm so sorry, William T.," Trish said. Trish was unflinching, tough with her husband and her kids, who were grown now and far away, but everything inside her dissolved when it came to dogs.

"She loves those dogs more than she loves me," her husband had told William T. once, in a resigned sort of way.

Some people distrusted their own kind and lavished all their kept-at-bay love onto the dogs that came into their lives. Trish was one of them. William T. had hung up and turned to Crystal. What to do? Tell Zach? He couldn't bear the thought of it.

Let her come to things in her own time. That's what the hospital social worker had told them, back when she first woke, after he'd asked her what "dark birds" meant. *Let her lead the way,* she'd said. Mallie looked up at them, another question on her face.

"Did they take my appendix out while I was sleeping?"

William T. frowned. "What? No."

"What's this from, then? This scar?"

She turned down the waistband of the pajama bottoms and showed them the silvery curve. Crystal paled. This? Now? Mallie's eyes went from Crystal to him, and he watched her body go completely still. She turned the pajama waistband back up. She tucked the top into the bottoms and hitched them a little higher, then stayed put. Waiting. Crystal was the first to speak.

"You didn't have your appendix out," she said.

"You were out of it for a long time," William T. said. "You couldn't make decisions. And during that time there were people trying to figure out what was best for you. Your mother and her church and your lawyer and the judge and family and friends."

"My lawyer? I don't have a lawyer. And I don't go to church."

"Factions," he said. He couldn't look at her. He focused on the kitchen door and talked to it as if he were talking to her. As if he were reading from a teleprompter. "That's the word for it, *factions*. Opposing factions. Your mother's church was one faction. The parking lot was full of marchers. Pro and con. You had a lawyer to protect your rights. Or supposedly to protect them."

He kept talking to the door. "Nobody knew what to do. Nobody knew for sure what you would have wanted. Zach and Charlie and Crystal and me, we all thought we knew what you would've wanted and what was best for you, but the others didn't agree with us."

"William T., what does this have to do with the scar on my stomach?"

Crystal held up her hand. "Let me," she said to William T., and she turned to Mallie. "The scar is from an operation."

"What kind of operation?"

They sat there, Crystal's eyes fixed on the floor and William T.'s on the door. Outside, the wind was a steady hum surrounding the house. Wind was invisible, but its physical force was audible. When Mallie was a little girl she had once taken an umbrella off the hook by his door and run out into a gale with it open above her head. She had stood on tiptoe at the top of the hill that led down to William T.'s broken-down barn and held on to the handle with both hands. A human bird waiting to fling herself into the wind and fly. When William T. came out of the barn, he watched for one second before he charged up the hill after her. It was a memory he'd never forgotten. The tiny creature she had been back then, holding tightly to both earth and sky, wanting up and away.

Now her hand was on her stomach, over the double thickness of cotton cloth, waiting for them to talk. He looked at Crystal, whose face was set, and dipped his head at her, as if to say, *Just tell her.* So Crystal did.

"Mallie, you were pregnant."

Mallie opened her eyes, her face blank, and then looked down at her hands, laced over her belly. His heart clenched. Then, to his shock, she looked up at them and smiled. Her eyes lit up.

"Zach," she whispered.

William T. turned to Crystal at the same moment she turned, stricken, to him. Neither of them had anticipated this, that she would have been happy, that she would have welcomed a baby with Zach.

"No, Mallie," Crystal said. "Not Zach's."

An enormous grief rose within William T. as he watched her face change in an instant from delight to confusion.

"Not Zach's?"

Crystal shook her head. Mallie rocked back and forth on the couch and William T. could feel her trying to put it together. Pregnant. Not Zach's. Then her breath caught and broke and she reared up, shouting.

"No!"

She raced across the room and then wheeled around like a trapped animal looking for a way out. She spiraled her arms, knocking down the lamp, the aerial photo of the house that hung on the wall, Johnny's stack of coloring books for when he was visiting, the salt and pepper shakers. She was a windmill come unmoored, wild and spinning and shouting one word over and over and over: *NO.*

She raced up the stairs and then slammed the door so hard that the old house shook on its foundations. The sound of her voice came from behind it, traveling down the upstairs hall, past Crystal who was now clinging to the banister, and down the stairs to the living room, where a wail made of *no no no* gathered itself and hung heavy in the air.

———

William T. didn't think he would sleep, but sleep he must have, because when he opened his eyes, it was nearly dawn. Crystal had turned onto her stomach with the pillow over her head, something she did only after a bad dream. He eased out of the bed so as not to wake her and went downstairs, where Mallie was sitting on the couch in jeans and a T-shirt, crushing a throw pillow between her hands. How long had she been there? She looked as exhausted as he felt. Shadows under her eyes, a slumping look to her whole body.

"You want some coffee?" he said. Stupid. But she nodded. He put the water on to boil and measured out twice the grounds, then sat down next to her. They were silent for a while.

"William T.?"

"Yeah?"

"When you told me what this scar was from"—she placed two fingers over her T-shirt—"I was for a minute so happy."

"Because of Zach?"

"Yeah. Zach and me and a baby. It was like the future had already happened, even though I didn't know it. Like fate. And any second Zach would walk in with our baby."

She sounded bewildered.

"William T., do you think abortion's wrong? Not legally, we both know it's legal. But in your heart do you think it's wrong?"

Where had that question come from? He opened his mouth to ask but then remembered that she was supposed to lead the way and he was supposed to let her say whatever she wanted on her own terms and in her own time.

"Wrong doesn't have much to do with what I think about abortion."

"What do you mean?"

He shook his head. He had never been able to articulate, even back when *Roe v. Wade* raged in the court and in conversations across the country, how he felt about abortion. It was not a wrong or right thing, it was not a moral issue to him. It was a . . . stopping of something that would have continued.

"I think it's a mystery," he said.

"How so?"

"I wonder where they go. What happens after"—he spread his hand slowly in the air before them—"they're sent away."

"Who's they?"

"Them. The"—he hesitated over the word, because *baby* and *fetus* and *embryo* and all the other words had never felt right—"spirits. *Spirits* is as close as I can come to what I mean. The exact word doesn't exist."

She nodded. Her hand was still tight to her belly. "Most abortions happen early."

"That's true."

"So was mine not an early one? Is that why they did it this way, through my belly?"

Over on the counter, the coffee was beginning to burn. He knew in that instant that forever after, when he thought about this conversation, how he had messed up, how they should have told her earlier, the smell of scorched coffee would come back to him.

"William T.?" she said. "Why do you have that look on your face?"

He turned away, helpless, to see Crystal standing at the bottom of the stairs, her hairbrush in her hand. She had heard the conversation, or the end of it.

"What?" Mallie said. "Is it the abortion? William T., you just told me you didn't think abortions were wrong."

"Mallie. You didn't have an abortion."

"You said last night that I was pregnant. That's what this scar is," Mallie said patiently, as if she were explaining something to a very young child or a very old person. "Remember?"

Her face darkened with another possibility.

"Wait. It died? The baby died and they had to take it out of me."

The smell of scorched coffee filled his nose. He needed to get up and turn off the goddamn pot. No one was going to drink it now.

"Mallie," Crystal said. "What we're trying to tell you is that you didn't have an abortion, and the baby didn't die."

Mallie looked from Crystal to William T., her face a puzzle. He could feel her thoughts churning on themselves: pregnancy, abortion, no, not abortion, dead baby, no, not dead baby. Crystal kept going.

"The baby was born early but healthy. It was a C-section. Your mother had custody and she was raising him when she died. Now he's living with a foster family in Utica, or that's what we were told, anyway. The custody hearing was confidential and closed to the media."

Crystal's words were calm and blunt. Exhaustion mixed with a kind of relief spread through William T.'s body. Now Mallie knew. She knew everything that they had dreaded telling her. He watched her head dip downward, the way it used to when she was small and working on a sheet of arithmetic homework. She was focusing, concentrating inward. He looked away because the tilt of her head, her neck, brought back to him the look of her in the emergency room, that first awful night. The dried blood, the brace that held her head rigid. Her closed eyes.

He and Crystal sat waiting for Mallie to look up. Waiting for her to say something. A long time passed. A minute? Five? Then Mallie leapt up from the couch. William T. reached out to her but words went silent in his throat at the look on Mallie's face and the words she spat at them.

"You're telling me that I was pregnant and then I wasn't and there's a baby out there that was in me but they took it out and that baby is alive and in this world?"

He nodded.

"A boy," Crystal said, and she turned to William T. as if to make sure that was right, that yes, the baby was a boy. He opened his mouth to back her up, Yes, boy, but Mallie turned on them both.

"What about *me*," she said. The words were nearly inaudible. "Did anyone stop to think what I would have wanted?"

Yes. Endlessly. They had thought and wondered and tried to figure out what it was that Mallie would have wanted, but in the end, in the end — the idea of telling her the entire awful sequence of events exhausted him.

"Because I would have wanted an abortion. One hundred percent."

The social worker's words came crawling back into his mind then, the words he had memorized and recited over and over and over again. *Let her lead the way.* She was leading the way now. She stood before them, her eyes on fire.

"Is that why Zach left? Because of the, the . . . because of it?"

"The baby? I don't know."

She flinched at the word *baby*. The baby, who was close to a year old now. A crawling, possibly walking child who lived near the playground, according to rumors, and was too young to know anything of his origins.

"When did he leave?"

"Zach left after the decision to proceed with the pregnancy," Crystal said. She sounded as if she were reading from a legal article. "He was here until then. He was here the whole time"—she was trying to reassure Mallie, William T. could tell, trying to tell her that Zach had been there all along. Which was true, but only until it wasn't. Zach was well and truly gone, with just that one phone call since. *It's complicated. There's a lot to explain.* No shit, Sherlock, William T. had thought, and waited for the explanations. But Zach had explained nothing.

"Where's that box?" Mallie said.

"What box?"

"The box that was on the table last night. Where is it?"

"The clippings," Crystal said, looking sick. "William T. collected a lot of articles and clippings for you. But they're not to, you shouldn't look at them until—"

But Mallie was already digging in the back of the closet, a homing pigeon with unerring instinct. "No," he said, "oh no," and he lunged for it but too late. She upended the sagging box on the table: clippings, transcripts, those same two photos over and over and over, high school yearbook and high school graduation party. Power of attorney. Transfer of guardianship. Attorney for the child. Mental Hygiene Legal Service. Guardian ad litem. Medical reports. Family Court custody hearing. Many months' worth of memory, messed up, turned inside out.

He should have burned them all up, because now look. Front and center before Mallie was the grainy photo full of shadows, the onlooker's photo that had gone viral, of a girl's body lying on the pavement. Dark pool beneath her head. Arms and legs twisted. Mallie looked up at him and he nodded, as if he were answering a question, which maybe he was. She stood on the other side of the table, surrounded by the wreckage of her life. Burning her up from the inside out.

"Where's the truck?"

"What truck?"

"*My truck*. Burl said it was still here."

William T. shook his head no. No, she could not get in that truck or any truck. She had just come back to the world. He would not let her go. It was too soon. She was defenseless yet. But she stood her ground. Her feet shifted. Maybe she could feel the clutch and gas beneath them, hear the turn and sputter of the engine. As if both she and the truck wanted to get going and be gone, *be gone begone begone.*

He crumpled before her, sagging the way the corners of the upturned box on the table sagged. *Please don't go, Mallie. Please. We just got you back.* She stood there, waiting. His hands gripped hers but she dropped them. She flipped the cardboard box right side up again, scooped up handfuls of papers and photos and official-looking documents, dumped them back in and then plopped the box of fortune cookies that she and Zach had collected on top of it. She turned to him.

"Key?"

He shook his head but she arrowed the force of her will at him and it was too strong for him, too strong for anyone. He hunched his way into the kitchen. The smell of burned coffee was repulsive. He opened the silverware drawer and fished a key—her silver key on the old green carabiner, her same key and same carabiner that had not changed or disappeared in all this time—and handed it to her.

"It's in the barn," he said, the words reaching her when she was halfway out the door.

He grabbed the cottage-cheese container from the table and went after her. No one but he had been behind the wheel of Mallie's Datsun since the night he'd backed it into the barn after it happened, thinking ahead to If ever a day came, please, God, let it, that Mallie would be alive and able to drive her truck again, then it would be easier for her just to pull straight on out. She wouldn't have to back it out wondering if there was enough room on the left side, where he'd propped the ceiling up with two-by-fours. Now that day had come, but he hadn't thought far enough ahead. He hadn't imagined a moment when she would be full of rage, full of fire, wanting only to flee. He had imagined everything wrong.

She had already flung open the double barn doors and was climbing up into the cab.

"Mallie!"

She turned but stayed suspended, one foot in the truck, the other on the running board.

"Take this," and he handed her the plastic container. The cow smiled up from the lid. "It's from Burl."

"I know. I heard. I was there when you were talking about me. Sitting right there and you never even looked at me until I made you."

She spat the words out. She tossed the container into the shapeless mess of cardboard boxes on the passenger seat, dredged the key up out of her shorts pocket and stuck it in the ignition. The engine sputtered to life and she looked at him with triumph.

"Mallie. Let me go with you. One of us should—"

"No. I'm not a defenseless little kid, William T. No matter what you or any of the rest of them think."

She was adjusting the seat now, looking in the rearview mirror even though there was nothing to see; the rear of the truck faced the solid darkness of the back of the barn.

"Here, then."

He dredged her old cell phone up from his pocket, the phone she hadn't used since the night of the attack, along with its charger. He had paid for the service all these long months and kept it fully charged, never let it drop below 95 percent. As if a fully charged cell phone might help keep her alive. He dug down in his other pocket for the spare key and the slip of paper he carried there. The name of that little Montana town was scrawled on it. Coburn, a town he'd never been to, and below it the name of a restaurant he'd never eaten at. It was all the information he had, relayed to him by Zach's cousin Joe a couple weeks after Zach left, when he'd gone up to Joe's repair shop and begged, begged him to tell him where Zach was. He handed her the second silver key. Was this the right thing to do? He had no idea. *Her life, her decisions.* The other line the counselor had repeated.

"This is the spare. Keep this one in your pocket in case you lose the other. Or lock it in the cab. Either of those keys gives you any trouble, just drill out the ignition. Take it to any garage, wherever you are, and tell them to drill the goddamn ignition right out. Then you can stick anything in there — a screwdriver, a butter knife — and she'll start right up."

He heard his voice speeding up, sentences blurring together in a big word ball of advice. Advice advice advice. *Stop*, he told himself. He tossed the dark oblong of the cell phone into the box-within-a-box on the passenger seat. It landed in the fortune cookies.

"That's your phone," he said. "Call us. Call us, Mallie."

The little slip of paper came last. He handed it to her without a word. She pushed it down into her pocket. She started to roll the window up but then hesitated, grabbed his hand and held it to her cheek.

"Thank you. For everything. For real, William T., thank you. But I have to go."

"Where to?"

She just shook her head. She put the truck in gear and drove straight out of the barn and over the rutted dirt of the barn driveway. She paused at 274. Right or left? She had always been a girl who put on her turn signal, no matter where she was. Not this time, though. The red Datsun gleamed in the sun — William T. had polished it and polished it, waxed and buffed it until it barely looked like the same dusty truck that Mallie and Zach Miller used to rocket around the back roads in. She pulled out to the left, a dark shadow behind the wheel.

From the Box

Utica Tribune

Decision Made in Williams Guardianship Case

The court battle between Lucia Williams, mother of Mallie Williams, who has been hospitalized and unconscious since a brutal assault nearly five months ago, and former friend William T. Jones, longtime neighbor in the rural hamlet of North Sterns, New York, where Mallie Williams was raised, has ended. As expected, the court granted legal guardianship of her daughter to Lucia Williams.

Many had deemed Mr. Jones's move for guardianship as both quixotic — it's fairly rare that a judge, without compelling reasons to do so, would grant guardianship to a non-family member when a family member is ready, willing and able to assume guardianship — and disrespectful. But public opinion on the court decision remains divided, with about half of the respondents to our poll believing that Miss Williams's mother was the obvious choice for legal guardian and the other half in favor of Mr. Jones, who had, in the words of another neighbor, "been part of that girl's life, a father almost, since her own dad died when she was little. I mean, we're all convinced that her mother's church is the one pulling the strings here."

That observation was roundly denounced by the members of Lucia Williams's church, who insisted that Mrs. Williams was not only "perfectly capable of making decisions on her daughter's behalf," but had the full support of her church community.

"She's the girl's mother," said Carol Farigant. "She's her only living relative besides her brother, Charlie, who is still a child. She is a woman of faith and strength, and this whole thing should never even have come up."

"I don't know this Jones character," said another church member, who requested anonymity, "but this is wrong. Maybe he thinks he's doing the right thing, but Mallie Williams has a perfectly good mother who is standing by her daughter. Everyone else should just butt out."

Mr. Jones disagrees.

"B — — —t," he said yesterday to a reporter who reached him at his home. "Those vultures never even met Mallie. They just want to use her as an incubator. As their pro-life poster child. They're not pro-life. They're pro-birth. And they don't give a s — t about what Mallie would want."

Ambulance driver interview from The EMT Diaries *podcast, transcript excerpt*

Do I remember her? Of course. You don't forget something like that. I don't forget many calls in general. It's not like an office job, or what I imagine an office job being like. There's routine in this line of work, but it doesn't come from the calls themselves. They're all different. You can't predict what will go down on any given call.

My advice is to make your assumptions, sure, whatever, but be ready to revise on the spot. The homeless guy in the doorway in February, you assume he's borderline hypothermic. Maybe malnourished, maybe an untreated mental illness, maybe drunk or strung out, maybe wearing all his clothes at once, layers and layers, maybe disoriented and exhausted. All these things you assume, and you'll probably be right.

But not always. What if his appendix is about to burst? What if it already did? That happened once. That's why you need to be ready to revise on the spot.

It was raining that night. I remember that too, because it hadn't rained in a while and I was concerned about oil on the roads mixing with the water. Hydroplaning. Everyone laughs at me because I worry about hydroplaning, but it's a real thing.

We got the call and I assumed that the girl was drunk. That's a normal assumption. But about a block away I had a feeling that it was going to be worse, much worse. Sometimes you get a feeling like that. Over the years I've learned to pay attention to that.

She wasn't conscious when we pulled up. Things were quiet. No sirens, just the light turning on the one car. The cops, they were quiet too. I think we all felt the same. I know that I was thinking of my own daughter. She's grown now but it doesn't matter. You always worry about them. It never goes away, the worry.

The darkness under her head, I knew it was blood right away. After a while you can tell the difference, even if it's dark. Rain, car exhaust, street oil, blood: I can always tell.

We got her braced and loaded onto the stretcher and into the ambulance and then we were off. That's when it got noisy. I flipped on the siren and I didn't let myself think about the hydroplaning. We needed to get her to St. John's as quick as we could.

It was a clay pot of some kind. I remember thinking that's what he must have bashed her head with, because there it was, right on the sidewalk, the bottom broken. Like someone took it by the neck and swung it against her skull.

I remember looking at the broken pot and looking at the blood and thinking I needed to make sure they kept as much focus on potential head injuries as on everything else. Because there was a lot of everything else.

Everything that happened after that, what all they did to that poor girl while she lay there unconscious, the way they fought over her like she was some kind of prize when she couldn't even speak for herself? Sickens me.

Do I remember who? The brother? Of course. I wish I didn't.

The way he stood there screaming. And the older gentleman, the one who got to the scene while we were loading her in? Him too. It's one of those things I wish I could get out of my mind, that look on his face. That sound that came out of his mouth when he saw her lying there. That's her father, I remember thinking. That would be me, if it were my daughter.

That he turned out not to be her father surprised me completely. But later on, when the story kept unfolding, it was clear that in his heart she was his daughter. Family doesn't have to be blood to be family.

Everybody knows her face now. For a while there you couldn't get away from it—TV, newspaper, online, billboards, you name it. She'll always be frozen in time that way. But when I think about the whole mess, to be honest, it's Mr. Jones I think about. You could see on his face how much he adored her.

I can still hear the sound he made when he saw her.

Central New York Daily

Area Woman Assaulted, Left for Dead

(UTICA) A 21-year-old woman waiting for her brother outside a party on Hawthorne Street was robbed, assaulted and abandoned nearby late Friday night. Police responding to an anonymous 911 call at approximately 10:30 p.m. confirmed that the woman, whose identity has not been revealed pending notification of family, was sexually assaulted and beaten by a blunt instrument.

The woman's handbag was found a few blocks away, her wallet missing. Based on further evidence, police hypothesize that the woman fought back and may have attempted to follow the assailant, who then drove a blunt object against her skull.

"A flowerpot," said Derek Hattering, who lives just down the block from the scene of the assault. "From my front step. Whoever it was picked it up and bashed her head in. Broken pottery all over the place."

The woman is currently in intensive care at St. John's. The hospital did not release any further information.

"This is an open and ongoing investigation," said Utica Police Chief Bruce Koloskey. "We encourage any witnesses or anyone who may have information relevant to the case to come forward."

Central New York Daily

Rape and Assault Victim Identified

(UTICA) The identity of the young woman assaulted on Hawthorne Street in Utica last Friday was released by the Utica Police Department. She is Mallie Williams, who grew up in North Sterns, New York, and now resides in Forestport, New York, a rural township north of Utica.

"With her next of kin's permission, we're releasing the victim's name in hopes of gathering more information that will aid us in our ongoing investigation," stated Utica Police Chief Bruce Koloskey. "As of this morning, no witnesses have come forth. We encourage anyone with any information to call our tip line."

Miss Williams is still in intensive care at St. John's in critical condition. Her prognosis is unknown.

Mallie Williams
10/10/2014
11:14 PM ED to Hosp Admission
MRN: 93648915

Description: 21 year old female
Encounter # 1305041041
Center

ED PROVIDER NOTES BY DARLEEN FITZGERALD CONNOR, MD AT 10/10/2014 11:58 PM

Author:
Connor, Darleen F

Service:
Emergency Medicine

Author: RESIDENT

Filed: 10/11/2014
1:09 AM

Note Time:
10/10/2014 11:58 PM

Note Type:
ED Provider Notes

Status: Signed

Editor: Connor, Darleen F, MD (Resident)

ST. JOHN'S HOSPITAL
EMERGENCY DEPARTMENT ATTENDING SUPERVISION NOTE

CHIEF COMPLAINT: BLUNT FORCE TRAUMA, SEXUAL ASSAULT

History of Present Illness

Mallie Williams is a 21 y.o. female with a PMH of N/A who presents to the emergency department after being both sexually assaulted and assaulted with a blunt force weapon.

Patient is unconscious. Patient was found unconscious and bleeding and transported to the ER via ambulance. Patient sustained blunt force trauma to the back of the skull with accompanying traumatic brain injury. Extent of injury and possible brain damage unknown. No spinal fracture. Regular heartbeat. No shortness of breath. Bruises and abrasions to pelvis. Slight gush of vaginal fluids, slight vaginal bleeding. Patient is not on blood thinners.

Patient's father, William T. Jones, reports no unusual medical history and no previous hospitalizations.

Discharge Medications:

Allergies: Patient's father reports no known allergies.

Active Medical Problems: Mild refractory psoriasis. Beyond that, there is no problem list on file for this patient.

PMH: History reviewed. No pertinent past medical history.
PSH: History reviewed. No pertinent past surgical history.
Social History:

HISTORY

Substance Use Topics

- Smoking status: Not on file
- Smokeless tobacco: Not on file
- Alcohol Use: Not on file

Family History: No family history on file.
Review of Systems: A 10-point review of systems was performed and is negative except as per HPI.

ED PROVIDER NOTES BY DARLEEN F CONNOR, MD
AT 10/10/2014 11:58 PM

Physical Exam

Vitals: BP 117/71 mmHg | Pulse 85 | Temp (Src) 98.3 F (36.8 C) (Oral) | Resp 16 | Ht 5'7" (1,702m) | Wt 52.571 kg (115 lb 14.4 oz) | BMI 30.83 kg/m2 | SpO2 99%

Primary survey: Patient is unable to speak, bilateral breath sounds. 2+radial pulses and dorsal pedal pulses. GCS 15. Pupils are equal, round and reactive to light and accommodation. Patient in c-collar.

Secondary survey:

General: Unconscious, unresponsive to sounds, touch or light

HEENT: pupils mid-sized and equally reactive, EOMI, conjunctiva clear, oropharynx without erythema or exudates, MMM. No periorbital, no mastoid. Bruising. No otorrhea or rhinorrhea. Patient has a 22cm laceration to the vertex of her scalp, fractured skull.

Neck: Midline cervical bleeding, no LAD, supple. No step-offs.

Chest/Pulmonary: Normal work of breathing, chest clear with equal lung sounds bilaterally, no wheezes or crackles

Cardiovascular: RRR with normal S1 and S2, no murmurs or gallops appreciated, peripheral pulses 2+ bilaterally

Abdomen: Soft

Back/Spine: No deformity, no midline abrasions/contusions, no step-offs

Extremities: Patient has some bruising to the medial aspect of her anterior mid right tibia tenderness. Patient has some bruising exhibited. Patient has some swelling over the lateral malleoli with inversion. Patient has some swelling to third digit on right.

Skin: Warm and dry, skin color normal, no rashes appreciated

Neuro: Unconscious

Psychiatric: N/A

Assessment:

TBI-SAH

Head laceration; skull fracture; suspected traumatic brain injury; possible brain damage

Plan:

Re-check vitals

Rape kit examination

Imaging: Plain radiograph(s): and CT scan(s): head

Counsel patient/family

Re-evaluate patient

Check response to treatment

Planned Disposition: Hospitalization

Medical Decision Making & ED Course

Ms. Williams is a 21 y.o. female who presents . . .

Diagnosis & Disposition

Diagnosis:

1. TBI (traumatic brain injury), with loss of consciousness of 30 minutes and more, initial encounter

2. SAH (subarachnoid hemorrhage)

3. Laceration of scalp without foreign body, initial encounter

4. Sexual assault with penetration; rape kit ordered

Author: Darleen F. Connor, MD

Electronically signed by Darleen F. Connor, MD at 10/10/2014 11:58 PM

Central New York Daily

Still Searching for Leads in Williams Case

(UTICA) Nearly three weeks after Forestport resident Mallie Williams was assaulted and left for dead on Hawthorne Street late on the evening of October 10, there are no clues as to who the assailant or assailants were.

"How many assailants, we believe one, but we're not sure," said Utica Police Chief Bruce Koloskey. "The investigation is ongoing and forensics is actively analyzing all evidence collected at the scene."

The victim's mother, Lucia Williams, 40, and members of her church (Faith Love Congregation) ask for ongoing prayers for the young woman. Chief Koloskey continues to urge any witness or anyone with information about the crime to come forth.

"Call the tip line if you have any information at all," he said. "Even if you think it's only remotely related, call."

Mallie Williams's neighbor, William T. Jones, interrupted Chief Koloskey at a press conference to ask what would become of the bystander who had posted a photo of Miss Williams, taken at the scene, on his Facebook page.

"Nothing," Chief Koloskey responded. "What he did was repulsive, but not illegal. And the photo has now been taken down."

Mr. Jones, visibly upset, began to argue with Chief Koloskey and eventually was led out of the conference room by armed police officers. Multiple telephone calls to his North Sterns home went unreturned.

The Adirondack Mountains Standard

The Story Behind the Story

BY JERRY TOWNSEND

No one can claim that William T. Jones, lifelong resident of rural North Sterns (about twenty miles northeast of Rome), is anything but persistent.

Remember when Jones's young neighbor and friend Mallie Williams was viciously attacked on the late-night streets of Utica and left for dead? Remember how the police department hasn't been able to figure out who did it? Remember how Mallie Williams has been unresponsive ever since? Remember how, early on, Mr. Jones sought legal guardianship of Miss Williams over her mother in a highly publicized court challenge because he believed Miss Williams would have chosen to terminate her pregnancy?

I'll go out on a limb and state that I'm pretty damn certain that no one with even a passing acquaintance with the nightly news has forgotten much of anything about Mallie Williams. Or about her mother, Lucia Williams, who was granted custody of her grandchild. At last report, however, Lucia Williams is fighting terminal cancer and hasn't been seen in public solo, without the surround-sound protection of the flock of the Faith Love Congregation, since days after her daughter was assaulted.

It's also not going out on a limb to state that most of us in these here parts remember William T. Jones, the neighbor who came out of the woodwork after the girl's hospitalization, claiming that he should be named legal guardian because "the goddamn right-to-lifers shouldn't be using Mallie as an incubator."

Not a kind thing to say, certainly, but set that aside for a moment and ask yourself this: Was he right? Was William T. Jones speaking the truth?

By all accounts, Mr. Jones, who is in his mid-60s, has been a father figure to the young woman for most of her life. Neighbors and friends describe him as fiercely protective of both Mallie and her underage brother.

It's possible that William T. was lying, or at least inaccurate, when he claimed to know what Mallie Williams would have wanted with regard to her child, conceived in rape and born while she lay unconscious. It's also possible that Lucia Williams, by all accounts a profoundly religious woman, was convinced that the decision to proceed with the pregnancy was in her daughter's best interests.

What's done is done. Hindsight is not foresight. But I am haunted by the decision and its ripple effects. I am haunted by the existence of a baby whose parentage and beginnings of life are so fraught. I am haunted by the fact that Mallie Williams is still alive, still breathing, still unaware of all that transpired without her conscious knowledge. And I suspect that I am not alone in my uneasy and troubled wonderings.

𝔖𝔶𝔯𝔞𝔠𝔲𝔰𝔢 𝔖𝔱𝔞𝔯

[EDITORIAL]

Ever since the news of Mallie Williams's pregnancy broke last month, rain or shine, snow or sleet, the protesters have shown up every morning at St. John's hospital in timeworn Utica. In separate circles they march, signs gripped in both hands. The difference between the signs, whether homemade or professionally printed, and the two separate circles of protesters, is clear. Half the signs bear photos of smiling infants, with black headlines below each:

LIFE BEGINS AT CONCEPTION

ABORTION STOPS A BEATING HEART

AT SIX WEEKS I HAD FINGERNAILS

The other half bear no smiling babies. Instead, photos of Mallie Williams—from her high school graduation, mostly — are posted above equally black headlines.

DON'T LIKE ABORTION? DON'T HAVE ONE.

KNOWLEDGE + CHOICE = POWER. MALLIE WILLIAMS HAS NEITHER.

WHAT WOULD MALLIE DO?

In some ways the scene in the parking lot of St. John's depicts a wearyingly familiar battleground of anti-abortion vs. pro-choice. You don't have to travel far in this country to find billboards advocating for either side. Churches with white crosses on their front lawns, abortion clinics with rings of protesters and equal numbers of security guards and volunteers.

But in a fundamental way, this is a different battle entirely. The fetus — product of a rape in which the assailant is unknown — whose future is being fought over is growing within the womb of a young woman likely never to gain full consciousness. It's equally likely that Mallie Williams, massage therapist and graduate of Mohawk Valley Community College, would not have imagined herself as a fixture on the nightly news.

In the absence of Mallie's decision-making capability, a grim battle is being fought over whether Miss Williams would choose to abort or carry her fetus to term. Attorneys for both Lucia Williams, Mallie's mother, and William T. Jones, the family's lifelong neighbor and friend, have laid out the case for guardianship of the young woman and, thus, decision-making ability about the pregnancy.

Mr. Jones has advocated that the fetus be aborted on grounds that a) no woman should be forced to bring forth a child conceived of rape, and b) it is morally wrong for a woman to be forced into motherhood. On the other side, Lucia Williams belongs to a church that is against abortion in any instance, no matter the circumstances, and that church has rallied around her and is providing support in the form of shelter and payment of legal bills. Time is closing in, though, and unless the judge shortly awards guardianship to Mr. Jones — a highly unusual outcome, according to legal sources — the advancement of Miss Williams's pregnancy will render Mr. Jones's argument moot.

Meanwhile, Mallie Williams's

face, familiar by now to anyone within reach of a newspaper, a television or the internet, hovers silently on signs hoisted high. What Would Mallie Do, indeed.

The decision must be made. But by whom? We believe that this is a decision best left to medical professionals. But public opinion, it seems, is not with us.

Central New York Daily
LETTERS TO THE EDITOR

To the Editor,
There has been a lot of back and forthing with regard to the young woman Mallie. In my view it doesn't matter how she came to be pregnant. She is carrying life within her and that life is innocent and deserves to be given a chance. Let life make the call.

— Martha Sorovich

▪

To the Editor,
Put yourself in the young woman's place. She is a vegetable in terms of brain, right? But the baby inside her is not a vegetable. If the young woman could still think, she would want her baby to be born. What's done is done and now they should do everything possible for the baby.

— Harrison L. Stupak

▪

To the Editor:
What bothers me about the whole Mallie Williams incident is all the articles that are being written about her. All the people asking for prayers for her, all the people claiming that they knew her, that they went to school with her, that they knew her when she was little, that they know her family, that they know her neighbors, that they know everything about it. Excuse my language but this is B———t. We are the ones who know Mallie. We in Sterns. We are the ones who should be asking the questions and getting the answers.

It is wrong that others who don't know anything about her are trying to take over her story.

— Sara Maggio

•

To the Editor,
With regard to the idiot who presumes to "put himself in the place of" the young woman in the coma, I'm putting myself in her place right now and you know what? I would say Hell No. My body, my life. Abort now, before it's too late. Keep stalling your way through the courts and the right-to-lifers will have left her for dead all over again.

— Hilda Borokovich

•

To the Editor,
If that baby was mine I would give it a biblical name. Like Matthew or Jesus.

— Makenzy Wilson

•

To the Editors,
"Abortion stops a beating heart." Yes, it does. Isn't that what it's supposed to do? I got pregnant when I was 18 and I had an abortion. This was not an easy decision. I was still in high school, living with my parents and my younger sister. My parents would have helped me, I'm sure, but I never told them

about the pregnancy. I didn't want to hurt them. My boyfriend at the time and I made a mutual decision and we went to the clinic together. Was it hard? Yes. Did I feel sad and do I still sometimes feel sad? Yes. Was it the right decision? Yes.

But here's the thing: As I see it, none of what happened to me, and none of what anyone might feel about a fetus's right to live, has anything to do with Mallie Williams. This whole horrible situation is not about abortion or a woman's right to choose whether and when she wants to have a child. Nor is it about the rights of a fetus, either. Both sides are using the baby as a means to an end. That poor girl is nothing but a lump of breathing meat.

What this is about is control. About who gets to decide someone else's future. I know that something has to be done, one way or another, but God help me, I don't know what that should be. Poor Lucia, poor William T., and poor, poor Mallie.

— Name withheld

•

To the Editor,
I would be very happy to give that baby a good home. I have wanted

a baby my whole life. I never met the right guy but I know I would be a good mama and I am wondering where is the sign-up list? I can provide references and I would like to be considered for an interview. Thank you.

— Name withheld

Obserber

Mother of Assault Victim Dies

Lucia Williams, 41, originally of North Sterns, NY, and current resident of Marcy, NY, died yesterday at St. Luke's hospital. At the time of her death, Ms. Williams was battling advanced pancreatic cancer.

Lucia Williams was predeceased by her husband, Starr, and leaves behind a son, Charlie, 16, a grandson, and a daughter, Mallie, who has been unresponsive since a brutal assault last October. Ms. Williams worked as an occupational therapist at Forever Home, an establishment for developmentally delayed children, for most of her adult life.

"She was a hard worker and she will be missed," said her former supervisor Eduardo Perez. "She had a beautiful touch with children who didn't respond to many others." Ms. Williams was interred next to the grave of her husband in the North Sterns Cemetery. There will be no public service.

Obserber

Williams, Lucia, 41 of North Sterns and Marcy, New York, died of cancer, last Thursday. Ms. Williams became nationally recognized after a vicious assault on the streets of Utica left her daughter, Mallie, near death. In the months immediately following the assault, an equally vicious legal battle ensued over the guardianship of Mallie Williams, who is currently a long-term patient in the rehabilitation wing of St. John's.

"Our sister Lucia has gone to

be with God," stated Carol Farigant, worship director of the Faith Love Congregation in Utica, NY.

"Lucia was a faithful servant of God," said Horace Worth, treasurer of the organization, "and we take comfort in knowing that she is in a better place now."

"In the midst of tremendous darkness, Lucia was led by God to our church, and it was here that she found light and faith," added Ms. Farigant. "We are pleased that we were able to offer her comfort and even though we are saddened by her passing, we know that she is now in a far better place, a place of everlasting light."

A private service was held over the weekend. No public funeral is scheduled.

ᛗbserver

[EDITORIAL]

"Foster parents play an essential role in providing temporary, safe, nurturing homes for children when their parents are unable to care for them. New York State continues to find permanent, safe and caring homes for our children."

This statement was taken from the home page of the New York State Office of Children and Family Services. We at the *Observer* reference it today in relation to the child of Mallie Williams, born last week and immediately transferred, by order of the court, into the custody of Lucia Williams, mother of Mallie Williams. Lucia Williams is the baby's grandmother, not foster parent, but given that there is a chance, however slim, that Mallie Williams may one day awake, we believe that the "temporary, safe, nurturing home" mission applies in this instance.

Despite the unusual and trying circumstances that have surrounded the Williams case from the beginning — a young woman assaulted and left for dead with a brain injury and subsequent brain infection; pregnant as a result of rape; the unwitting subject of both anti-abortion and abortion rights groups; the fate of both herself and her unborn child fought

---

over bitterly—we believe that this custody placement represents the best outcome for the child.

We recognize the strong emotions that have influenced public opinion, perhaps unduly, over the fate of both Mallie Williams and the child. But in our opinion, the fraught testimony and painful events have all along obscured the heart of the matter: the victimization of a young woman unable to speak for herself, and the fate of a child we may never know if she would have wanted.

Now is the time to put aside acrimony. Now is the time to let go thoughts of religion, politics, victims' rights and the wishes of those closest to the victim. Now is the time to focus on the innocence of a child born into circumstances beyond his control. Let us all set aside our differences, that this child may enjoy the rights and privileges of normal life.

The Adirondack Mountains Standard

The Story Behind the Story

BY JERRY TOWNSEND

Before she was a name in the headlines, before her photo was plastered in newspapers and on television and computer screens nationwide, before she became a symbol for the religious right and the feminist left, Mallie Williams was a girl who lived a quiet life in the rural hinterlands north of Utica.

Many of the residents who call the picturesque Sterns Valley home are Amish. They tend their small dairy farms quietly. Barefoot Amish women can be seen hanging laundry—blue, gray and white—on clotheslines, Amish children can be seen trundling reel lawn mowers back and forth on the lawn or weeding enormous vegetable gardens, while Amish men are usually in the fields or barns. They coexist peacefully with their non-Amish neighbors, many of whom are also dairy farmers, while others work as teachers, small-town bankers, insurance salespeople. Others eke out livings as housecleaners, Adirondack guides, handymen. A typical rural mix.

To a casual passerby, it's an idyllic scene, rural upstate New York at its pastoral finest. Dig deeper, though, and secrets reveal themselves.

A wooden sign nailed to a telephone pole at the intersection of a nameless dirt road and Route 274: LIFE BEGINS AT CONCEPTION. Another wooden sign nailed to a fencepost at the intersection of two also-nameless roads a mile north of the first sign: SAVE MALLIE'S LIFE. And a third, on a stick driven into the soft earth in front of the Sterns Town Hall: WHAT WOULD MALLIE WANT?

Mysterious signs, to be sure, at least to those who don't know the story of Mallie Williams, who grew up here and is now hospitalized 20 miles south in Utica, New York. But one would be hard-pressed to find a soul here who doesn't know Mallie Williams, and not just her story, but Mallie herself.

"Of course I know Mallie," said Edwina "Eddie" Beckey, when a reporter approached her in the aisle of the Sterns pharmacy. "She's one of my best friends. I grew up with her."

When asked her opinion of the controversy raging in the media and in the courtroom, however, Eddie refused comment. "Enough people have said enough s—t about Mallie," she stated. "I'm not about to let you take something I say and twist it into something else and then put it out there for the whole f— —g world to see."

Others were not so reticent.

"Mallie was a good student," said Harold Chelms, former biology teacher at Sterns High School, where the student body numbers 500 total and draws from a 15-mile-wide radius of surrounding towns and countryside. "Well liked. She loved birds. Really had a thing for birds."

"Smarter than she ever let on," added Kathleen Dominguez, whose teaching duties are split between art and Spanish. "You know that old saying 'Still waters run deep'? That was Mallie."

"She'd already gone through a lot," said a coffee-drinking patron at Crystal's Diner, the town's only eating establishment. "Her dad died when she was nine and her mother was way overboard into her church, if you ask me. The whole church thing, if you're religious, fine, but don't shove it onto others, you know? Especially your kids, which is what Lucia tried to do. Not fair this had to happen to Mallie now too."

He pointed at a large plastic jar next to the cash register. Mallie's face, unsmiling in a tattered photo taped to the front, stared out. "We try to help," he said, "but nickels and dimes and dollar bills aren't going to do a hell of a lot. Even though they waived all the hospital and rehab fees. Felt sorry for her, I guess."

A woman came from behind the counter bearing a fresh pot of coffee and refilled the patron's coffee mug. He emptied three packets of sugar into it and added cream. "It kind of feels like it's beyond us, now," he added. "Once the lawyers get into it, you can kiss your ass goodbye. That's my feeling anyway."

When a reporter asked the woman behind the counter if he could ask her a few questions, she just shook her head and retreated into the kitchen.

And so it goes, here in a place where, it can reasonably be assumed, no one ever expected to be a regular feature on the nightly news. A place where protesters can still, after all this time, occasionally be found marching in circles on the village green, placards and signs held high. A place where long-simmering beliefs regularly erupt into impassioned debate, if not outright shouting matches. A place where that third sign, WHAT WOULD MALLIE WANT? attains a haunting power, given that its subject is unable to speak for herself.

"Right for her?" said the anonymous coffee drinker at Crystal's, before he refused to say anything else. "Or for them? It's easy to talk for someone else if you don't think they're ever coming back, isn't it?"

Good question. For in some ways the fate of the young woman thus far has had little to do with her and everything to do with religion, politics and the intersection thereof. Google the name Mallie Williams and take your pick of hundreds of articles, opinion pieces, photos and letters to the editor.

"You could spend the next week glued to your computer screen and you wouldn't get through half of them," said Ms. Dominguez, the teacher. "But you know what? You'd never get to Mallie. Mallie the girl, the person, she's nowhere in any of those articles."

The only one who could answer these questions and that other one — WHAT WOULD MALLIE WANT? — remained unable to communicate for nearly a year and a half. But that, readers, is about to change. For the central figure at the heart of this tragic story has awakened.

PART TWO

William T.

T HAD BEEN THREE DAYS. THEY SAT ON THE PORCH, WATCHING THE sun as it dropped below the pine woods across the field. Somewhere out there was Mallie, behind the wheel of the old truck she'd learned to drive in.

"You heard from her?"

"You know I haven't, William T."

"I call and I call but it goes right to voicemail."

"That means the phone's turned off. Either that or she's talking to someone else."

How Crystal knew this he didn't know, but she was attuned to the modern world; it was she who had taught him how to use the computer. This was as bad as when Mallie was in and out of consciousness. No, it was worse than that, because at least then they knew where she was. No, it was better than that. For God's sake, she was alive again.

"She's in charge now, William T.," Crystal said, as if she could read his mind. "It's her life now."

The words coming out of her mouth sounded tired, as if they had been used beyond their capacity. Maybe Crystal repeated them to herself, the way he said, *Mallie, please call,* over and over to himself. Willing the little phone in his pocket to buzz. They hated thinking of her out there alone in the truck, with the box of pain riding shotgun.

"I'll tell you what I'm most afraid of," he said. "That she wants it back."

He expected her to ask what "it" was. Or to say that it was impossible; the baby had been placed by court order with a foster family and it was time to leave it alone, stop wondering and worrying. But she hesitated. Then, "I think about it all the time," she said. Her voice was almost a whisper. "I torment myself about it. It's in the back of my mind. I see a baby in the diner and I think about it."

"Crystal, would you have wanted to keep it?"

"We couldn't. We had no legal rights. You know that."

"But if somehow we could've. If we'd kept fighting. If we'd kept on, if we'd made a stink about it, gotten more lawyers, different ones, found some way?"

She shook her head. No. The thought of it all—courts and lawyers and depositions and arguments—was too much. Even now, nearly a year later, it was too much.

"We were hanging on by a thread as it was, William T."

Which was true. Reporters, pro-life protesters, pro-choice protesters, headlines and the phone that didn't stop ringing until it did, which was even worse. And Charlie, angry and heartbroken. They had all dealt with so much. William T. pictured the little gray house in Utica, his secret trips to the playground, where he sat on the bench, inspecting every baby in sight.

"Listen, Crystal. Sometimes I go by the attorney's house."

She was still and small next to him but he felt her instant alertness.

"Whose house? Aaron Stampernick's? The attorney for the child?"

He nodded. "They're foster parents too, you know," he said. "They might even be the ones the judge assigned the baby to."

The second Family Court custody hearing, after Lucia's death, had been closed by order of the judge. Records confidential, no media allowed. But William T. had heard rumors that the attorney for the child, Aaron Stampernick, and his social-worker wife, Melissa, were the ones raising the baby. He had no way of knowing for sure. The one thing he did know was that the Stampernicks knew exactly where that baby was.

"Have you actually seen the baby, William T.?"

"No."

"Good," she said, with a vehemence that startled him. "William T., do not tell me where the Stampernicks live. And if you find out they *are* the ones who have the baby, don't tell me that either. Don't ever make me see that baby."

"Why? Because you're afraid that if you look at him, you'll see the rapist?"

She stared at him, bewildered, and shook her head. "No. The opposite. What I'm afraid of is that if I ever saw that child, I would see Mallie. And I would want to take him and keep him and never let him go."

When they took the baby from her, William T. and Crystal and Charlie weren't allowed to be there. But the nurse, the kind one who had always liked the two of them, had left an anonymous voicemail from an unknown number the day before. This was a serious violation of HIPAA rules, and she had left neither name nor number, but, still, they knew it was her.

"They're going to deliver the baby tomorrow via C-section," she said. "The fetal heart tones have decreased, which means that the baby is in distress or Mallie is in premature labor. It's kind of miraculous that the pregnancy's made it this far, anyway. And since she's uncooperative, she can't deliver vaginally."

"*Uncooperative?*" William T. had said to Crystal, after playing the message three times. "What the hell does that mean?"

"It's a medical term," Crystal said. "Not a reflection of personality."

How she knew that, William T. didn't know, but Crystal usually knew more than she let on. Neither of them slept that night. At dawn the next morning William T. made coffee and he and Crystal sat on the cool cement of the porch and drank it. They had woken Charlie but he had just stared up at them—"No"—and pulled the blankets up over his head.

At St. John's they drove into the rear parking lot, the one used by employees. They sat in the truck, windows rolled up, and looked at each other in a *What do we do now?* sort of way. A gray unmarked door opened and the young orderly, Beanie, stepped out. He shook a cigarette out of a pack and put it to his lips but didn't light it.

He leaned against the building and kept taking the cigarette out of his mouth and putting it back in, going through the motions of smoking.

"You think he's trying to quit?" Crystal said.

Beanie suddenly looked in their direction, as if he had overheard. Impossible. They were too far away, and the windows were rolled up. But he was looking directly at them. After a minute he raised his hand.

"Does he want something?" Crystal said.

Beanie put the unlit cigarette back in his mouth. He pointed at them and nodded. Just once.

"I think he knows why we're here," William T. said.

"You think so?"

"Yes. I think he's trying to tell us the surgery went okay."

That was a guess. Back when William T. had still been allowed in the hospital, William T. and Beanie had never talked. Now they watched as he returned his cigarette to the pack and waved a pass in front of the door sensor. They sat there another while, not knowing what to do, and then they drove home, where another anonymous message was waiting from the kind, HIPAA-violating nurse. The surgery had been a success. *Success?* The word had no meaning in this situation. William T. had waited for the anger to gain force and traction, propel him forward, but he was too tired.

———

The custody arrangement had already been in place before the baby was born. Mallie's attorney had done what her guardian ad litem suggested and recommended custody go to the child's grandmother Lucia. The Family Court custody hearing, with Aaron Stampernick, Mallie's attorney, Mallie's guardian ad litem and Lucia all present, was, in William T.'s eyes, a mere formality.

Custody. What did the term mean, exactly? "The control or care of a person or property" was the first dictionary definition, but there were other, darker definitions as well, such as "the state of being detained or held under guard." Slogans and signs and billboard images from the past months ran through William T.'s mind.

A PARENT IS THE ONE WHO RAISES YOU

ADOPTION IS AN OPTION

I WAS BORN NOT UNDER YOUR HEART BUT INSIDE IT

William T. kept picturing how the documents had tumbled out of the box when Mallie upended it on the table. Everything that had happened to her, around her, above her, while she lay sleeping—it was all in there. Piecemeal, scraps, fragments, parts of a whole that people who didn't know Mallie had woven around her.

He remembered the first time, long ago, that she had ventured to his house on her own. It had been early morning, and he was sitting on his porch with a cup of coffee, watching an unfamiliar machine make its slow way up the hill in his direction. Some new Amish contraption? It was still far enough away that, whatever it was, it posed no threat, and he watched with interest. The kitchen door opened and Crystal joined him, the coffeepot in her hand.

"What is that thing?" she said, squinting.

"That I cannot tell you. I'm taking a wait-and-see approach."

"It looks like a giant lame bird. Maybe it heard about your lame bird sanctuary."

It was about a quarter of a mile away and they both kept their eyes trained on it. Another few seconds and then, all at once, the slow labor of the creature on the road resolved itself in William T.'s vision and he jumped up and off the porch.

"It's Mallie Williams," he said to Crystal.

Down across the lawn and then down the road he went. He could still run in those days—almost fourteen years ago now—and it took him only a minute to reach her.

"Mallie? Mallie?"

She looked up and smiled. Nine years old, pulling her little brother in the wagon behind her, all the way from their house, a full half-mile down the hill. She was wearing overalls and the Mao cap she wore all the time back then because her father, Starr, who had died only months before, had loved China. It was the Mao cap that got to him most. That and the fact that Charlie, wrapped in a blanket and sitting

in the wagon, seemed perfectly content. Her face was flushed from
exertion.

"Hi, William T."

This was in the early days of her conviction that otherwise, people would confuse them, seeing as they shared the name William,
partly anyway. Which had made him laugh out loud — big, rough
man that he was and scrawny little girl that she was — but she had
persisted. Mallie Williams was nothing if not persistent. And now
he was known only as William T., even to Crystal.

"What are you doing out on this fine summer morning?"

Instinctively, he kept his voice calm and conversational. He smiled
down at her, this little girl who had so recently lost her father.

"We're coming to visit you."

"Well, I'm glad to hear that. It's very neighborly of you. Want to
hop in the wagon and I'll pull you the rest of the way?"

She looked up at him and back at the wagon, considering. A car appeared from around the bend at the bottom of the hill, and he posi-
tioned himself between the road and the wagon. Best to put something, even if it was just his big body, between the oncoming car and
these two little kids.

"You could keep your brother company," he said. "He's sitting by
himself back there."

That was the right thing to say. She frowned and nodded — there
should be no lonely brothers in this world — and he picked her up
and set her down behind Charlie and tucked the blanket around them
both.

"Your mother know where you are, Mallo Cup?" he said, and
looked back to see her not looking at him. "No?" She shrugged. This
was before most people had cell phones. He pictured Lucia, frantic in
the house, calling around to see if anyone had seen her babies.

"She's still asleep," Mallie said. "We decided to go on an adventure.
Right, Charlie?"

"Right, Charlie," the boy echoed.

"Once upon a time there was a sister," Mallie said, and, "Once upon
a time there was a brother," Charlie echoed.

"I'm teaching him the Once Upon a Time game," Mallie explained to William T., who had never heard of the game but nodded anyway. Mallie was known for making up games, and he approved. Games were a good distraction from grief. So were knock-knock jokes, his personal specialty.

William T. pulled them up the hill, the wagon wheels rumbling behind. Crystal was waiting for them in the kitchen, having already called Lucia to tell her the children were safe — Mallie was right; she had been still asleep — and she and William T. made them some scrambled eggs and toast. Afterward, Crystal taught Mallie how to make hummingbird nectar.

"It's a four-to-one ratio of water to sugar," she said. "Bring it to a boil and let it cool."

The four of them had sat on the porch and watched the humming-birds. They were like giant bees, thrumming and buzzing, long beaks dipping in and out of the bright-red feeder. It was birds from that point on, with Mallie Williams. With Lucia's permission, she walked up the road whenever she wanted, always with a new bird fact in hand. Did he and Crystal know that some cultures viewed birds as the spirits of recently dead? Or as harbingers of death? Did they know that hummingbirds could hover upside down? That they had to drink more than their own weight in nectar every day? That every night when they were asleep they slipped into a torpor?

"What the hell's a torpor? Never heard the word."

"It's a kind of hibernation," she had said patiently. "An overnight hibernation."

Mallie had been the one to spot the hummingbird nest in the young willow next to the garage one morning, as they sat on the porch. It was spring, a cool day, and she was wearing the red jacket she always wore back then because hummingbirds loved red. He watched her eyes narrow, then widen, then she leaned forward and held herself still.

"William T.," she whispered, and he followed her pointing finger. "A nest."

He squinted. "That's a knot," he said. "A nestlike knot. Your eyesight's going, Mallo Cup. Poor kid, only nine years old, with failing eyesight."

"Wrong. It's a nest, and it's a hummingbird nest."

He got up to prove her wrong but she was right. "Well Jesus H. Christ," he said. "That's a hell of a camouflage job. Guerrilla fighters, these hummingbirds are, aren't they?"

She nodded. Did she have any idea what a guerrilla fighter was? Look at her, willing to go along with him, come what may and come whatever he said. If he had ever had a daughter, he would have wanted her to be like Mallie. He and Crystal had told themselves they were like Mallie and Charlie's uncle and aunt, a second home, a refuge, if need be. That was one reason he had fought Lucia for guardianship.

———

Three days after the C-section, after one more anonymous message from the kind nurse, William T. and Crystal had gotten back in the truck and headed to the hospital at dawn one more time. They had vowed to witness whatever they could. They were doing it for Mallie. Charlie had stayed home again. He wanted nothing to do with it.

They parked three long blocks away this time — they didn't want to risk anyone seeing them — and made their way through the woods on the shortcut path between the hospital and the strip mall. It was quiet that early. Faint fluorescence glowed through the propped-open employee door in back of the Thai Garden as they walked past, and the *chop-chop-chop* of a knife, a machete from the thunk of it, came to their ears.

Crystal walked ahead. She was light of foot and incapable of walking slowly. When they hiked, sometimes she got a switchback or two ahead of him before she noticed.

The scrubby patch of lawn next to the employee lot was quiet when they arrived. All the cars familiar to them from many months of visiting were there: the white Ford, the rusted-out Buick, the gleaming Honda Accord. And the same battered red bicycle was locked to the bike rack. The marchers, if there were any, would be out front with their signs. The news crews too, if there were any. But maybe William T. and Crystal were the only ones, thanks to the kind nurse, who knew that today was the hand-off day.

It happened fast. Like this: the back door opened and a man and a woman, along with Lucia, backed out. Aaron and Melissa Stampernick, family law attorney and social worker, husband and wife. And Lucia. She looked thinner than the last time William T. had seen her, her cheekbones prominent. She cradled a blanketed bundle that could only contain her premature-but-healthy grandson. She walked in a protective, carrying-a-baby way toward a blue sedan, whose lights winked on and then off: one of the Stampernicks must have pressed a remote. Aaron glanced right, left, and then his eyes fastened on them. He drew himself up, ready to speak if he had to. To fight, if he had to. Crystal's breath was quick and light but she said nothing.

Lucia was standing in front of the car door, which was open. Aaron Stampernick stared at William T. and Crystal, then turned to his wife and Lucia and pulled something out of his pocket. A cell phone. The man held the phone before his eyes and said something to Lucia, who was bending over the baby, and she stood straight and smiled for the camera. An imaginary book of imaginary photos swam up in William T.'s mind, a book full of photos of a baby and a toddler, first day of school, last day of school, birthday parties and Christmas trees bright with ornaments.

Crystal brushed tears away with the back of her hand. He put his hand on her elbow. There was nothing they could do about it. The baby was in the world now, and Lucia would raise him as her own. The days and nights and months would pass and Mallie would be unaware of them. That baby would grow into a boy, and then a man, separate and apart from the woman who had given birth to him, and all the people besides her mother who loved her.

Unless things were different now. Unless, with Mallie back, the rules had changed.

Mallie

MALLIE SAT CROSS-LEGGED ON A MOTEL BED ON THE OUT-skirts of Utica. White walls, white bedspread, white pillows. She had loosely organized the contents of William T.'s box into four piles that rose around her on the bed: Mallie, Darkness, Time, Pain. She was Mallie, the rapist was Darkness, Time was a long sky filled with dark birds, all the months she had slept through. And Pain was everywhere, laced throughout the letters to the editor and newspaper articles piled in William T.'s cardboard box, in lines like *Everybody knows her face now.*

Which was a lie.

The face that everybody thought they knew was the face they had seen online and in newspapers and on the television screen. But there were plenty of other photos of her. There was a photo of Lucia pregnant with her. A photo of her father, Starr, pushing her down the sidewalk in front of Crystal's Diner. A photo at the end of the driveway, waiting for the school bus, on the first day of school every year. On tricycles. Bikes. Ice skates. In her purple and gold robe at high school graduation. A photo of her and Charlie holding hands in front of a Christmas tree bright with lights.

She pulled out her phone and called her brother. No answer. This was the fourth time she had tried him. She pictured him staring down at the blinking screen of his phone, out there wherever he was in Pennsylvania. *Pick up pick up pick up,* she willed him. *I need to talk to you.* But he didn't.

When Charlie was three years old, she had made up a game called Questions, trying to keep their father's memory alive in him. What had their father liked to eat, what had he spent his days doing, what was the song he used to sing to them? Questions upon questions, and Charlie would recite the answers. She had been a child herself, nine years old. Back then she used to wonder about spirits, and if the spirit of a person could still be in the world after they were dead. She had wondered about reincarnation: If it was real, could you be reborn as another human being? As an animal? A bird? Was her father's spirit somewhere in the sky, migrating above her?

Then the game of Questions morphed into the game of Once Upon a Time. Charlie had been a quiet, reserved little boy. It was hard for him to talk about things that he worried or wondered about. Making up a story together—eight words per sentence because he liked to count on his fingers—became a means to improvise their way through hard times.

She had always been his protector, his confidante, his translator to the world. But now he wouldn't pick up the phone. Her connection to her brother: one more thing that had disappeared. Charlie was gone and Zach was gone and William T. was so on edge she couldn't stand being around him. And the baby—the fact of him, his existence in this world—that was something so big, and so bewildering, that she couldn't get her head around it all. Piles of documents, evidence of all the months she had slept through, rose around her on the bed, boxing her in with all the answers they didn't contain.

Who: An unknown male. Based on DNA evidence, no known previous criminal record.

Relationship, if any, to the victim: None. None of the men she knew and loved in her life or from her past, none of the MVCC classmates she had sat next to and studied with, bought coffee with, laughed and talked with, would ever hurt her. Unless?

Age: Young. But maybe not?

Occupation: Something. But maybe not?

Family: No. No one who did that would have a family. No one who did that would look a parent or a sister or a brother or a girlfriend or a wife or a child in the eye and be able to keep on living. Unless maybe he would?

Physical description: Strong. Not weak. Because if she could have, she would have fought. She would have fought him for her life.

So Darkness was a mystery. Faceless and placeless. Dark bird hiding in the heart of a man. It made her skin crawl to think about. This motel room made her skin crawl too. It was too white. Too quiet. Too much like St. John's rehab. Who could she talk to?

Just then her silenced phone flashed bright with an incoming call, like an answer to her quandary, and she snatched it up. WILLIAM T. JONES.

She let it flash until it stopped. She couldn't talk to him even though he kept calling. William T. was too heavy, too worried. He had been through too much. He was too *invested*, was the word that came to her. Too close to her. Hurt by proximity. His old flock of lame birds came back into her mind and how he used to shoo away the mean rooster to keep him from pecking at her. How he and Crystal used to scramble eggs for her and Charlie on sunny mornings. How he used to call their names in that giant voice of his from the big green John Deere across the field. All the knock-knock jokes he had kept telling her, years after she'd outgrown them, his big body bent double with laughter.

Was there anyone in the world she could be an ordinary girl with, have an ordinary conversation with? She fished Beanie's number out of her pocket.

SO HOW'S THE STAND-UP GOING?

After a minute the screen flashed.

COULDN'T BE BETTER. KNOCK, KNOCK.

WHO'S THERE?

WOODEN SHOE.

WOODEN SHOE WHO?

WOODEN SHOE LIKE TO HEAR ANOTHER JOKE?

She laughed. It sounded strange in the quiet motel room, just her and the phone and the laugh. Wooden Shoe was the oldest knock-knock joke in the world. It was one of William T.'s favorites.

KNOCK, KNOCK. She tapped the letters in one by one.

WHO'S THERE?

DEWEY.

DEWEY WHO?

DEWEY HAVE TO GO THROUGH THIS EVERY TIME?

DAMN FINE JOKE THERE, M.W. AND, YES WE DO. IT'S CALLED WARMING UP THE CROWD.

Beanie's flashing grin, his yellow hat, the white worms of his mop wiggling over the shining floor, were among her strongest memories from St. John's.

BEANIE?

YEAH?

HOW AM I GOING TO GET THROUGH THIS?

Dammit. That was not something that an ordinary girl having an ordinary conversation would say. She looked around the white room again, white walls, white bedspread. She suspended the phone above her head with both hands and waited. *Keep working*, they had said. *Your recovery will be consistent with your determination.* She lowered the phone and raised it, lowered it and raised it, waiting for Beanie's response.

I DON'T KNOW, he wrote. ABSORB IT, I GUESS?

BUT HOW?

MAKE UP SOME KIND OF STORY, MAYBE. A STORY THAT LETS THE MESS IN BUT LETS YOU OUT. YOU KNOW?

JUST MAKE UP A STORY? LIKE ONCE UPON A TIME?

MAYBE. WHY NOT?

But where to begin? *Once upon a time a girl was assaulted. Once upon a time a girl got pregnant. Once upon a time a girl gave birth to a baby who was alive and in the world. Once upon a time the girl's boyfriend left her. Once upon a time dark birds surrounded the girl.* What could she make up to counteract any of it?

She left the piles of papers in the stale motel room and stepped outside into the cool air of late afternoon. Across the street was Beautiful You Wigs, tucked between Trusty Hardware and the China Garden Buffet. *Everybody knows her face now.* Oh, hell no, they didn't. She crossed the street and checked out the wigs: A Dolly Parton–like platinum mound of curves and waves. A jet-black pixie. A tousled strawberry-blonde, a snowy cap of white. A swingy blue-green bob. She pushed open the door.

A heavy woman behind the counter, a pencil in her hand, looked up from a dark grid of columns and numbers.

"Help you?"

"How much is that blue-green one in the window?"

The woman laid the pencil down and hauled herself up. She eased the wig up off its faceless Styrofoam head and peered inside.

"Twenty-six ninety-nine. Want to try it on?"

Mallie stood in front of the mirror and pulled her own hair back with the elastic the woman handed her. Shiny, synthetic blue-green hair swished around her jawbone. The cursed bangs were hidden.

"Not trying to drive off business," the woman said, "but your hair is real pretty just the way it is. Why a wig?"

Because everybody knows my face now. But this woman didn't seem to recognize her.

"Can I ask you a question?" she said, disregarding the woman's question. "If you saw me on the street wearing this wig, would you recognize me?"

"Honey, I don't know you to begin with."

Which was proof. Right? Mallie handed the wig lady two twenties from Burl's stash and watched as she folded the wig in half — it was unsettling to watch, as if she were squeezing a human head into something much too small — and put it in a Beautiful You plastic bag. Mallie pushed the door open and emerged onto the cracked pavement.

"Mallie? Oh my God. Mallie."

A girl stood in front of her there on the sidewalk in front of the wig store. Charlie's old friend Amanda. Mallie's legs went shaky and she sat down on the curb. Amanda used to relax her hair but she'd let it go natural, a beautiful highlighted cloud around her oval face. A tiny stud glittered just below her lower lip. She and Charlie had been friends since middle school. The two of them used to share saltine and butter sandwiches at lunch; they loved the way the butter spiraled up through the tiny holes in the saltines. Now Amanda sat down next to Mallie. Her fingers were covered with rings, huge and black and spiked and leather.

"It *is* you, right?" she said again. Shyness, confusion, recognition flitted across her face. "Don't worry," she said softly. "I won't tell any-one."

Amanda had been a shy middle-schooler, and that shyness was still in her despite the rings and the haircut and the gold stud.

"When it happened I cut your picture out of the paper and I taped it up above my desk," she said. "Not the horrible photo, not that one," she added quickly. "I mean the good one. The pretty one. And I prayed for you every night. I mean, not *pray* pray, I'm not a religious freak like all the ones that were fighting over you, but just, you know. Charlie and I texted all the time when it happened. And for months, I mean, we still do."

The girl was babbling. Her hands worried themselves together in her lap.

"Do you talk to Charlie?" Mallie said.

"Yeah. I mean, we . . ." She looked away, then back. "We hung out a lot. When it happened. Which maybe you didn't know."

"Charlie lives in Pennsylvania now. I don't really know why, though."

"Well," the girl said, uncertainty in her voice. "I mean, you talk to him, don't you?"

Mallie shook her head, but Amanda was talking again.

"I'm just so glad you came back from the dead. I mean not dead, obviously, but from wherever you were. I won't tell. But it must be crazy, right? To find everything out. Like to find out about the baby, and know he's out there? Would you ever try to get him back?"

Mallie closed her eyes.

"I'm sorry," Amanda said. "What a stupid thing to say."

"Charlie doesn't pick up when I call."

"I know. I tell him he should. We text all the time. But, guilt. Like if he hadn't gotten drunk, he wouldn't have called you, you wouldn't have driven down and the whole thing would never have happened. The same story he goes over again and again."

"He has to get through that. Because I'm still here. I'm still *me.*"

Her voice cracked. Next to her, Amanda was quiet. Mallie kept her eyes closed so she wouldn't have to see pity on her face. But the girl surprised her. "Charlie wants to talk to you," she said. "He wants to get through this. He just doesn't know how."

———

Back at the motel, Mallie gathered up the contents of William T.'s box and put them back into it and closed it up as tightly as she could. Worn-down corners and sagging sides. The box that told the whole story and none of the story. Next to it sat the box of possible futures. It hadn't seemed right to leave it in the truck, where someone might steal the fortunes that belonged only to her and Zach. It didn't seem right to have it here in the motel room either. The box of possible futures belonged on its high shelf in the cabin mudroom, ignored until there were more cookies to add to the pile.

She lay back on the motel bed and put her hands on her stomach. If she were not herself but a client, she would place her hands on her shoulders and breathe in deeply and let it out slowly. She would oil her hands and rub them together to spark warmth, then begin. First the heavy egg of the head, cradled in both her hands. *Relax the muscles of your neck and let me support your head,* was how she usually began. People were not used to letting go. Not used to letting their heads be supported by another's hands. She would press her fingers hard into the client's scalp. In the beginning her teacher had told her to press harder than seemed right, that harder was better than light, and the teacher had been right. Mallie had learned to hold a client's head in her hands, fingers pressing tight, until the first deep exhale came. Sometimes it took a long time, minutes, even, but that was all right. She was patient. She would wait.

From the skull, she would move to the face, fingers pressing and smoothing the forehead. The rim of the eye sockets. The cheekbones. The jawline. By now the client's eyes were usually closed. The deeper letting-go had begun. This was when the stories could be drawn out of the body, spun slowly into the quiet air of the massage room. It was not a fast process. It took time.

You won't be able to do it to yourself, the teacher had warned them. *Sad, but true. You can only work your magic on someone else.*

The reports said that the police hypothesized that she had fought, that she had tried to chase the attacker down the block before he hit her with the clay pot. Charlie had seen her after the fact, splayed on the sidewalk, when the first responders arrived. Poor brother.

And poor William T. The media must have tracked him like a bloodhound. She would have been able to figure that out from the locks on the door alone, the changed home phone number, the existence of a cell phone—William T.? A cell phone?—and the way he looked around before he got out of his truck, before he walked into a place like the diner, the way he had jumped to his feet at Burl's late-night knock. It must have been hard on him, watching her head out alone in the Datsun. No, not hard. Awful. Panicky awful.

How that night had happened, every step of it after she got out of the truck and walked down the shining sidewalk, was a series of questions without answers.

Maybe she had gotten tired of waiting for Charlie. Maybe she'd decided to go for a walk in the rain while she waited. She had walked down the sidewalk. Her truck had been found parked in front of the apartment building where the party was, where she must have parked it, because it was still locked and the key had been in her pocket.

She remembered the sidewalk, gleaming with rain under the streetlight, and a rainbow swirl on the street. Exhaust, or oil, or a combination of both. She must have stepped over the sidewalk cracks because she always did, so as not to break her mother's back if she could avoid it. Seen the rainbow swirl on the street beneath the streetlight at the end of the block and stopped to admire it. Then what?

Then nothing.

Then nothing, nothing, nothing, nothingnothingnothingnothingnothingnothing, on and on an endless *nothing*, until a touch on her arm and the sound of a familiar voice. William T. Jones, who insisted she had said something about dark birds. The invisible dark birds that lived inside a person and ate away at their soul? Or real-life dark birds? Like the ones that had appeared to her when she was a little girl. She had come across the young willow next to William T.'s garage, quivering and quaking with darkness against the reds and yellows and oranges of its neighbors. She had stood and stared at the tree, convulsing against a blue September sky, until she realized that birds had engulfed it and blotted out its original shape.

This had happened just as William T. was beginning to teach her about birds, when she was obsessed with the hummingbirds that flitted to the feeder that hung by his porch. She was full of questions about birds, migratory birds, in particular. Soaring birds like raptors, birds that depended on thermals to lift them and carry them away, migrated during the day. Most land birds that migrated long distances, like thrushes and sparrows, tended to lift off at night. They sometimes congregated in a single tree, waiting for the wind, waiting for a signal, waiting for a flicker of something only they could understand, until they lifted off en masse.

She had stood watching that tree made of birds, filled with wonder and then horror, because it was the hummingbird nest tree.

"William T.! William T.!" she'd screamed, but she hadn't waited for him to hear her and come running. The nest was in danger and she ran straight at the tree, windmilled her arms and screamed at the dark birds. "Leave those babies alone!" She had watched as they whooshed into the sky, a hovering cloud that vanished down the valley.

And now she herself had flown away to a motel on the outskirts of north Utica and gotten herself a room.

In the past year and a half, the blinking *e* in the neon sign of Crystal's Diner had been replaced. A stretch of Route 274 had been repaved. There was now a handicapped ramp winding along the walk to the front door of a little green house on Elm Street. The people she loved looked the same, but older. Careworn. Lines at the sides of Crystal's eyes fanned out wider, and two grooves ran from the sides of William T.'s nose to the corners of his mouth. Her brother, Charlie, was now *Charles*. Zach had moved to Montana.

Once upon a time there was a girl
who was the same, except that she wasn't.

William T.

_____

THE DAY ZACH MILLER HAD TAKEN OFF, HE HAD PULLED INTO the driveway and left the engine running and the door open. He walked straight up to the porch, where William T. was waiting. For what, he didn't know, but he had woken up with the sense of something invisible changing then and there, and out to the porch he had come to wait until he knew what it was. Zach's truck shook slightly, there in the driveway, as if it were being held on the gravel against its will.

"William T.," Zach said. "I came to say goodbye."

So this was the something invisible. Something else William T. didn't want to happen — Zach Miller leaving — was happening. Another thing he couldn't stop.

"Where you going?"

"Away. I can't stand not being with her and I can't stand what they're making her do. They keep insisting this is what she'd want but they don't know shit. This is what *they* want."

William T. had felt himself nod against his will. But did Zach think the nodding meant that William T. was giving him his blessing to abandon Mallie? Because he wasn't. Zach turned to the truck and whistled. Out came Sir, bounding onto the porch, dancing and nosing William T.'s legs in the delighted way he always greeted him.

"Can you and Crystal take care of Sir?"

"You're not taking him with you?"

"I don't know what kind of life it'd be for him, wherever I end up."
Words pushed up against the back of William T.'s throat, battling to get out. What more kind of life could a dog want than a life with Zach, who, along with Mallie, had taken care of him since the night they had hauled him out of that dumpster? What the hell was wrong with Zach that he couldn't see that? *You can't just abandon the creatures who love you,* he tried to say, but the words wouldn't come out.

"No?" Zach said, and William T. nodded. No. He and Crystal couldn't take Sir. Not because they wouldn't want him and didn't love him. But because Sir was a symbol of Zach and Mallie, their past and present and future. Taking Sir would be messing with fate, somehow. Zach leveled his hazel gaze at William T. and waited, but all William T. could do was shake his head.

"Okay," Zach said. "I'll take him to Trish's, then. She always told us if he ever needed a new home"—his voice trailed off. Sir was looking up at him intently, his tail moving back and forth in a searching way. Trish the dog sitter. Trish the dog lover.

"Mallie could still get better."

There. Finally some words had come. He squinted up at Zach Miller. Damn the sun and its pitiless glare. Zach just looked at him.

"That's a long shot at this point," Zach said. "And even if she did, look." He pulled his wallet out of his back pocket, flipped it open and held it out like an offering to William T., pointing to an empty slot in the wallet. "See that space? That's where that photo was."

"What photo?"

But even as he said the words, William T. knew. Mallie, dancing in the sun at her graduation party, the photo that was everywhere, that would live forever in the heads of strangers. So this was where the beautiful photo used to live, in the calm darkness of Zach Miller's wallet.

"They stole it from you?" William T. said. Those bastards. Vultures, going into a grieving boy's wallet and stealing the photo of his girlfriend. But Zach was shaking his head.

"I gave it to them."

"No, you didn't." William T. handed the wallet back to Zach, Zach Miller, who was a profoundly private person, Zach, who would never give something so intimate to the vultures. "You wouldn't do that."

"I did, though. They were working on her and I was standing there and you were talking to the EMTs and they wouldn't let me near her and they found out I was her boyfriend and they came swarming over and they asked me if I had a photo—they said it would help—"

"How. How would it help."

"They said it would. I figured the police, maybe? The investigation? I was too stupid to think it through, that they wanted her for their property like everyone else. And that if I gave the photo to them, it would be there forever, for anyone who punched in her name."

Zach stood in front of William T., not trying to apologize or excuse. That dark night on that dark street flung itself up in William T.'s mind, followed by the drive to the hospital and the fluorescent-lit hospital hallway that came afterward, where he had talked with the cops and then the EMTs, while Zach, a rigid shadow, had stood against the wall. He looked now at the young man before him, standing there with his arms at his sides, and his anger disappeared.

"It's not your fault."

"It's none of our faults," Zach said. "But when does it stop? That's my question."

He and Zach and Crystal had within months been turned into shadow people, the silent, off-to-the-sides witnesses, while their girl was fed upon by people who didn't know her and didn't love her, all with Lucia's permission. Charlie had turned into a man, a fierce and angry man, when up until then he had been a reserved and gentle boy.

"I love her," Zach said.

"I know you do, son."

That—"son"—undid the both of them. William T. put his arms around the boy, who started to weep, the first time William T. had ever known Zach Miller to cry. After a while Zach got back into his truck, which had been shuddering impatiently the whole time, and disappeared down the road.

———————

After dinner, William T. lowered himself onto the front step, the scent of cut wood rising from the pile next to him, and fished the little phone out of his pocket. The tiny screen glowed and he fumbled for the right button. A single push and her name came shining up.

He pressed her name and watched the green phone symbol light up.

It rang and rang and he sat there and let it. The night would come when she would pick up, wouldn't it? When the "call fail" symbol appeared, he slipped the phone back into the recesses of his pocket and sat there. The last time he'd spoken with Charlie—Charles— the boy had been impatient.

"William T., listen to me," he had said. "Maybe you think you're helping Mallie by spending every minute of every day worrying about her, but you're not. All this worry and panic and darkness, it's like a disease. It does her no good."

"You turning New Age on me, Charlie?"

"Charles. And she's tougher than you think. She'll call if she wants to," Charlie said. "She needs to get her life back, William T., and so do you, and so do I."

The boy had changed. Was it Amanda's influence? Amanda, with the dark cloud of hair and the many rings and the shy way that hid a core of steel; Amanda, who'd been his friend since elementary school; Amanda, who had become his sounding board in the absence of Mallie. Had Charlie and Amanda fallen in love? Because love could do that to a person, make you fierce and strong in ways you hadn't known before. Now William T. looked up at the sky and arrowed his thoughts and sent them winging over the land to wherever Mallie might be: *Bless her and keep her safe.* William T. had given up on the idea of a benevolent God, because what kind of benevolent God would let such misery exist? He still believed, or tried to believe, that there was something beyond himself. Because he himself was not enough. That had been proven.

The kitchen door opened and then Crystal eased herself down onto the step next to him. He put his arm around her.

"What are you doing out here, William T.?"

"Talking to God."

He sensed surprise travel through her body. "I didn't know you talked to God."

"I don't even believe in God. But I talk anyway."

She leaned against him and put her cheek against his so that they were looking up at the same angle. The stars were brightening now, as night deepened, and the Milky Way was visible, a dusty veil drawn over part of the sky. Headlights blinked and stuttered their way along Williams Road. There was a time, only weeks ago, when he would have assumed they were coming for them. For a statement, an update, maybe hoping he would get angry and start cursing on camera, the way he had in the beginning. Back then they had chased him down whenever a new crisis arose—Mallie's pregnancy, the birth of the baby, the news of Lucia's diagnosis—but now no one appeared in person. Dozens of unanswered messages left on the home voice-mail, yes, but no cars. No television cameras. Maybe they were all afraid of him.

"William T., I keep thinking about what if she wants the baby," Crystal said. "What then?"

He shook his head. If she wanted that baby, if she was going to try to get that baby, wrest it away from its foster parents, he did not know how he would cope. He did not have the strength it took to contemplate the idea of Mallie ending up with the child he had been so against from the beginning. Let alone what it would take from him to look at that baby and not imagine, every single time he did, how the child had come to be.

––––––––

When Crystal had gone inside to bed, William T. opened up his phone to call her again but stopped at the sight of his outgoing calls: Mallie. Mallie. Mallie. Mallie. Mallie. Mallie. Mallie. Mallie. Mallie. Mallie. Mallie.

Jesus.

She needs to get her life back, William T., and so do you.

His life was worrying about Mallie and watching over Mallie and wondering what Mallie was thinking about at that very moment. Maybe Charlie was right and he was driving himself and everyone around him nuts. The image of Crystal by herself, dancing in the late-afternoon air of the diner's kitchen, came into his mind. The Vienna waltz.

He opened up the search bar on the phone. Crystal had shown him how to use it, but goddammit, these tiny phones were a pain in the ass. He poked at the letters with his thick, slow index finger:

W and A and L and T and Z.

Shouldn't this phone be easier by now? Shouldn't he have mastered at least the basics of typing on it? He kept on typing. HOW and TO.

How to Waltz Dance for Beginners.

Learn to Waltz.

How to Dance Waltz — Basic Beginner Routine.

How to Waltz — Swing and Sway.

How to Do a Waltz Ladies' Underarm Turn.

Was it possible to teach yourself how to dance?

Mallie

WHEN MALLIE WAS FOUR, AFTER A SERIES OF INFECTIONS, the doctors told her parents that her tonsils had to come out. *All the ice cream you want*, they had told her, *all the Popsicles, all the ice chips*. When she woke up, though, it was impossible to eat the ice cream and Popsicles they brought her. Her throat was on fire. It hurt even to open her mouth. All she could do was shake her head. There had been nothing between the memory of *All the ice cream you want* and the new memory of waking up with a fiery throat in a small bed next to a window.

But in all the years since they cut the tonsils out of her, had her body secretly carried inside it the memory of a slicing knife? And in all the months between the night of the shining sidewalk and now, did her body secretly know exactly what happened to it? What if every muscle and bone and artery and cell, somewhere way deep down, remembered?

The facts of the past were known. The reasons behind them weren't. And now that she was back, neither was the future. Making up a story from it all was like solving an algebraic equation, which was something she used to love doing.

Their high school math teacher, Ms. Bailey, had told them to use their imaginations when it came to solving word problems, algebraic equations and geometry proofs. That there was more than one way to solve a problem, even if at first inspection, it seemed unsolvable. Everything could be resolved, according to Ms. Bailey, even if the solution was unexpected, ungainly and messy. No matter how hard it seemed, if they only used their imagination and their knowledge, they could figure out a way to make it work.

Pretend the problem is a mystery that doesn't want to be a mystery, she had said. *The problem wants to be known. It wants to be seen. It wants to be understood. Help it be not a mystery.*

One late night two years into her practice at Northwoods Therapeutic Massage, Mallie had explained her work to William T. in terms of stories and secrets. That everyone's body contained them. That it was possible to understand those secrets and stories by the laying on of hands.

"The laying on of hands?" he said. "Isn't that a religious thing?"

She shrugged. "I don't know. I'm not religious. There's a lot of hard stories out there, William T.—that's what I do know."

She had begun at that point to volunteer as massage therapist at the women's shelter in Utica. Those women's stories were the hardest, both to listen to and to ease. Violence and fear ingrained itself into muscle memory, even into bone, and the women were often afraid of even gentle touch. They had to learn how to re-enter their own bodies, how to inhabit their own skin, how to own themselves. How to shake off the dark birds.

That conversation with William T. haunted her. Her own body must hold an impossible story now. A dark bird had gained entrance to her. They waited everywhere in the world, invisible, ready to invade someone's body and spirit. When a boy marched into a school spraying bullets, dark birds watched from above. When a man stood behind a pulpit and proclaimed to know the only truth, dark birds beat their wings over the congregation. When a man pushed a girl down on the pavement, dark birds were there, gathered on the man's shoulders.

The piles rose around her on the bed: Time and Pain and Darkness and Mallie. An unknown man had robbed her and raped her and bashed her head with a flowerpot. She had been taken to the ER with a head injury. She had been unconscious far longer than expected because of a subsequent brain infection. She had been pregnant. Despite passionate arguments to abort the fetus, the pregnancy was allowed to continue. At thirty-six weeks the baby had been delivered via C-section and placed with her mother, Lucia, and, upon her mother's death, and as a result of a sealed custody hearing, with unknown others. Months later, she had emerged from unconsciousness and begun her recovery. In all these things, she'd had no say in the matter. No choice. And it was too late now to have any choice. Wasn't it?

KNOCK, KNOCK.

WHO'S THERE?

ANNIE.

ANNIE WHO?

ANNIEBODY READY TO HEAR A NEW KNOCK-KNOCK JOKE?

DAMN, M.W. THAT'S A HELL OF A JOKE. WHERE'D YOU HEAR IT?

WILLIAM T.

NO SHIT? NOT SURE I'VE EVER SEEN THAT MAN SMILE.

Oh, but William T. had smiled. He used to smile all the time. He'd had a hundred and more knock-knock jokes, back when she and Charlie were little. Now they were coming back. But the William T. of her childhood, bellowing with laughter at every one of his knock-knock punch lines, was not the William T. of today. She sat on the bed, the phone warm and glowing in her hand.

She was already living in a future world. A world she'd been dropped into, a fate she hadn't chosen, in which a man she barely knew had given her a new nickname, and a man she knew better than almost anyone had turned grim and laughless. It was hard to remember fun. It had been a long time since she'd done anything but regain her strength. What was fun? Eating soft-serve from the Kayuta. Driving at night with the windows down. Playing Sequence with Charlie and Zach. Eating dinner with Charlie and Zach. Putting on music late at night and dancing in the living room with Zach while Charlie played DJ. She loved to dance. As if Beanie could read her mind, a little dancing-woman emoji appeared on the screen, and then he was gone.

She wanted to dance. She wanted to move. She wanted to work. She wanted to walk into the massage room and stand at the head of the table and feel the power of her own muscles and intuition to draw out the tired in another human being, to pull out the stress and tension and let it dissolve in a quiet room. She didn't want to be one of the women at the clinic, bruised and raw and hurt. She spread the fingers of her left hand and flexed them.

————

Charlie's name suddenly blinked up on the screen and she snatched up the phone. He spoke before she could say anything.

"I'm sorry, Mal."

"For what?"

"Not picking up. Not texting. I didn't know what to say. I still don't."

She was struck again by how much deeper and older his voice sounded.

"It's okay."

"It's not. Amanda called. She told me she saw you in Utica. She told me to call you. She told me you looked sad when she said my name."

"I *am* sad. I miss you."

"Well, I miss the way it used to be."

"It still feels like it *is* that way to me. Every day I wake up and remember that it's not. But in my head Mom is still alive and you and me and Zach are still in the cabin."

There was a pause, and then his voice came in a rush. "Mal. If I could, I would go back in time. I would make it so none of it happened in the first place. I would make it so nobody would know our names the way they do, and all those jars with your picture on them wouldn't exist, and there would be no baby out there. And Zach would still be Zach, not the asshole he turned out to be."

"Charlie. Don't call him an asshole."

"Why not?" His voice was shaking. But the word made her flinch. It was not possible to think of Zach Miller and the word "asshole" at the same time. She was caught between her brother and her boyfriend, the two she adored, and suddenly she was exhausted.

"How did you make it through this, Charlie?"

He barked a joyless laugh. "I didn't. All I did was get the hell out. I applied to Braxton and they gave me a full scholarship and I just . . .

left. And I'm going by "Charles" now. But that's as far as I've gotten. I haven't made it through anything."

"That makes two of us, then."

She pressed the phone to her ear and pictured her brother, wherever he was in Pennsylvania right now, with the glowing screen of his phone pressed to his own ear. Charlie didn't say anything for a minute. When he spoke again, his voice was soft. He sounded like himself. *He sounds like the Charlie you remember,* she corrected herself. *But he's changed. He's in a new life too.*

"You know what I think about, Mal?"

"What?"

"The nights you and Zach would be dancing and I'd be sitting on the couch playing DJ. That's what I think about the most."

"Yeah," she said, "me too."

She was afraid to keep talking because she might cry. And she didn't want her brother, there in his new life, to hear her crying. They *were* good nights, those nights at the cabin in Forestport when the future seemed wide open. It was too hard to think that those nights were over now, too disorienting to picture the cabin empty and dark, Zach and Charlie far away, so she didn't. Instead she conjured up the feeling of Zach's arms around her, their bodies moving together, her little brother searching his playlist for the next good song. The rule was that any song he played, they had to dance to, and they did. Smokey Robinson was Charlie's favorite. Any Smokey song. The three of them, the cabin with the strings of white lights they draped around the walls, she and Zach swaying around the room, each holding a beer, Charlie smiling to himself on the couch, calling up the songs.

William T.

T WASN'T EASY, TEACHING YOURSELF HOW TO WALTZ. HE TRIED watching some of the dance shows on television, but they were too intimidating. He wasn't some former celebrity trying to make a comeback with his dance moves, nor was he some teenager hoping for a showbiz break. He was a sixty-five-year-old man trying to learn how to waltz so that he could surprise his girlfriend with something that was new. Something new and uncomplicated and good. A good thing that had nothing to do with Mallie. A thing that would not drive her insane, if in fact he was driving Crystal insane. Charlie had told him that he needed to get his life back and he was trying to get his life back.

Practicing the waltz was easier when Crystal's nephew Johnny was visiting from his group home. A cord wrapped too tight around his neck at birth had given Johnny cerebral palsy, a slowed mind, few words. And an army of people who loved him and who he loved back. Crystal had raised him from infancy, and from infancy, Johnny had loved the color red. On Johnny weekends, everything red came out in force: red crayons, red throw pillows, red bowls and red spoons, red Popsicles. He sat at the table now, eating oatmeal out of a red bowl with a red spoon. William T. held his arms out to him.

"You want to try, Jonathan? Give it a whirl?"

Johnny laughed soundlessly at the sound of his proper name—Jonathan—and shook his head.

"You'd have to follow, because I only know how to lead. Correction: I'm *learning* how to lead."

William T. turned the volume up as loud as it could go on the computer and pulled up The Waltz Boss's channel on YouTube. The orchestra's waltz music swelled through the tinny speakers. He plucked up a couch cushion, clutched it to his chest like a dance partner and copied the Waltz Boss's motions as best he could.

"Did you know that waltzing originated with the peasants, Jonathan? True fact. The upper class favored the minuet. Or so says the Waltz Boss."

The Waltz Boss was William T.'s favorite YouTube instructor. The sheer number of how-to-waltz videos out there had been overwhelming at first. But they were easily weeded out, beginning with voice. Too high or too low, forget it. The Waltz Boss, although he was rotund and barely five feet two, had a striking baritone voice. He also always wore a bow tie clipped to his T-shirt, and each lesson included a Waltz Fact of the Day. William T. waltzed his cushion dance partner around the table where Johnny sat with his oatmeal. The cushion was square and dense and not at all like a living person in his arms, but he persevered.

"Am I getting better, Jonathan? Has the Waltz Boss worked his magic on me yet?"

Johnny laughed through a mouthful of oatmeal. Johnny's greatest laughs were both soundless and infectious, like now, when William T. started laughing in spite of himself. It felt strange to laugh, and wrong. How could he laugh when Mallie was somewhere out there, who knew where, and not calling him back? *She needs to get her life back, William T., and so do you.*

Start at the top of the box. Step forward with the left foot, then side with the right, then close with both together. Repeat. Repeat. Repeat. If you could just keep going like that, back and forth in a single small box, the waltz wouldn't be so bad. But no, you had to then rotate a quarter of a turn with every single combination.

"It's harder than it looks, Jonathan. But as the God in whom I have no certainty exists is my witness, I will waltz your aunt Crystal around this living room and this kitchen or else. Or else, I tell you, or else."

Johnny laughed while William T. danced on with the cushion in his arms. It was a workout, trying to learn to waltz with a burdensome couch cushion instead of a live human being. But he was getting there. Maybe.

"I'm trying, Jonathan," he said. "I'm trying."

He hadn't spoken to Charlie since the boy had told him that Mallie needed to get her life back. *And so do you,* Charlie had said. *I'll talk to you later.* He hadn't, though. Neither Charlie nor Mallie had called him. Burl had taken him aside at the post office this morning.

"Look, William T.," he had said. "Crystal told me that you go by the Stampernicks' house sometimes. You're going to drive yourself crazy with that. The hearing was a long time ago. The decision was made. And that baby will always be in the world. You have to come to peace with that."

"How?"

"However you can."

But the how eluded William T. It was hard to reconfigure your life. All the months that Mallie lay sleeping, he had been single-minded: Watch over her. Protect her. Don't let them do anything else to her. But where did that energy go, now that Mallie was back?

"She doesn't want to talk to you, old man," he said out loud. Johnny looked up inquiringly. "Not you, Jonathan. I'm not referring to you. You're a young man, remember?"

If Mallie had come back to the same world, maybe it would be easier to let go. But the cabin in Forestport was empty. Charlie was in Pennsylvania. Zach in Montana. And the baby somewhere in Utica. A familiar anger and sorrow washed through him. Had he messed it all up? If he hadn't told them in the beginning that Mallie was his daughter, so he could watch over her, would it have gone better for them all? Maybe if he hadn't lied, the court would have ruled in their favor. Crystal and Burl had told him over and over that he had done what seemed right at the time. That there was no going back. But the question still haunted him.

"Not everything comes down to blood and paper!" he had shouted

in the courtroom on the day of decree. "Take your goddamn docu-
ment and shove it!"

They should have listened to him. The lawyers and the judge and
Lucia and the flock that surrounded her should have thought things
over long and hard and answered honestly, from their hearts and
their consciences instead of the goddamn letter of the law. Did any
of them ever play it out in their minds, the way William T. did?

The image of Lucia Williams, pale and emaciated in her last days
on the television news, swam up into his head, that look on her face
when the reporter asked her about the decision to keep Mallie pregnant, about her impending death, about what would happen now
to the baby. Surrounded by the Faith Love flock, several of them
pressed close to her as if they would rather take the question. But the
reporter had kept the focus on her.

"I'm sorry," she had said.

"You're sorry about what? That you decided against terminating
your daughter's pregnancy?"

"I'm sorry about fate."

"The fate of your daughter? The fate of the baby? Your own fate?"

The reporter's voice was tight and serious, as if much depended
on the answers to these questions. William T. had sat forward on the
couch, watching. Anger and frustration filled him. It was too late by
then, wasn't it? Hadn't the future already been decided?

"I'm sorry," Lucia had repeated. Then the flock shepherded her
away and the same loop, that endless old loop, of dueling protesters
in the hospital parking lot filled the screen again. The thought had
come to William T. then that life was about more than protest. The
idea appeared to him like a mirage, and he tried to grasp it, but it
flew away. Lucia had died weeks later, when the baby was only three
months old.

From the house he drove south, up and down the giant hills of Glass
Factory Road. At the crest before the final downslope, a small fiery
panic of *Where is she? How is she?* rose up within him. He gulped it
back but there it stayed, a hurting lump in his throat.

"Why do you want to see Aaron Stampernick, William T.?" Crystal had said.

"Don't *you* want to see him? He's the one who caused all this. He's the one who knows where the baby lives now."

"He's *not* the one who caused all this. That was the rapist. Aaron Stampernick was appointed attorney for the child and he most likely did the best he could. And no, I don't want to know anything about the baby. That would only make it worse."

He took his foot off the gas and let the truck gather speed on its own, heading down toward the Utica floodplain, spread out flat and marshy below. Was Crystal right? Which was harder, to know that the baby was in this world, breathing the same air that all the rest of them were breathing, but have no idea what he looked or sounded like, or to see him in the flesh and forever after carry around the image of his face?

William T. didn't know. Maybe he was being dumb. Maybe he was playing with fate. Maybe he should just stop, but he couldn't. This was his ritual.

He eased onto Route 12 south, past the turnoff for the mall and then onto the side streets that brought him to the Foothills playground. Busy today, a cool early summer day. Parents and babysitters and babies and children all circled the equipment and the benches like bees in search of the last nectar. He sat down at the end of a bench in the shade of a mulberry tree and cast his glance around. Parents pushed their children on swings, an older couple was setting up a picnic on a picnic table, teenagers played Frisbee on the baseball diamond, toddlers stalked one another with plastic shovels in hand at the sand pit. A young man, his hand shading his eyes from the sun, half crouched to hold the hand of a small girl making her way to a bouncy-seat cricket.

The young man stood up and William T. saw his yellow cap. It was Beanie. Beanie, in that unnerving way that sometimes happened, must have sensed his presence, because he turned and met William T.'s eyes. When the little girl was settled on the bouncy cricket, he walked over and sat down by William T.

"My daughter," he said, nodding toward the child. "Danielle. How you doing, Mr. Jones?"

"I'm all right," William T. said cautiously. There was no reason he couldn't be here at the playground. It wasn't as if he were some kind of predator. He had every right to be here. *Stop being so defensive*, he silently lectured himself. Beanie was young to have a daughter. Was he married? Or was he co-parenting with a former girlfriend, as they did these days?

"How have you been, Mr. Jones?"

There was something preternaturally calm about the man, young as he was. Beanie must have seen a lot, there at the hospital, days and nights spent cleaning up after everyone who passed through those halls. He must have listened and watched and observed.

"Call me William T., okay?"

Beanie grinned. When he smiled, everything about his face changed. Everything about his being. It was a grin with magical, transformative powers that instantly eased William T.'s spirits.

"You talked to M.W.?"

"No," William T. said. "She took off and she won't return my calls."

"How many times you called her?"

"Dozens. Maybe a hundred."

"Ha," Beanie said. "Maybe that's why." He tilted his head and looked at William T. in an examining way. "What are you doing at this playground, anyway?"

"It's on my way. I'm just taking a break."

Beanie looked at him. Waiting. He knew it wasn't the real answer. The man was a psychic ninja orderly. He was willing to wait as long as it took. William T. felt himself giving in.

"The real reason I come here is because I keep thinking I might see him. The attorney, Aaron Stampernick. He knows where that baby is. It supposedly lives close by. And the fact of its existence torments me."

"Him," Beanie corrected him. "Not 'it.' And the fact of his existence isn't his fault. Right?"

"Maybe you haven't heard that Bible verse about the sins of the father."

"*The sins of the father shall be visited upon the child.* Yeah, I've heard it. He's just a little kid, though, William T. Like my girl over there."

"It's a hell of a lot more complicated than that. What if Mallie wants him back? You ever think how unbearable that would be?"

"It'd be *hard.* Hard, maybe. Not unbearable."

But Beanie was wrong. William T. could not get his mind around the idea of that child in their midst. That child with its genes. Child born of pain and cruelty and violence. He thought back to the days when Mallie and her brother were small, how he and Crystal had welcomed them into their lives. How they had played games with them—those mind-numbing childhood games of Candy Land and Chutes and Ladders and Mouse Trap—and told them jokes. Or William T. had told them jokes, anyway, mostly knock-knock jokes.

"You remember telling Mallie knock-knock jokes in Saint John's?" Beanie said suddenly. Jesus H. Christ, was he reading William T.'s mind? William T. shook his head in denial. Beanie was unnerving.

"You did," Beanie said. He chuckled. "I used to come in there to mop and there you'd be. 'Knock, knock, Mallo Cup, knock, knock.'"

"I don't remember that." And it was the truth. The only knock-knock jokes William T. recalled telling were from long ago.

"Oh, you did, though," Beanie said. "You used to whisper them to her. Like you were hoping she'd wake up and say, 'Who's there?'"

Mallie

S HE PINNED HER HAIR BACK AND PUT THE WIG ON.
"Nice," the motel clerk said.
"Does it look natural?"

"If you wanted it to look natural, you wouldn't have dyed it like that, would you? I mean, blue-green hair?"

But his voice was kind, and he smiled. She got in the truck and drove to her mother's church, Faith Love, next to a Friendly's ice cream and across the street from a While U Wait oil change. To the left of the steps was a fake cemetery of tiny white crosses. A lit-up sign listed times for Sunday and Wednesday services, and the sermon topic for that week: WHO DOES THE GRATEFUL ATHEIST THANK?

The church was little and white and tired-looking. She stood at the foot of its painted bright-green steps, trying to picture her mother and the congregants filing in and out. How could something so small have wielded so much power?

Lucia had joined the church in Mallie's first year of high school, when Charlie was in third grade. She began driving down to services every Wednesday and Sunday, took adult Sunday-school classes, took turns leading Bible Study every Friday evening. Mallie had been in favor of all this churchgoing at first, because it was clear that the church brought comfort and relief to Lucia. Once, at Lucia's urging, she had gone to a Sunday service with her mother. The minister talked softly, then loudly, then softly, about how Jesus had died for them, and how once they felt that, truly felt it — that kind of encompassing love—their lives would never be the same. Heads had nodded throughout the congregation. Mallie remembered the scarf her mother had knotted around her throat that day, orange and bright blue, like a parrot.

For a second, she missed her mother so fiercely that her knees buckled and she sank to the first step of the church.

It was awful to think that she hadn't been with her mother when Lucia died. She hadn't been there to hold her mother's hand, Charlie on the other side of the bed holding the other one. The three of them had not had a chance to come together, to find peace with one another, after the years of drifting apart. Mallie looked up at the closed doors of the church. A cross hung above them. That Jesus had died for them and their sins had always felt wrong to her. Like cheating. Weren't people supposed to take care of their own sins, by not committing them in the first place or atoning for them afterward? Had Jesus died for the man who raped her and left her for dead?

The first year or so of Lucia's newfound religion hadn't brought much change to their family. Mallie and Charlie had always been a united front, each more important to the other than their mother. When that had started, Mallie wasn't sure, but maybe in early childhood, after their father died. He had been the one who intuitively understood each of them. He had been lightness and laughter, whereas Lucia's personality was heavier. Solemn. Those had been the days of invention and escape: the Once Upon a Time game, the Questions game, the endless knock-knock jokes from William T.

As Lucia's faith deepened, though, things changed. Mallie thought of them as the Don't years. Don't forget to thank the Lord before you eat. Don't forget to say your prayers before bed. Don't dress immodestly.

"Don't dress *immodestly*, Mom?" Mallie had said. "Are you kidding me? Have the Amish rubbed off on you that much?"

"Don't take the name of the Lord in vain, Mallie."

"Good Lord, Mom. I didn't even mention the word *Lord*. Until right now."

The look on Lucia's face, grim and prim simultaneously, made her want to scream. What was her mother turning into? "Lord!" Mallie said. "Lord, Lord, Lordy Lord Lord." And watched as her mother steepled her hands together, lowered her head and began to pray for her daughter.

"It's like a scene out of a mockumentary," Mallie said to Zach later. "Next she'll be telling me to save myself for marriage."

Which is exactly what Lucia did, a week or two later.

"That train left the station a while ago," Mallie had informed her mother, and then watched as Lucia turned away in sorrow or revulsion—it was impossible to tell. For God's sake, her mother had been barely nineteen when she gave birth to Mallie. And she had adored Mallie's father, Starr. Surely she had had fun when she was young. Why turn to such a restrictive religion, so full of rules and judgment, at this point in her life? It was a few months later that both Mallie and Charlie, unable to stand what felt like their mother's rigidity and harshness, moved into the cabin in Forestport with Zach.

And yet her mother had found some kind of comfort, however unfamiliar to Mallie, in her church and her version of Jesus. Mallie wanted to understand that, if she could. She walked up the steps and pulled open the door to the church. Immediately inside was a little vestibule with bulletin boards on either side. Notices of church meetings, quotes from Scripture, photos from church picnics and celebrations.

And her. Mallie Williams.

There she was, in a special photo box that someone had nailed right into the cork bulletin board. That graduation photo and another photo of her in a hospital bed, bandages wrapped around her head and tubes snaking around her face and neck and arms. She'd never seen that one. William T. must not have seen it either, or he would have printed it out and stashed it in his cardboard box.

PRAY FOR OUR MALLIE AND HER UNBORN BABY, read the caption beneath it.

Slam.

She hit the box with the flat of her hand. She pounded it with the side of her closed fist, then tried to pull the whole box off the wall. *No. No. You don't get to see me like that anymore.* The box stayed firmly on the wall, and there was the sound of hurrying footsteps.

She turned then and tried to pull open the door. Yanked and yanked until a voice behind her said, "Miss, what are you—" and she shoved at the door instead and it opened. There was a hand on her shoulder, a hand that must have belonged to the voice, but she slapped it and spat, *Get your hand off me.* She took the steps two at a time and then she was back in the truck, tires spitting gravel.

———

Hassan's Superette appeared a few blocks away. William T. used to bring her and Charlie down to Utica for the brewery tour when they were little, and afterward he had brought them here. Hassan's hadn't changed. There was the row of tall glass candy jars where she used to buy sticks of root beer candy, twenty-five cents apiece. The money had come from William T., who would pay them a quarter apiece for small chores: sweeping the front porch of his house, picking peas and beans from his garden, polishing the banister with an old T-shirt.

"Child labor! I could be arrested for this!"

Mallie used to laugh when he said that but it had scared her. If William T. got arrested, what would they do? He was family. At night, if her mother and Charlie were asleep but not her, she used to look out the window into the darkness, up the hill in the direction of William T.'s house, to make sure that his always-on porch light was still on.

A television mounted high on the wall behind the counter was muttering in a background-noise sort of way. Ads. A green lizard inclined its head and danced across the screen. A shiny car roared up a mountain road and came to an instant stop at the edge of a cliff. A bottle of beer was yanked out of a cooler, beaded with condensation. Then a news anchor's mouth moved inaudibly against his fake-tan skin. Closed-captioning appeared across the screen below a photo —her graduation photo—self-correcting as it jerked along: "Assault victim Mallie Williams was recently released from long-term rehabilitation, raising questions once again about the identity and whereabouts of her assailant. New questions are also being raced . . . *raised* about the rolls . . . *role* of the Faith Love Church in the initial struggle over laggard . . . *legal* guardianship of Miss Williams. And the possible . . . *ultimate* question of all—What would Mallie have done, had she been awake to make the decision—remains unanswered. Miss Williams is unavoidable . . . *unavailable* for comment." The news anchor shook his coiffed head and pursed his lips, and then the screen cut to a commercial for erectile dysfunction.

"Help you?"

Hassan must have asked the question several times already because he was glaring at her from behind the cash register. She hadn't moved from the door way. Some people changed when they got older, as if they exchanged one body for another one, a shorter, slumpier, worn-in version. But Hassan was aging in place. His dark eyes and cropped black hair were exactly the same as she remembered. It felt as if she were hiding something, standing there with the blue-green bob pulled over her head. *You* are *hiding something*, she reminded herself.

"Sorry. I used to come in here when I was a little kid and it's weird to see it again after so long."

He nodded. No smile. He was a serious man. She walked over and picked a stick of root beer candy out of the glass jar at the far end.

"Thirty cents, miss."

When she was a child he had called her "kiddo." Now she was "miss."

"They used to be a quarter," she said.

"And now they're not."

She dug down in her pocket and hauled out a bill.

"A Benjamin? You're kidding, right?"

Heat flushed her face and she pulled out more bills. They were all hundreds, fifties, with a single twenty at the bottom of the pile. His face darkened but he said nothing.

"Sorry. Someone gave me a lot of money."

"I can see that."

He held the twenty in one hand and rang up the root beer stick in the other. The drawer popped open and he stepped back a half-step just before it hit him, the exact way he had done when she was a child. Then she saw the plastic jar to the right of the gum display. HELP BRING MALLIE BACK! EVERY LITTLE BIT COUNTS! Hassan began briskly counting out ones but his tone softened when he saw her staring.

"Local girl," he said. "You hear about her?"

Everybody knows her face now. Mallie touched her head, the blue-green wig, and shook her head.

"She used to come in here once in a while when she was a kid. It was an awful thing, what happened to her. First she gets raped and then she gets pregnant from the rape and she's in a coma and she almost dies and in the middle of the whole thing they force her to have the kid when she's got no idea what the hell's happening."

"But didn't she . . . didn't I hear . . . isn't she . . . she's okay now, right?"

He shrugged. "It's my opinion that once something like that happens to you, you're not ever going to be the way you were before."

He picked up the jar. Coins rattled at the bottom of it.

"Her friend came to collect the money but I'm still keeping the jar on the counter. It's a neighborhood thing at this point. Something like what happened to her? After a while, everyone's affected. She belongs to all of us now."

He held out the sheaf of ones.

"No," she said. "Put it in the jar."

That brought a smile. It changed his whole face, that smile, changed him from a stern, wary man into a person who could see something new that made him happy.

"See what I mean?" he said. "God help her, wherever that girl is now and whatever shape she's in; she belongs to you now too."

———

Mallie lay in the dark motel room, hands clenched on the blankets, little electronic lights blinking here and there: television, bedside clock, sliver of hallway light beneath the door. She looked up at the ceiling and wondered if birds were flying high in the night sky above the roof of the motel. On a late-fall day long ago, when she was a child, William T. had pointed out a flock of geese winging their way south. They were sitting together on his porch drinking hot cider made from the windfall apples in Burl's orchard, the ones he put through his apple press.

"They're on the wing, Mallo Cup," William T. had said. "No upstate New York winter for them. Sayonara, suckers. That's what they're saying up there."

"But how do they know where to go?"

"They're born knowing."

"How, though?" she insisted, but he had no answers.

After their day together in New York City, when William T explained about migratory birds, she read about their patterns. That, when they were on the move, they would ride the wind higher than the highest skyscrapers. They swooped into the current and let it carry them above everything human-made. Everything nature-made too, but for the invisible wind itself. During migration, many of the birds were invisible too, but invisibility didn't mean they weren't there. They *were* there, high in the sky, higher than the Empire State Building, bound for somewhere they could not see but trusted was there.

Some cultures believed that birds carried messages from the world beyond this one. Some believed that the spirits of the dead lived on in the bodies of birds. Was there a life before and after this one? Were the spirits of her mother and father somewhere in the world still?

She fell asleep and dreamed that Zach Miller was walking toward her down a road made of sand, smiling. Something was in his hand and he held it out to her, waiting for her to come take it, but when she tried to walk toward him, her legs wouldn't move. She tried to talk, but no words came out. Panic filled her and she tried to hold her arms out to him, to wave, to let him know she was on her way, but her arms were too heavy to lift.

She woke drenched in sweat and crying.

A tiny red light blinked on the ceiling above her: the sprinkler system, ready to go off if there was a fire. Today was Thursday. Thursdays used to be her day to work at the women's shelter. She had only to walk through the door of the shelter to be hit with the sadness and pain and fear that the women carried in their bodies. She had always felt so different from those women. It had been impossible to picture herself as one of them, as someone who had been through the fire and managed to emerge, a scarred and torn version of her former self.

"Picture a place in your mind," she used to tell them at the start of a session. "Think of a place where you feel safe, and peaceful, a place where nothing bad can happen to you."

Now, in the darkness, Zach appeared again in her mind. Charlie had said that Zach turned out to be an asshole. But she could not feel it. It made no sense to her. Zach was a Miller, and Millers were said to be crazy, but they weren't crazy. What they were was wild, a quiet kind of wild. Millers weren't meant for sitting still. Zach had worked days cutting and hauling giant pines for the lumber mill in Boonville, while she worked days and some evenings at the clinic and the shelter. They were building up their savings so they could head out once Charlie was grown. Bust their lives wide open, see what the future might bring. They were the masters of their fates, the captains of their souls, at least that's what Zach used to say.

She gave in and let herself remember a night with him, a Thursday night when she had driven back from the shelter. Up and over Glass Factory, up and over Potato Hill, Starr Hill, all the way to Forestport and the cabin.

When she had gotten home, she had leaned against the truck's warm hood for a minute to feel the ticking heart of the engine, then walked up the wooden stairs and eased the door open so it wouldn't wake either Charlie in the sleeping loft or Zach in their bedroom. The spidery red lines of the old stereo glimmered behind the bed. Brandi Carlile, still singing, even though Zach was asleep. She crossed her arms and pulled off her black T-shirt, her soft leggings.

The cotton sheets were cool. She laid her cheek against Zach's flung-out arm and breathed him in. When he slept, it was like everything in him soothed itself out into a single flowing current. As if anything that had broken or unraveled during the day wove itself together again when he was asleep. He pulled her over and wrapped himself around her, as if he had been waiting for her in his sleep.

When he was awake, Zach Miller moved lightly and fast, like he wasn't bound to the same rules of gravity as most people. But at night, gravity pulled him back down, made him heavy and dark. The earth reaching up and claiming him for its own. He had swung his leg over her.

"Too heavy?" he whispered.

She shook her head against his. In the beginning, when they were first together back in high school, those long afternoons with the sun coming through the window and the sheets damp with sweat, he would sometimes push himself up on his elbows so that he was suspended above her, afraid that he was crushing her. But she would pull him down again. She wanted his full length stretched out on her, covering her.

It was just the two of them back then, skipping school to be alone in his house while his parents were at work. Later, after Zach's parents moved to Alaska, she and Charlie moved into the cabin that Zach himself had built. Some might say they were young, too young to be taking care of themselves like that, let alone her brother. But they weren't.

"Hey," he said that night, that Thursday night when she returned from the shelter, and she flipped over so that her face was against his and kissed him. Soft. His body was still slow, but he was returning from wherever it was that sleep took a person.

She stroked his hair back from his brow, there in the darkness where she couldn't see him. It had been three years since they began living together. There was nothing she didn't know about his body, his skin and muscles and bone. They made no noise. His fingers tugged her underwear down over her legs and then they were pressed together. He slept naked, something else she loved about him. Some might say they were too young to know for sure how they felt, but that too was wrong.

Now, in the motel, she pulled the blanket tight around her like a sleeping bag and laced her hands over the silken silver scar. They had cut a hole in her and pulled a baby through it. She couldn't think about it. But she had to think about it. She had to figure it out. None of it made sense but she had to make sense of it. She remembered one young woman at the shelter, her eyes staring up from the table, face and body rigid with worry. Two kids in the shelter, no family to turn to.

"Think of a safe place," Mallie had told her. "Where nothing bad can happen to you."

"I don't have a place like that," the young woman had said.

"Make one up, then," Mallie had told her, and waited, her hands cupped beneath the woman's heavy head, until her face relaxed and her eyes went soft. In the end she must have dreamed up a place where she could truly feel safe, because by the end of the massage, the young woman had fallen sound asleep.

Mallie had never had to make up a place where she felt safe, because she had Zach. Zach Miller had been the place where nothing bad could happen to her.

William T.

THE LITTLE PHONE BUZZED DEEP IN HIS POCKET AND HE dropped the armful of birch he was holding. The chunks scattered, one narrowly missing his foot.

"Mallie?"

A man on the other end cleared his throat and said, "It's Zach."

Dust motes danced and twirled in the golden air of the last rays of the sun, slanting through the door of the storage barn. A large spider skittered away from the orderly row of wood he had stacked in the last hour. The boy's voice sounded lower than it should. *He's not a boy*, William T. reminded himself. It had been more than a year since he had last seen Zach Miller. All this flew through his mind in an instant, as a dark arrow of fear rose inside him. Why was Zach calling? Beyond the faint static of the connection he heard a bark, a loud woof that ended in an upward yip.

"That dog has a bark like Sir's," he said.

A pause, and then: "It *is* Sir."

"It can't be. Sir disappeared from Trish's."

"I took him. Which is something I should have told you a long time ago."

"You couldn't have taken him, Zach. You were in Montana when he disappeared from Trish's."

William T. sounded teacherlike to himself, as if he were explaining a geography problem to a not-bright student. Here's Montana, see, and here's Sterns, and there's a very long distance between the two places. But Zach was talking again.

"I took him when I went back," he said. "When Mallie had the, that . . . operation."

Zach must be talking about the C-section. William T. saw the day clearly in his head: A cool day in June. The hospital employee parking lot with him and Crystal, Beanie watching from the back door. No Zach. Unless he had hidden himself away. *Stay calm*, he told himself. *Be Switzerland.*

"You were there? Why?"

"Because. Someone needed to be there. Someone who knew her, who knew who she was." The boy's voice turned hard on itself at the end of the sentence, angry, but he kept going. "I was in the woods behind the hospital."

"Just standing there?"

"Yes. Until I knew it was over."

"But Crystal and I were there."

"I know." Zach's voice was quiet, laced with apology. So Zach Miller had been there at the same time, he had seen William T. and Crystal, but he had not come forward. *Switzerland*, he told himself. Zach was talking again, as if he could hear William T.'s thoughts.

"And when I knew it was done, I drove up to Trish's and I waited until it was late and all the lights were out and then I went through their back door into the dog yard and I took Sir."

"What do you mean you went through their back door? How?"

"Broke in. Kind of, anyway. Trish keeps the key under the welcome mat."

William T. felt the ghost of a smile flit across his face. The whole valley knew that Trish kept a key under the welcome mat. His free hand began to peel the parchment bark off a piece of white birch. Zach Miller had returned. He had been there, watching from the woods.

"How's Sir?" William T. said. An inane question, but a neutral one. He was trying not to judge. He was being Switzerland.

"Good. He's good."

Screw Switzerland. Anger rose up in William T. and he couldn't hold it back.

"Look, Zach. Why didn't you tell us you had him? We loved that goddamn dog too."

"I know. I'm sorry. I punched in your number a bunch of times. But I kept imagining the sound of your voice if you picked up and it would've made me too sad. When I left home I had to shut it all down, William T."

Too sad didn't sound like Zach Miller. Zach Miller was not a sad person. But it had been a long time, William T. reminded himself, and none of them were the same people they had been. He held the phone to his ear with one hand and began chunking wood onto the stack with the other. A steady, even row, cross-hatched on either end. He had been stacking wood his whole life. Repetitive motion neutralized anger and brought calm.

"Have you talked to her?" he said. "Since she left?"

"Since she *left?* Isn't she with you?"

"No. She took off a week ago in the Datsun."

"How can she be gone? Can she drive? Does she have—"

"Her brain is fine, if that's what you're talking about. I told you that already. She gets tired. Maybe a little confused sometimes. Who doesn't?"

Chunk. Chunk. Chunk. The orderly row of wood grew higher. Zach was silent on the other end of the line. Not that it was a line. Cell phones had no lines. They had, what? William T. didn't even know. He wondered if the endless television loop from the early days of the vigil played in Zach's head the way it did in his: the protesters in their circles, the billboards with Mallie's smiling face receding behind grim black letters: MY HEART WAS BEATING AT 9 DAYS AND SO IS MY BABY'S. FINGERNAILS AT 19 DAYS. LET ME LIVE!

"Zach, how are you?"

What he meant was how was Zach Miller, *really,* in his heart and soul? How was he surviving, in the midst of the ghosts that swirled around them both? But Zach must have understood, because he answered right away.

"I'm trying to figure it out, William T. What I should do."

"About Mallie? Jesus, Zach" — he could hear the tension surging in his voice and he fought it back down — "she loves you. There's no one who means to that girl what you do."

"She's in the dark about a lot of things, William T."

"Like Sir?"

"Like Sir, yeah."

There was a tone in the boy's voice — *he's not a boy*, William T. reminded himself — that made him uneasy. Did he have a new girl-friend? Zach Miller was a young good-looking boy — man, he re-minded himself, man — with a big heart, and he had gone a long, long time without Mallie and without the hope of Mallie. *Don't ask*, William T. told himself. *Don't say a word.* And he didn't. He didn't think he could bear it if Zach Miller had fallen in love with another girl.

"Does she talk about the baby, William T.?"

"No. Not to me, anyway. She knows she had one. She knows it's with a foster family somewhere in Utica."

"*Him*, William T. Don't call him 'it.'"

Who are you to tell me what not to call that baby, William T. thought, *when I'm the one who can't get the fact of him out of my head, when I'm the one who keeps driving down there and driving back*, but again he kept quiet.

"Call her, Zach. If there are things she's in the dark about, like you say, then she deserves to hear about them from you."

————

The rules:

1. Drive past the little gray house and look once, casually, the way anyone might glance at a house he was passing.

2. If no one was going into or coming out of the front door, then drive around the block and turn down the alley. Wil-liam T. knew which garage belonged to the little gray house — white with green trim — and he could putt past and take another casual glance.

3. If there were no signs of life either front or back, then he had to drive on down to the end of the alley, take a left and drive straight out of the neighborhood.

Those were the rules William T. had made for himself. But no rule said he couldn't drive as slowly as he wanted, and today he crawled along, no more than three miles per hour. No one was going into or coming out of the back door. He crept by the garage, the small, tired backyard with its flowerbed filled with marigolds and weeds, a laundry-less clothesline, a sandbox covered with a small blue tarp. The chain-link fence sagged in one section. It was an ordinary house on an ordinary block that belonged to an ordinary attorney for the child and his social-worker wife.

Should he break his own rule? Should he go around the block and the alley one more time, just on the off chance?

"No," he said aloud.

But he did anyway. And there they were.

Aaron and Melissa Stampernick were unaware of anyone but the child between them. Each held a hand. One, two, three, *wheee*. William T. could still feel that motion in his own hands, from long ago. The abrupt tug of muscles in his arms and shoulders and the weight of a small body swung up into the air.

Tiny. Slight. Pale. Overalls and a hat. William T. could not see the color of the child's eyes. He rolled down the window as if he were an ordinary man who wanted some fresh air, when what he really wanted was to hear the child's voice.

"One, two, three . . ." Aaron and Melissa singsonged, then, "Wheee," came the small voice in response.

He put his foot down on the gas and drove away. He'd seen them. And maybe the baby too. One of their foster children, for sure. Aaron and Melissa Stampernick were also religious, deeply so. Christians. He knew that from the newspaper articles. But had that stood in Aaron Stampernick's way when it came to the baby they'd made Mallie give birth to? It had not. What about the separation of church and state? Didn't their religion, and Lucia's, prejudice them against making a fair decision? William T. thought so, and he had made his thoughts known. But "it's not a crime to be religious," he had been reminded. "Many people are religious."

Now he'd seen the Stampernicks close up. Aaron Stampernick knew where that baby was living. It was maddening, watching him and Melissa coming out of their house, swinging a child down the steps, knowing that they held information William T. needed but were bound by law not to give it to him. Did no one understand that he, William T. Jones, needed to see that baby? Even once. Just to settle his mind.

Him, *William T. Don't call him "it."* Zach's voice, stern on the phone. Beanie's voice at the playground. It? Him? Everything was too complicated. Was he, William T., in the wrong? He pictured the cardboard box that he had tossed all those clippings into, the indistinct slump of it in the closet, the psychic weight of his obsession. Did he in fact have some kind of borderline mental illness, an illness that kept him doing the same thing over and over, with nothing to show for it?

But maybe he did have something to show for it. Because Mallie had come back to the world.

How did you let go of things that kept eating away at you? How was it possible to let go of his anger, and his grief, and his worry? *Should* he even try to let go of those things? He thought of Burl, who every time William T. saw him seemed light and happy, proud of all the money he had raised for Mallie and glad that she had taken off on her own. "She needed to get out of Sterns," he had said to William T., "and none of us should hold her back."

He thought of Crystal, so quiet next to him on the porch. Dancing alone in the kitchen of the diner. Would he ever get good enough at dancing to waltz her around the living room? Big, clumsy man that he was. Was he holding her back? Holding all of them back?

Mallie

―――――

S HE PUT ON THE WIG, CHECKED OUT OF THE MOTEL IN THE LATE afternoon even though it was paid through the following morning, and headed north on 12, then right onto 28, into the Adirondacks, ticking off the towns and the signs as she drove.

Thendara. Old Forge. Inlet.

Fly-tying. Shear Madness. Taxidermy. Deer hides.

At a bend in the road just north of Inlet was a bar with little white lights strung up around the windows and door and pickups and old cars parked here and there in the gravel lot. A man with a dish towel in hand, bartender, from the looks of him, stared out the window as she passed. The wig, maybe. Its unearthly blue-green color.

Twilight was approaching, the time when deer waited just beyond the shoulder of the road to cross. Mallie slowed and kept watch for the shine of their bright eyes. She drove one-handed and slipped the other one under her T-shirt, over the scar. Over the space that stayed stubbornly blank in memory, even though it had happened to her. Had they given her a drug? Was anaesthesia involved? Or maybe they just cut into her and lifted the baby out. Maybe they thought that because she was unconscious, it wouldn't hurt.

Zach's cousin Joe once had emergency surgery after a car hit him when he was changing a tire by the side of the road. The surgeons had removed his lacerated spleen and part of his intestines, which necessitated lifting some of his internal organs out of his body and then replacing them when they had finished. But once your insides were displaced and then returned, your body could not ever be the same. That's what Joe said. Strange pains came and went. Food felt different once it was eaten. He felt hungry and not-hungry in unfamiliar ways. Even the way he walked had changed.

"I don't care if everyone says I look just the same," he had told Zach. "I'm not just the same."

Even if you had not had your insides displaced and rearranged, and even if you hadn't been living in limbo for a year and a half while the world went on around you, you couldn't remain the exact same person you had always been. The difference between Mallie and other people was that others had been conscious through the process of changing. She pictured herself in that hospital bed, unaware of the world revolving around her, coming into light and turning away from light. And her clinging to the surface like everyone else, carried into darkness and carried out of darkness.

A little diner appeared in the distance. She put on her blinker and pulled in and made sure her wig was on straight. That diner smell of pancake syrup and a hot grill and frying hamburgers and wet-mopped floors and flannel and coffee and butter. Booths with two adults crowded in on each side, tables with tired parents and two or three kids bouncing on the chairs. Each tabletop held a miniature jukebox. *Don't look at the cash register, Mallie; don't check to see if there's a plastic jar there*, but she looked anyway: No jar. No photo of her former self, staring out at the world.

"Sit wherever you want, sweetheart," said a voice behind her. "Coffee?" Without waiting for an answer, the waitress flipped a mug right side up and filled it from the pot in her hand. Then she fished a quarter out of the deep pocket of her apron and put it on the table, nodding at the little jukebox.

"Here you go, honey. Play yourself a few songs."

The waitress was a *honey sweetheart darling* kind of person. Three for a quarter. Three songs. She flipped through the selection and punched in the numbers for Johnny Cash, Hank Williams, and Glen Campbell. *These are for you, William T.* Music filled the tiny booth — "I'm So Lonesome I Could Cry," which was William T.'s favorite song — and she pictured Hank's voice swirling up into the sky and

over the miles to North Sterns. Hovering in the sky above the house
where William T. and Crystal might already be asleep.

"I grew up listening to these guys," the waitress said. She was
back, her order pad in her hand. "In this very diner, as a matter of
fact. That jukebox is older than I am."

"Did you ever go away?"

"Once. I started college at MVCC, down in Utica. I didn't like being away from home, though." The waitress lifted her shoulders and
dropped them in a *What can I say?* sort of way. "I know it's not my
business, but are you okay? You look kind of sad."

Mallie reached up and touched her wig. Was her real hair showing? Did the waitress recognize her? *Everybody knows her face now.*

"Can I ask you something?" Mallie said. "Do you have any kids?"

"I do. Three of them."

"Did you want them?"

"If by wanting, you mean were they planned, then no. My husband
and I are not poster children for contraception." She laughed. "But do
I want them now? Yes. Even if I want to kill them sometimes. Which
I don't. That was a joke."

"Do you believe in abortion?"

"No. I don't believe in abortion."

Mallie looked down at the paper menu, which doubled as a place
mat. Hank was still singing above the clinking silverware and grill
sounds of the diner. The waitress touched her arm.

"For me, I mean. I don't believe in it for *me.* But sometimes it boils
down to a bad choice and a less-bad choice. You know what I mean?
It's a hard, hard thing."

A bad choice and a less-bad choice. A hard, hard thing. The space
beneath the scar was still empty and blank. The waitress finally said,
"Do you know what you want, honey? If not, the special's a good
choice."

Ham steak with peas and biscuits. The waitress returned with the
plate, a long oval with a green border, and the low hum of conversation washed up on the shore of the booth and lulled her. When she
scooped up the last bite of peas, the waitress brought over a piece
of pie on the house, strawberry-rhubarb with a cloud of whipped

cream. Mallie ate that too, then she added up the bill in her head, including tax and a big tip, and left some of Burl's cash under the empty coffee mug.

Back in the truck, she felt around for the little black phone, invisible in the bottom of the box of fortune cookies. Her link to the people who knew her. Three missed calls from William T., along with one unheard voicemail.

". . . Mallie? It's . . . me."

Zach Miller. Her heart stampeded in her chest. Around her, in the parking lot, people entered the diner, left the diner, opened and shut car and truck doors. Engines revved to life and tires crunched on gravel. Blinkers blinked left and right, flashing silently in her rearview mirror. There was noise in the background of the message, noise and static. Banging, of pots, maybe, and indistinct voices.

"Mallie, I'm so sorry. I should have called you earlier but I didn't know what to say. I still don't. Everything is complicated."

She clutched the phone to her ear while the voicemail played itself out and then she bent over the steering wheel. It felt as if he were there in the truck with her. She pressed play on the voicemail again and listened to his voice, indistinct, hesitant, but his. She pressed play again. And again.

William T. had told her that Charlie had left the cabin and moved in with him and Crystal after it happened. So Zach had been alone. She pictured him in the hospital room, driving back and forth from their cabin in Forestport by himself, throwing tennis balls for Sir by himself, eating by himself, by himself, by himself. Panic suffocated its way up her throat and fogged her head.

My God, my God, why hast thou forsaken me?

Long ago, the Sunday-school teacher's eyes had filled with tears when she told them about the crucifixion and the resurrection. "Can you feel God's love for you?" she used to say, and hands around the small yellow-painted room would rise. "He loves you so much."

Mallie's hand had stayed down. The story had meant nothing to her. It still meant nothing. What was God and where was God and what was heaven and where was it? She hated the idea of the heaven portrayed in the paintings on the old Sunday-school wall, with the angels and haloes and golden harps, a place where light streamed down from an endless unseen sun.

Where, in that heaven, was Zach Miller's hand holding hers? Where was the cabin where she and Zach lived, where on summer nights the crickets were wild, their song rising from the woods and the creeks that ran behind it? Where was their old bed that sagged in the middle, quilts and pillows piled high? Didn't heaven hold anything familiar? Her heaven had been right here on earth, lost now in all the days that had passed since the night of the shining sidewalk.

She had known Zach Miller since she was five years old. Her earliest memory of him was from school Picture Day. The school secretary stood at the head of the line of children, a basket full of cheap plastic combs on a stool next to her. The Olan Mills photographer ducked under an umbrella-like canopy by his camera, which stood on a tripod. His butt stuck out, which they all wanted to laugh about but didn't. Second graders, first graders, and Mallie's kindergarten class, three separate lines, everybody single file.

"Next," the secretary would say, and put a finger under each of their chins, tilt their head up and look at them appraisingly. Sometimes she nodded and gave a little push, and that child advanced to the white backdrop and sat on the stool and smiled when the Olan Mills man said, "Cheese."

Most of the time, though, the school secretary tilted her head and squinted.

"One second," she said, and she would pick up a comb and turn the children into sober, formal versions of themselves. They bent their heads and submitted. But that day, one week into kindergarten for Mallie and second grade for Zach, Zach Miller didn't.

"No."

"Just a quick comb."

"No."

"Excuse me, Zach"—all the teachers knew the Miller boys' names; they were a legendary family, multiple branches extending throughout North Sterns—"but your mother would want you to look nice for the photo."

"No, she wouldn't."

Mallie was in the line right next to his, so she saw the whole thing. He tilted his head back and looked up at the school secretary—way up; she was a big, tall woman—and held her gaze.

"Of course she would. No mother wants her child looking like a ragamuffin in his school photo."

"My mother doesn't care about stuff like that."

Everyone was watching at that point. Even the Olan Mills man poked his head out from behind the big black-draped camera to check out the back-talking second grader.

"Every mother cares about stuff like that, Zach."

"Not mine."

His eyes. That's what she remembered most from that day. They were small children, so those eyes of his had been in the world only a short while. Like hers. But in her memory his eyes were dark hazel, like green-flecked smoke, and completely steady on the secretary's. Zach Miller was fearless. All of them, all the little kids waiting in line behind both of them, could feel it. They watched as the secretary hesitated. She finally lowered the comb and nodded at him.

"Okay. Go on, then."

She smiled the kind of smile that didn't mean happy. Her smile was the period at the end of a drifting sentence, an *I'm lost* kind of smile.

When the pictures came back, Mallie snuck a peek at Zach's photo. He was sitting in the seat across the aisle from her on the school bus. Zach looked exactly the way he always did, gazing out from behind the clear pane on the front of the packet, whereas she looked like a scrubbed, intimidated version of herself. He saw her looking, reached across the aisle and touched her face in her photo, through the glassine window.

"I like your picture," he said.

"You do?"

"Yeah."

That was all he said. But he looked at her and smiled. Zach Miller in that Batman T-shirt, those hazel eyes the color of the foothills in March, calm even back then. She and Zach were small and then they weren't and they were children and then they weren't, and where was he now? Had he given up on her? Had the fact of the baby, how it had come to be, that it was in the world, driven him away?

When she tried to think about the baby, tried to imagine it as a living, breathing being, there was only emptiness. It felt as if she were on the bank of a great river and the baby was living his life on the other shore. Out of sight, out of hearing, out of feeling. But shouldn't she feel something? Shouldn't she sense the baby somehow, if not the presence of him, then the loss of him?

She put her hand over her stomach again, the place where the baby had grown. The place where they had opened her up and taken him out. If she were on the massage table, one of her own clients, she would put her hands on her stomach in just this way, and her body would speak to her. Not in words, but in feeling. In memory. In history.

What if the baby were Zach's?

At the thought, all the emptiness instantly filled itself in with sound and laughter and crying and a baby's face, asleep and awake and smiling. A baby's hands. A baby waking in the night with her and Zach next to it. A refrigerator covered with photos that looked like a miniature Zach, who on his school Picture Day, wore jeans and an old Batman T-shirt that was probably a hand-me-down from one of his cousins. Just then her phone buzzed and she picked it up with shaking hands, her heart racing again.

But it was Beanie.

KNOCK, KNOCK.

She didn't text back. The screen went dark while he waited, then leapt to life again.

WHO'S THERE?

She watched the familiar words appear on the screen and heard William T.'s voice saying them, the way he had said them so often to her and Charlie when they were little. Beanie wasn't waiting for her to respond. He was telling the joke one-sided.

HOWARD.

HOWARD WHO?

HOWARD YOU LIKE TO HEAR ANOTHER KNOCK-KNOCK JOKE?

In her head, William T. could barely get out the punch line because he was already laughing. He had always laughed harder than anyone else at his knock-knock jokes. It was his laughter, rather than the joke, that had made her and Charlie laugh. Now she pictured Beanie, telling jokes to his daughter. Beanie would be a good father.

The custody hearing after Lucia's death had been closed and confidential, according to William T. and Crystal, and the baby had been placed with foster parents. Were they good parents? If they felt sick at the thought of how he had come into existence, did they suppress it? Was that part of their training? She already knew how William T. felt about the baby. His repulsion was clear from the way he stiffened and turned away at the mention of him. How did Charlie feel? Crystal? Zach? None of them could feel the blankness that she did. She had lost time, but no one else had. Even if they'd wanted to, there had been no way to press pause and wait for her. No matter how much they loved her, they had moved on without her. She would always be behind, behind, behind.

She clicked the phone off and sat there in the truck. Everything used to be easy, didn't it? She and Zach were easy, she and Charlie were easy, she was easy in her life and so was everyone around her. It couldn't have been smooth, all of it, but when she looked back now, it seemed that way. Images bathed in golden light. Late nights with Charlie smiling over his playlist, she and Zach swaying around the living room with their beers. Their bodies doing what the music told them to do. She pictured Zach holding their imaginary baby against his chest, dancing him around the living room. It was a dream she hadn't known she had, until now. Herself a mother, Zach a father, their baby whoever he would be. Crystal had told her once how, when Johnny was a baby and crying all the time, she used to waltz him around the trailer in the middle of the night.

"It soothed him," she said. "Not much soothed him back then, but that did."

"Do you still dance, Crystal?"

"No. I wanted to take lessons once, with William T. But he said he was too big and clumsy to dance. So I didn't bring it up again."

"Maybe you could dance by yourself?" Mallie offered. She hated to think of Crystal not dancing. Not doing something she loved to do because she didn't have a partner to do it with. But Crystal had just smiled and shrugged.

William T.

───────────
═══════════
───────────

THE PHONE IN HIS POCKET BUZZED AND CHIRPED LIKE A TRAPPED bird.

"William T.?"

Zach again. William T. pressed the phone against his ear and ordered himself into neutrality. No anger. No blame. He would be Switzerland.

"Hi, Zach. You talk to her yet?"

Silence. Was Zach still there? It was impossible to tell with these tiny phones. There was no definitive click of a conversation ending, the other phone replaced in its cradle. There was only dead air.

"I left her a message," Zach said.

A message? A message wasn't enough. *Switzerland*, he reminded himself. The boy—the *man*—was talking again.

"William T., I need to talk to you. Remember how none of us knew if she would ever come back? Remember how they told us that she was going to be like that for the rest of her life?"

"Of course I remember. Why bring it up now?"

"Because it factors into something you don't know, William T., which is that before I moved to Montana I tried to get custody of the baby."

"*The* baby?"

"Yes."

Zach Miller with a baby? A baby whose biological father was a demon? What the hell had he been thinking? He nearly snapped out the words but stopped himself in time.

"But it wasn't your baby."

"I know that, William T. We both know they tested my DNA, seeing as Mallie was my girlfriend. But when she didn't die and they decided to make her go through with the pregnancy, I tried to get custody instead of Lucia."

Exclamations and questions and objections thickened his tongue and he couldn't get the words out. The image of Zach Miller roaring around in his truck with a baby in a car seat next to him sprang into his mind.

"What about a car seat?" he heard himself say.

"What are you talking about, William T.?"

"A baby has to have a car seat. You can't have a goddamn baby without a car seat. They won't even let you leave the hospital until they make sure the car seat's properly installed. They watch you like a hawk, Zach."

"William T., are you crying?"

"Hell no!"

Hell yes, though. He was crying. It was stunning, the idea of Zach Miller trying to raise that baby. Who had he talked to? Had he filled out forms? Had he told anyone? Had he gone through some kind of foster-parent training? Images appeared in his mind one after another: Zach in a huge store, comparing car seats; Zach leaning over a Formica counter in a courthouse somewhere, filling out forms; Zach sitting in a classroom taking notes alongside other would-be foster parents; Zach in the hospital with deathly ill Mallie, whispering to her his plan to raise the baby; Zach with a bottle of formula, Zach with a box of diapers, Zach in the truck alone, driving off to Montana. Alone. Alone was the feeling that rose up in William T., and he brushed the tears away but they kept on coming.

"I'm sorry, Zach," he said when he could keep his voice steady again.

"What are you sorry for, William T.?"

"That I didn't know." That he had assumed Zach couldn't take it any longer and just took off. Zach had been banned from the hospital, just like William T. and Crystal. And yet William T. had blamed him anyway. Blamed him for leaving Mallie alone, with the vultures and the flock as dark guards.

"Yeah. I tried. I wanted that baby."

"But why?"

Unspoken was *He wasn't yours* and *Half his DNA comes from a rapist* and *Could you ever raise a kid knowing he wasn't yours?*

Zach answered all the questions, though, without William T.'s having to ask. "Because half of him is Mallie, William T."

His voice sounded tired. Old. Much older than twenty-five, which was his age. He was still talking. "I thought about names, even."

Names. A name was a thread that stitched a child to the earth. A name made a child definite. Against William T.'s will, a small boy began forming himself in William T.'s head. A small boy with dark hair like Mallie's, a small boy with a wagon like the one Mallie used to have, a small boy fascinated by birds the way Mallie used to be, a small boy who liked red grapes, not green, cut into quarters, the way Mallie used to like them. A small boy in a car seat strapped into a car. A small boy holding a stuffed penguin to his cheek like the stuffed penguin Mallie had carted around everywhere when she was a small girl. A small boy who would swing between his parents' hands while they all sang, *Wheee.*

The child and the ghost of the child Mallie used to be hung inside William T.'s head, and it felt unbearable. It must have been unbearable to Zach too, but he had gone as far as thinking about a name.

"Did you come up with one?" he said.

"Yeah. Maybe. I talked to Lucia about it, even."

"Did not."

"We talked about a bunch of things, William T."

Another thing that William T. had not known. He himself had cut ties with Lucia after she was awarded guardianship. He had been so full of anger and frustration at the wrongs he felt she'd inflicted on her unconscious daughter that he didn't trust himself around her. Not even in the end, sick and dying though she was. It had not been Christian of him, but then again, he wasn't much of a Christian.

"The baby's in this world, William T., like it or not. He's part Mallie. You ever think about that?"

"It's part rapist too. You ever think about *that?*"

"More than you can imagine. And I already told you: Don't call him 'it.'"

William T. could barely wrap his head around the fact that Zach had wanted custody. From the minute the decree came down that the pregnancy would proceed, Zach must have been planning. Going back and forth, considering the options and the ramifications of the act. Zach was a Miller but he was not, unlike his cousins and his parents, an impulsive man. Zach must have been working behind the scenes. He had been to see Lucia, which was more than any of the rest of them had done. The two of them had come up with names, a boy name and a girl name.

"What happened, Zach? Did they laugh you out of the court? How far did you get?"

"Not far. Big surprise—it turns out that a devoted grandmother has a much better shot at custody of her grandson than a twenty-four-year-old single man. When I said they should give me a shot, that I had been with Mallie for years, that I loved her, they just looked at me."

"You sound tired, Zach."

"I feel tired, William T."

"She's back. Remember that."

"But I'm not the same person I was. None of us are."

———

William T. sat for a while on the porch after they hung up. It was late afternoon and Crystal was at the diner, closing up for the day. Soon she would get in her car and make the five-mile drive north. How long had it been since he had sat here and waited for her to pull into the driveway with a sense of happy anticipation instead of weariness? Not since Before, which was how he sometimes thought of it. The Before, when Mallie and Zach and Charlie lived in Forestport, and The After, when everything fell apart and they were thrust into the confounding world of medical intervention and politics and religion and legal rights versus what was best for Mallie.

He forced himself just to sit. Feel the cement step beneath him, the air cooling as the sun sank lower in the sky. Breathe in the smells: cut grass, manure from the farm fields up the road, peonies in full bloom. When was the last time he had been aware of the scents of North Sterns in the early summer? Not since Before. The sound of tires humming on the macadam of Route 274 came floating on the air now, punctuated by crickets and the rustle of squirrels in the oak tree. Crystal, slight behind the wheel, not bothering to put on her blinker as she turned into the driveway, parked and shut off the ignition.

"William T.? What's wrong? Is Mallie—"

She stood on the other side of the car, her door still open, headlights still on. Alarm on her face. In that moment he knew how he had neglected her. How he had forged on alone, blind in his anger and the knowledge that he was helpless to change what they were doing and had done to Mallie. He had left Crystal behind. He had left Charlie behind. He had left them all behind, following his own obsessive routines—the baby, the playground, the box of pain—and forgetting that he was not alone in his sorrow. He looked at her now, his quiet Crystal.

"I didn't know what to do, Crystal," he said. "And now I don't know how to fix things."

She tilted her head and looked at him. Then reached into the car, turned off the headlights and came to him on the steps. Her tread noiseless, as always, on the driveway. Crystal floated instead of walked, as if she weighed nothing. She sat down next to him, a wraith of a woman—she had lost weight and she did not have weight to lose— and he put his arm around her and pulled her to him.

"I got stuck," he said. "Didn't I?"

"Yes. Like a lot of us."

"No. I'm the one who's stuck. I was holding her back, wasn't I? That's why she took off."

"You pulled her through, William T. Sometimes I think it was the sheer force of your will that kept her alive."

"But I have to let her go now. She's back and I have to let her go. It's her life now."

"Why do you say that?"

"I talked to Zach."

"How is he?"

"He told me he tried to get custody of the baby initially, instead of Lucia, but they wouldn't hear of it. Did you know about that?"

He could tell from her tiny flinch that no, she had not known. She shook her head, a brief back-and-forth.

"Why didn't he tell us?"

"Maybe he would've, but . . ." Her voice trailed off, so he finished for her.

"But he probably thought I'd hate the idea. Which is why he didn't bring it up with you either."

She nodded against his shoulder. He imagined the two of them, Crystal and Zach, discussing the idea of Zach raising the baby. Crystal would have listened without speaking. She would have absorbed everything Zach said. She would have let him talk through the whole idea, the reasons for and against, the ramifications, the various scenarios. One of those scenarios would have been "What would William T. think?" Clearly, Zach had known what his reaction would have been. Even now he could hear his own voice thundering forth with all the reasons why it wouldn't work, the awful weight of history that the child, and by extension all of them, would carry on its shoulders. The force of his anger had made it impossible for Zach to talk about it with them. Sitting there on the porch, with Crystal tired and sad against his shoulder, he waited to feel the flush of fury at the idea of that baby in their lives forever, which, only a few months ago, would have flooded through him.

But all that came was a feeling of regret, that he had somehow let Crystal down. That he had let Zach down. That he, William T., had missed something he should have seen all along, which was that his love for Mallie did not exist in a vacuum. They all loved her. They all wanted to do right by her. He had thought that he knew what was best for her, but had he?

Mallie

Y OU COULD GO A LONG WAY IN UPSTATE NEW YORK. A LONG, long way. What you had to do was stop thinking and just drive. No GPS, no map. Little frame houses and camps, some with propped-open doors and signs in the front yards.

People said it was impossible to hide, in the age of cell phones and internet and voice and facial recognition, drones and security cameras and GPS software, but it wasn't. The trick was to skim along the surface of the world. Have no permanent home. Not answer your cell phone. Stay away from computers. Give a different name when you checked into a motel. Wear a wig. Use only cash. Leave no trail. Stand in a different way. Move in a different way. Consciously confound your body. If you had good posture, slouch. If you slouched, stand up straight. If you walked fast, stroll. If you slept on your side, turn on your back.

PREGNANT? WE CAN HELP.

It was a homemade sign on a building just off the road at the far end of a long curve north of Saranac. The words were carefully painted, using a stencil, but the WE CAN HELP slanted slightly downward. The parking lot behind the building was painted with wobbly lines, as if whoever was holding the can of spray paint had been unsure. A single car huddled next to the entrance as if it were scared to be alone. Mallie pulled into a far spot, where the road couldn't be seen. In the distance came the whine of a semi as it downshifted.

Once, before Zach, when she was new to sex, Mallie had been afraid she'd gotten pregnant. She missed her period and fear grew inside her. She had been barely sixteen at the time. She had driven to Utica, to a drugstore where no one knew her, and bought a pregnancy test: negative. She had bought another, and then another: negative. But her period hadn't come and her fear had grown. What would she do? She would have an abortion. The answer was instant and immediate: drive to the women's clinic in Syracuse and have an abortion.

But in that time, in those three weeks of believing she was pregnant and despite knowing that she would choose an abortion, she had changed the way she lived. It was winter, and she had walked carefully on the ice. She had not drunk a single beer, even though it was a go-to-parties-and-drink-beer time of life. She had eaten leafy greens every day. She was sixteen, and if she was pregnant she was going to have an abortion, and still: instinct had made her act like a mother protecting the baby growing inside her.

Then she had gotten her period, and the plan to abort had evaporated.

Later came Zach, and with Zach came love and care and constant birth control and a lack of fear. Now she put her hands on her belly, took a deep breath and exhaled slowly. Took another deep breath and pushed it down through her fingers into the imagined blank space of her womb. Did the baby's spirit still linger there? Was she somehow still connected to him?

Nothing.

Shouldn't she feel something?

She was a mother, wasn't she? Somehow?

She thought of her own mother. Not the mother of her later years, the mother lost to the rules of her strict church, but the mother that Lucia had been when Mallie and Charlie were small. The mother who held their hands and walked them down the dirt road to the blackberry patch. Who made them macaroni and cheese and read to them before bed. Who tried to help them, as best she could, when their father died. Who took them to the Jersey shore. Who signed their report cards and drew smiley faces next to her signature. She had been proud of her children, hadn't she? She had loved them. She had done the best she could.

Mallie bent her head to the steering wheel. The later years were what they were — years of pain and confusion and sorrow — but the early years were what they were too. The early and the late, indivisible and eternal. Unsolvable equations.

"Mom," she whispered. Not "Lucia," the name she had called her mother those last years, but "Mom." "I hope you're at peace now."

She lifted her head and her mother appeared before her. Right there, right in the air in front of the truck, here in this bleak parking lot in the high peaks of the Adirondacks.

"Mom?"

Lucia floated closer. Her hands were held out as if she wanted Mallie to take them. She was smiling. Her hair was long and brushed and her teeth were white and her eyes were clear and filled with love. When was the last time Mallie had seen her mother like that? Was she, Mallie, dying? Was her mother here to welcome her to whatever world lay beyond this one?

Her mother shook her head, still smiling. She wasn't dying. Her mother was not here to welcome her to that other world. She had come back from it to show her . . . what? That she was still here? That her spirit was whole now? That she loved her daughter? That things would be all right? That some connections could not be broken? That there was a way to solve the unsolvable equation?

Tap, tap.

A woman standing outside the window smiled apologetically at how Mallie startled in fear. She made a roll-down-the-window motion with her hand, peered in at the box of fortune cookies riding shotgun and nodded, as if she approved.

"Sorry," she said. "Didn't mean to scare you. Do you want to come inside? Can I get you some coffee or tea?"

Mallie's mother had vanished, replaced by a smiling unfamiliar woman here at the forlorn-looking PREGNANT? WE CAN HELP place. At the top of the cracked gray cement steps and inside the door, was a linoleum floor, wood paneling, a waiting room to the right.

"Are you cold?" the woman said. Her graying black hair was pinned back haphazardly with bobby pins and a single bright yellow barrette. She held out a lidded container of cookies.

"They're oatmeal raisin. Although I noticed you have enough fortune cookies out there to feed an army. Have a seat. What brings you here?"

"I'm not pregnant, if that's what you're asking. I haven't had sex in more than a year and a half."

The woman smiled. "Well, no sex in a year and a half is definitive. It means that pregnancy would be a miracle, wouldn't it?"

"It's not always a miracle."

"It can be messy. Getting pregnant, especially when you didn't plan to, can sure be messy. That much I know. For evidence, I present to you the existence of my two youngest kids."

"But you still think it's a miracle?"

"My kids? Well, sometimes it's harder than other times." She rolled her eyes in a motherish way, a way that Mallie could tell was a habit, meant to bring herself closer to the person she was talking to.

"Don't joke," Mallie said. "This is a real question I'm asking. Do you think that life is always a miracle?"

The woman paused. She took a breath and started to speak, then reconsidered and sat for a minute, thinking.

"Yes. I do. I do think life is a miracle," she said finally. "And I also think that miracles sometimes begin in messy circumstances, circumstances that no one planned on or wanted."

Somewhere in the building, a grandfather clock chimed. Such a formal sound in such a simple little place. The woman was quiet, waiting for Mallie to say something because it was her turn to say something and this was how conversation was supposed to go. How had it gone when she was unable to talk for herself? Had everyone talked back and forth right over her body, making decisions for her? Or had those conversations taken place somewhere else, in lawyers' offices and courtrooms, in churches and at rallies, on television screens, where talking heads looked into the camera and talked sideways with other talking heads.

Mallie pictured William T. and Crystal sitting on the couch in their house, holding hands and watching as Lucia and others decided her fate. She pictured Zach Miller driving west to Montana, escaping the scene of the crime, driving and driving and driving with the windows open and the wind drowning out his thoughts. The woman leaned forward.

"Do you want to tell me about it? There's no rush. I have all the time in the world."

"What if somebody raped you and you got pregnant and you were unconscious and you couldn't speak for yourself and others decided you would have the baby and you had no choice in the matter? Is that still a miracle?"

The woman shook her head, but it wasn't a shake that meant *No, that's not a miracle.* It was a shake of *I'm sorry.* Then the woman's eyes filled with tears. "You've been through something awful, haven't you?"

Darkness + Time + Mallie + Pain. Yes. Something awful.

Then the woman put her hand over her mouth. "Wait. You're not her, are you? You're not—"

Mallie shrugged and met the woman's eyes.

"I heard you had woken up." The woman's voice was a whisper. "Are you . . . how do you . . . what do you . . ."

"How do I feel about the pregnancy?"

"Yes. What would you have done, if you had been able to think for yourself?" The chatty-counselor attitude had disappeared and the woman rushed on. "Would you have carried the baby to term? Or would you have gotten an abortion? Now that you're back, do you think you'll try to—" She caught herself and stopped talking.

"Get the baby back?"

The woman looked away. Maybe she was thinking, trying to come up with the right answer. But what if there was no right answer?

"What would *you* do?" Mallie said. "Would you still want a baby if its father was the man who raped you and left you to die? Would you feel like, Well, the baby had no say in the matter, it was just an innocent baby? Or would the thought of raising that baby make you sick?"

The woman said nothing.

"Say you *did* want the baby," Mallie continued. "What about the baby himself? Would you think, He has a life with his foster parents, and how horrible to take a child from his parents?"

Silence.

"And what about the girl? Would you think about her? If you did, would you look at everything she already lost—her mother, her boyfriend, a whole huge stretch of her life, her privacy, the right to make up her own mind, the right to abort the baby or keep the baby or adopt the baby out—and would you think, That girl should get to do whatever she wants now? Whatever feels right to her at this point?"

The woman said nothing for a long time. Mallie sensed her trying to collect her thoughts. Then finally the woman said, "Does something feel right to you at this point?"

Mallie shook her head.

What she was thinking about, when she left the small white building with the gray cracked cement steps, cookies in a plastic bag that the woman had insisted she take despite the army-feeding box of fortune cookies on the passenger seat, was her tonsils. What she had wanted to say to the woman at the PREGNANT? WE CAN HELP place, was, "Have you ever had your tonsils out?" Because maybe then the woman would have understood what she was trying to say about pain, and the memory of it.

William T. would have understood. She pictured him sitting on his porch steps, nodding. He would have put two and two together and known what she was really asking, which was, Did she remember, somewhere within, everything that had happened to her that dark night? In that moment, she wanted to talk to him. But the thought of his grim face, his worry, his hovering, exhausted her.

———

Make up a story. Use your imagination. Solve the equation so that you can figure out how to live now, Mallie.

The four known variables of the equation are A, B, C and D. A = Time and B = Pain and C = Mallie and D = Darkness. Put them together in different ways and see what happens. $AB = CD$. $AC = BD$. $AD = BC$. No matter how she worked the equation, the outcome didn't change. Time × Pain = Mallie × Darkness. Time × Mallie = Pain × Darkness. Time × Darkness = Pain × Mallie.

There was no way out. However she solved the problem, the answers would always be Mallie multiplied and divided by Time and Darkness and Pain. All her futures were the same: unbearable. But what if she used her imagination? In her mind, Ms. Bailey stood at the head of the classroom, telling her to solve the equation a different way. That every equation, no matter how confounding it appeared to be, wanted to be solved.

She drove west, into the fiery rays of the sinking sun, and tried to puzzle her way into the heart of the problem. Mallie was the girl. Darkness assaulted and raped her and left her for dead. Time stretched on for sixteen months, while others made decisions for her. Pain was present then and now.

None of these variables could be changed, but Darkness was the great unknown. Could she manipulate him so that something unbearable became bearable? *Make him something you can somehow live with*, she thought. Make him a young man. A boy, even. Twenty years old. Make him drunk? Make him strung out? Make him not remember what he'd done? Make him horrified when he found out?

If doing so would solve the unsolvable, then yes.

Turn him into a real person. Give him a name, call him Darkness. Give him a job, make him a roofer. Give him a mother. Give him a sister, a little sister. Give him friends. Give him a dream, call it college, call it a trip to New Orleans, call it a girlfriend, call it kids, call it a future.

Make him human, if making him human is what helps *you* live with what he did to you. If regret and self-hatred make him human, then give him regret and self-hatred. Give him a dark night on a dark street in upstate New York when it was raining and he did something he can't ever undo. Give him shame. Give him self-hatred. Give him nightmares. Give him a life that is time and pain.

Give him a life that gives you back yours.

If A, B, C and D are constants, then:

Time × Pain = Mallie × D.

D lives in pain.

And Mallie figures out a way not to.

PART THREE

Darkness

EVERY NEW JOB BEGAN WITH THE STARTER ROW. ANYONE ON the crew could do it, but he was usually the one. If he put down the starter row and then the ridge shingles and the flashing around the chimney stacks and vents, he could look at a roof and know that he'd seen the job through start to finish. No one on the ground looking up could tell who did what, but that didn't matter to him, because he knew. Nights he couldn't sleep he sometimes eased out of the house and walked around looking at his roofs.

That was how he thought of them: his roofs. He knew every house he'd shingled over the past two years. Most were within a couple miles of his house. His mother didn't know he was out and walking around in the middle of the night. She wouldn't like it. She was a worrier.

It had taken him a while to learn how to use the air gun right. The compressor couldn't be set too high or the nails would sink too deep through the shingles, and shingles were neither thick nor strong. Roofs might look tight and solid, but the look was deceptive.

He had gotten the job right out of high school. He graduated from Proctor High School and he thought he'd go to Mohawk Valley Community College and get his associate's degree, but no. He didn't mind roofing. It was hard work. He was up on someone's house all day, crouching along with the nail gun, nailing down square after square, and there was a rhythm to it. Hunched over, working at a slant, a couple or three stories above the ground. His back hurt pretty much all the time, but still. There was something about that kind of work that people who'd never done it couldn't understand.

He always wore a cap. A Yankees cap, usually. He had a bunch of them, a collection, that began with a single cap that his little sister had given him on his birthday a long time ago. Now everyone gave him Yankees stuff: caps and shirts and key chains and shot glasses. And so on. The thing was he didn't really even like the Yankees. Too full of themselves. But it was too late to let everyone know that now. They'd look back on all these years and all their gifts and think, *All this time and I never even knew?* He didn't want anyone to feel dumb. So he just kept quiet.

Roofing was dangerous. How could it not be? He was way up there, and even though he nailed up the supports, they wouldn't keep him up there if he fell. It was a long way to the ground. The nail gun itself was dangerous. When he first joined the crew, he'd put two nails right through the palm of his hand. He still had the scars. Little white knots.

He lived at home. Once he got out of high school, the plan had been to live with Mack and a couple of the others in an apartment, maybe in Whitesboro, maybe even Clinton, but that fell through. Actually, those guys did all live together, over on Genesee in a triplex, but he didn't hang out there much. Correction: he didn't hang out there at all.

When he was on the roof it was almost like he was in another world. Only twenty, thirty, forty feet above the ground but everything was different. The wind sounded different. Steadier. He was closer to the tops of the trees. Sometimes branches drooped over the roof and he had to ask the homeowners if they wanted them pruned back. "Prune" sounded better than "chop off."

He was closer to the birds. That there were so many birds at the tops of trees was something that surprised him when he first started out. Sometimes they hung out on the roofline, watching him and the rest of the crew, or they perched on the edge of a skylight. He hated skylights. They felt wrong to him. A roof should be solid, impenetrable. No light should come through a roof. A skylight reminded him of the soft spot on a baby's head, something that scared him. He remembered when his little sister was born and he used to watch her brains pulsing up and down through that soft spot.

"What if we drop her?" he had said to his mother. "What would happen to her brain?"

His mother had laughed. "No one's going to drop our baby girl."

He had been nine years old then, and his mother in her forties. She carried his baby sister around all the time, holding her like a football or propped up against her chest. His mother didn't seem scared at all, and neither did his baby sister.

But he was. What if he dropped her? He was afraid for a long time, until she started to crawl. Then things seemed safer, somehow, although when he thought about it, they weren't safer at all, especially for a girl.

William T.

H E WAS BEGINNING TO GET THE HANG OF IT. HIS FEET WERE finding the rhythm, and for the heck of it he had added a little arm swoop on the tricky quarter turn.

"Let me tell you something, Jonathan," he said to Johnny, who was washing the kitchen table with the red sponge. All Johnny's tasks took him a long time, and whenever he was home for a visit he went at them with patience and determination. "Not all YouTube videos are created equal. Thank God we found the Waltz Boss."

All the online waltz instructors, no matter where he found them, seemed to be male, which in a way made sense, because they led and their partners followed, but in another way didn't make sense. Why shouldn't the female lead? And what if the partners were same-sex? Did they take turns leading? That would be egalitarian, but it would also mean learning both how to lead and how to follow.

"Who's to say who should lead and who should follow? Know what I'm talking about, Jonathan?"

Johnny looked up from the table and smiled. He was working on a hardened drip of candle wax. William T. began to hum "Moon River," which, although he had never known it until now, was a waltz. Another factoid from the Waltz Boss: many well-known songs were actually waltzes.

"*One* two three, *one* two three," William T. sang to himself. "Moon river, wider than a mile."

He concentrated on the quarter turns, dipping and swaying with his arms clutched around the couch pillow, imagining that he was dancing with Crystal. At one point he glanced up to see Johnny standing at the end of the table, smiling.

"We'll get there, Jo-o-o-na-than," William T. sang, to the tune of "Moon River." "We'll dance across the room, someday."

At that, Johnny laughed, sponge in hand, soapsuds trickling down his arm. What would become of Johnny, when he and Crystal and Burl were gone from the earth? Who would watch over him? Would he understand, when the day came, that they hadn't chosen to leave him but that this was just the way life worked? Crystal and William T. had taken care of him as best they could in their wills, and so had Burl. But wills were about money, which made things easier but wasn't the living, breathing presence in Johnny's life of the people who loved him.

What more could they do but try, though? Just as they had tried with Mallie. They had fought the church, fought Lucia, fought the decision. But the baby had been born anyway.

"What do you think's going through Mallie's mind, Johnny?" he said now. "What's she thinking about the baby? You think there's any chance she might try to get it back?"

At the word *baby*, Johnny looked up again, smiling. He loved babies. If a family with a baby came into the diner, Johnny would shuffle his way over to their table and hold out a finger for the baby to grasp. He sometimes brought over a coloring book and crayons too, no matter that a baby in a car seat or sling had no use for a coloring book.

"I know you like babies, Johnny," William T. said. "I'm not antibaby myself. But Jesus H. Christ, what a mess that would be."

Charlie's words — *She needs to get her life back, William T. And so do you* — haunted him. And so did Burl's: *She can get away from here. From them. From us. From the ghosts.* William T. didn't want to be a ghost. He didn't want to hold her back.

———

Later, after he'd dropped Johnny off at the group home, he drove to the playground again. It was a kind of compulsion at this point. If that baby lived somewhere nearby it was a near certainty that it would come to this playground. He parked under the mulberry tree and went straight to the bench. Burl had told him he would have to come to peace with the baby being in the world, but who was Burl to dictate how William T. should live?

Maybe it would be this way from now on, with the people he trusted most telling him to move on, to get over it, to be more help and less hindrance. The worst part was that Burl was right about one fundamental fact. That baby would always be in the world. Whether Mallie ended up with it or not, there was no way to avoid the fact of its existence.

All the parents, all the children. Their voices blended together. *Don't throw sand. That's not nice. There you go. Wait your turn now. Don't budge the line. Give me a hug.*

"Mr. Jones?"

A tall young man stood next to the bench and gestured to it, then said, "May I?" William T. nodded automatically, then flinched when he realized who it was. It was him. The attorney for the child. The man who had approved of Lucia getting custody, the man who had been present in the second, closed custody hearing upon her death, the man who knew everything. Aaron Stampernick. His thoughts crawled in a panic inside his head, the way ants did when their ant-hill was disturbed.

The young man sat down and William T. started to get up, then sat back down. Had the attorney for the child seen him driving by their house all those times? Had he and his wife seen him from the porch that day? He had never been this close to Aaron Stampernick. The young man was looking intently at William T., as if he were sizing him up. As if he knew something about him.

"I'm Aaron," he said, and he held out his hand.

William T. shook the hand. He was touching the hand of the man who had seen the baby, who had overseen its care, helped decide its fate.

"William T. Jones," he said, and the man smiled as if he had said something amusing.

"Yes, I know." He cleared his throat. "We, my wife, Melissa, and I, wanted you to know how sorry we are. We know how hard this has all been on you."

"No, you don't."

Aaron Stampernick bent his head in a churchlike sort of bow. Anger rose inside William T. He could just picture him in church, he and his wife side by side, the baby on one of their laps, a bag of crayons and paper in case it got bored. No, the baby was too young to color. The baby was not even a year old yet. Coloring would come later.

"You have no idea how hard it all was on me," William T. went on, "On all of us, me and Crystal and Zach and Charlie. And Mallie. How hard it all still is. The way you and Lucia and the guardian ad litem and the attorney for Mallie—what a joke—and the judge acted as if you alone knew what was in Mallie's mind."

His words spilled out, tumbling like Nine Mile Creek in the spring thaw. He was not being Switzerland. He was not calm. Aaron Stampernick stared at him and nodded. Why was he nodding?

"What do *you* think would have been best for her, Mr. Jones?"

Did he not see that this was a question that couldn't be answered? What happened to Mallie never should have happened to her. This was where William T. always got stuck. This was why he went first to abortion: get that thing out of her. Because the fact of the pregnancy was the sum total of all the hideous events of that dark night.

"My wife and I struggled with it, to be honest," the young man said. "We used to go over it and over it."

"That church of Lucia's had the answer," William T. said. "They proclaimed it loud and clear."

"Not all of them. Not all of them were sure what the right thing to do was. Some of them contacted me."

"If that's true, then you're guilty of silence. You should have been more vocal about their concerns. You let her be led off like a lamb to the slaughter." Biblical images from his childhood Sunday school rolled through his head, shepherds and stars and lambs and men in white robes with staffs.

"I'm sorry, Mr. Jones. For your troubles and Mallie's troubles and Zach's troubles. And for Lucia's troubles too. But I'm not sorry about how the baby situation worked out. He's healthy and he's happy and that's something for all of us to be glad about."

Worked out? Not one thing had worked out. The young man was talking again.

"Have you heard from Zach?"

"Why do you want to know?"

The young man sighed. It was a long, deep sigh and he didn't try to hide it.

"Because he's a good man," he said simply. "And I hope he's all right. I understand he's a private person and he needed to get away and start over, but still. I haven't heard from him in a long time."

As if he had any right to ask about Zach. But something about Aaron Stampernick's presence, his quiet, his lack of anger, had an effect on William T. He shifted on the bench so he could study the young man. He was older than William T. would have thought, maybe thirties instead of twenties, and thinner than he had looked across the parking lot that one awful day, or across the lawn that day last week.

"I hope he's all right too," William T. said, surprising himself.

The young man nodded and got up off the bench. He stood in front of William T. and the sun shone off his sandy hair. "You're a good man too," he said. "I'm sorry you had to go through this."

"*Have* to go through this," William T. corrected him. "For the fore-seeable future."

"Not necessarily. Everything changes."

Aaron Stampernick reminded William T. of Burl. Set on moving ahead, letting the past be the past. Maybe that was the way he had to be, given the fact that as attorney for the child, he had been le-gally obligated to oversee the care of the child of a rapist. Maybe, given his situation, Aaron Stampernick had to believe that every-thing would change, and for the better. The young man held out his hand and William T., after a moment of hesitation, shook it.

Mallie

WHEN SHE HAD WORKED WITH WOMEN AT THE SHELTER, SHE sometimes closed her eyes. It was easier to channel energy through her hands that way, easier to find the knots, the crunchy places, as her teacher used to call them. When her fingers found those places, a story came with them. Vigilance, fear, trauma, all held in the silent body of the woman on the massage table. Images sometimes stole into Mallie's mind as she worked: A car or a bed or a kitchen or a couch. A baby, a child, a man. A silent story that directed her fingers and guided her touch, a story that helped her draw the tension out of the woman on the table, a story that helped bring her calm and peace.

If she could bring peace to others, maybe she could bring it to herself. If not with her fingers, then with her mind. Maybe she could once-upon-a-time herself to some kind of resolution.

She thought about her *Therapeutic Massage for Trauma Survivors* textbook, how it described all physical bodies as keepers of stories, and how trauma survivors were often unaware of the stories trapped inside their own bodies. Maybe they shut down the memory of those stories because of the violence inherent in them. Maybe they did so instinctively, for reasons of survival. But when the immediate crisis had passed, it was crucial for survivors to unearth these experiences and learn how to absorb them into their present and future lives. Otherwise there was a chance they wouldn't be fully present in their bodies. This might manifest as difficulty in sexual relationships, emotional and even physical numbness, an inability to recall the events surrounding the trauma and a higher rate of depression.

Back in class, Mallie had studied the text dutifully, written papers and passed her exams. She and the other students at that point practiced massage only on one another, and under supervision. It was only when she began working with the women at the shelter that the idea of a story trapped inside a body became real. Sometimes, under her fingers and palms, a knot would gather and then recede, gather and then recede. The muscles and blood and tendons and bones of the woman's body were trying to bring something to the surface. She could sense it. In the beginning, it was almost impossible to release whatever was trapped. Call it trauma, call it tension, call it story: whatever its name, it was lodged far and deep.

It was Zach who had helped her come up with the idea of the dark bird.

"What if you pictured it—everything that had happened to the women—as if it were an animal?" he said. "Some kind of animal that attacked them?"

"And then do what?" she said. "Imagine I was fighting off the animal?"

"Maybe. Why not?"

She tried. A snarling dog with a vicious bite, a crocodile erupting out of a swamp, a rattlesnake's fangs. None of them worked. The imagined noise and motion and ferocity distracted her from the silent stories trapped inside her clients' bodies. It was only when she pictured their pain as a bird—a dark, hovering bird—that she was able to draw it forth.

The man she had named Darkness was alive in her mind now, but he kept morphing. He wouldn't stay put in the story she had constructed for him: roofer, meth-head, self-hatred. He kept spilling out. A life was growing up around him. She saw him standing on a roof. She saw him talking to his mother and his sister. She saw him wandering the aisles of Hassan's Superette. She saw him bent over a row of shingles on the steep pitch of a tall house next to a playground. She saw him dreaming menacing dreams, reliving the crunch of the clay pot on her skull. The story had taken on its own life.

"Something hard, something impossible, something good," Zach used to say when she came home from a night at the shelter. "Go."

It was a routine they had started back in the beginning, when she was new to massage and would come home wrung out from the tension and suffering of the women. She hadn't yet learned how to shake it off. The body memory these women held inside them was invisible and everywhere, and in the beginning, remnants would attach themselves to her.

Their teacher had warned them of this.

"Everyone in the world is connected," she had said, "and sometimes that connection can be dangerous."

People who cut hair, people who gave massages, therapists who talked others through their haunted pasts: all were at risk. You had to figure out a way not to get stuck in others' pain, the teacher said, and there was no one way to do it. A haircutter might set up a mirror at a certain angle, so that her clients' stories would refract off it and not be absorbed by the haircutter. A therapist might follow a ritual after each session — wash her hands, splash water on her face, open a window and breathe in the outside air.

"It's tricky for those of us who give massages," the teacher said, "because our skin is literally connected to another's skin. We absorb others' experiences and we have to figure out how to release them not only from the client but from ourselves."

"Look, Mal," Zach had said after a few weeks. "You got to figure out a way to stay sane here, or this is not going to work."

She had lost weight. She was pale. In her dreams she couldn't make her legs work, she couldn't scream; she couldn't get away from nameless and faceless men who were trying to hurt the women she worked on. She had nodded — yes, she needed to figure it out, but how?

"Was there anything good that happened tonight? Even one thing?" Zach said. "Because if there wasn't, then there's no hope."

It was late. Charlie was asleep in the loft. Mallie had pulled her knees up to her chest on the couch and wrapped her arms around them. She was a small ball of curled girl, sadness and pain ricocheting around inside her, brought all the way home to Forestport from the shelter in Utica. Three women tonight, each of them silent until the end of the massage, when their faces shone with tears and the stories came out of years of fear, years of trying to keep their children safe, years of being worn away until they barely knew who they were anymore.

She shook her head. No, there was no good thing.

"Something hard, then," Zach said.

"Everything's hard."

"One hard thing. Just one. Say it."

"The cigarette burn on the last woman's arm." She didn't want to see it in her mind, or how the woman had flinched when her fingers got close to it, but there it was. Deep and round and angry-looking.

"Okay." Zach nodded. "Now one impossible thing."

"Everything there is impossible, Zack."

"Just one, Mal. One impossible thing."

She clenched her arms tighter around her knees. Her stomach hurt. She tried to breathe into it and exhale it out, but her muscles were too tight and rigid.

"That the second woman I worked on is sixty years old and only just got the hell away from the husband who's been beating her up for the last forty years. Forty fucking years, Zach."

When Mallie had asked the woman—Jodie, it was a fake name, like most at the shelter—if there were places on her body where she should be very gentle, or avoid entirely, the woman had looked up at her. *Everywhere,* she had whispered. *Everywhere.* Next to her, Zach put his arms around her and she closed her eyes. She had barely touched this woman Jodie, and everywhere she touched, Jodie flinched.

"It's too much," she whispered into Zach's hands, which were covering hers. "There's too much awfulness. I don't think I can bear it."

"Think of one good thing, Mal. Just one. One hard thing, one impossible thing and now one good thing."

He laced his fingers through hers and waited. Zach was good at waiting. He was good at silence. He would wait as long as it took.

"That she left?" Mallie said, finally. "Forty years in, but she left?"

Zach's fingers pressed into hers. *Good job,* was what that pressure meant. She had done it. She had thought of one good thing. His fingers moved on to her shoulders, kneading and releasing, then moved over her head, pressing and holding. She let her head droop onto her knees, still drawn up to her chest, and concentrated on breathing. *She left. She left. She left.* The breaths grew slower and longer and deeper. Finally, her legs and arms unclenched and she lay back against Zach.

One hard thing, one impossible thing, one good thing. She pulled out her phone and texted her brother —

ONCE UPON A TIME THERE WAS A SISTER

and then stared at the screen, willing him to start typing, willing the little moving dots to appear. She waited and waited, but nothing. Come on, Charlie. Please. Make up a story with me, a story to get us through.

Left hand on the steering wheel, right foot on the gas, left foot on the clutch, right hand on the gear stick, heading west at seventy-seven miles an hour in a part of the country that stretched ahead like the sea. Enormous swells of ranchland, like waves rolling in, over and over and over. The way they did on the Jersey shore the time that Lucia took her and Charlie there when they were little, the week that the huge seagull swooped down and stole the block of cheese.

No people on this highway. No houses, no cars. Nothing but a four-lane ribbon of road leading straight ahead until it blurred and dissolved into the sky. She had not seen a single cop car since she passed through the western edge of Minnesota into the eastern edge of North Dakota. She pushed her right foot down.

Seventy-eight. Seventy-nine. Eighty-one. Eighty-seven.

The engine hummed and whined.

Ninety-two. Ninety-five. Ninety-nine.

The steering wheel shook. She gripped it tightly with both hands and dug her fingernails into the ripped vinyl. Wind roared outside the closed window. How much could the engine take?

A hundred and one. A hundred and three.

The Datsun shuddered around her but the engine throbbed and held its own. No sirens behind or ahead. No twirling kaleidoscope of red and blue in the rearview mirror. Nothing. She eased off the gas.

A hundred and one. Ninety-six. Eighty-eight. Seventy-six. Sixty-eight. Fifty-five.

The sound of the engine turned into a muted groan. The roaring wind quieted to a murmur. She and the truck trundled along at fifty-seven miles an hour. The road rolled and dipped and shimmered in the distance like a mirage, as if it ran out of itself up at the horizon and turned into water.

Another seventy miles gone. *See, Mallie, you're getting there.* The river of "there" was a far-ahead promise. The river of there held Zach Miller. If she could just keep her foot on the gas, keep the tank full, not give in to the tiredness, she would get there. *And once you're there, he'll help you figure it out.* Those were the words she used to muffle the dark birds hovering around her, keeping pace with the truck, invisible birds straining to open their beaks and call out *Baby*, and *Darkness*, and *Pain*, and *Zach.*

The sun was the yolk of an egg simmering in a pot of water. The truck was the pot of water and she was the swimmer at the wheel. Sweat stung her eyes. Then the golden yolk slid off the top of the truck and began its slow arc through the sky to her left. Long rays slanted through the open window, fingering their way into the wind-rushing cab.

NO SERVICES FOR THE NEXT 158 MILES, said a highway sign.

The gas stations in the Dakotas weren't gas stations the way she thought of gas stations. These were more like little general stores in the middle of nowhere. She pulled off on a ranch access road and clattered over a cattle guard.

"Gas on pump two please."

Forty-two dollars and fifty-eight cents. She handed the woman three twenties.

"Got anything smaller, miss? We're short on ones. And fives. We're short on everything, actually."

"I'm sorry. I don't."

The woman smiled, a big white-toothed smile. Little stud earrings marched up and down both earlobes. It was a tiny store and every shelf was packed. Groceries and candy and miniature cans of drinks that promised five hours of this and ten hours of that. Diapers and tampons and paper plates and napkins. Condoms and aspirin and cough syrup. Mosquito repellent and fishing poles and bobbers and lures. Tire pressure gauges and atlases and keychains and flashlights.

"Where you off to on this fine day?" the woman said.

"Montana."

"Nice. Big Sky country. Where are you on your way from?"

"Upstate New York. The Adirondack mountains."

"Adriondack Mountains," the woman said, pronouncing it the way many people did, *A dri on-dack.* "What brings you out west?"

"I'm running away."

The woman nodded, as if running away out west was nothing new to her. "From what?"

"The last year and a half. A lot of bad things."

"Well, good luck to you, then," the woman said approvingly. "Go westward, young woman. You want some gum?" She held out an open pack.

"No, thanks," and then something leapt in the woman's eyes, a flicker of recognition, and Mallie thought of the wig that wasn't on her head.

"Wait a minute," she said. "Upstate New York. You're not *her*, are you?"

It was the way she said "her." Her eyes were bright with discovery, with the kind of intuitive leap that defied rationality. Mallie shook her head, but that was a mistake, because how would she know who "her" was if she wasn't her? The woman tilted her head.

"You're not the girl who"—now she was faltering—"was, that story that was all over the headlines, you know, that girl, that photo of that girl, that cute boyfriend, the baby, it happened in upstate New York . . ."

Mallie said nothing. There wasn't much anyone could do, if you just stayed silent and kept shaking your head in a *No, not her, no, that girl is not me* sort of way. The other person would start to think they were crazy to have leapt to that conclusion.

She got back in the truck and drove and drove, and when she could drive no farther, she pulled over and stilled the engine. She stretched out as far as she could on the front seat and lay on her back, looking through the window up at the stars. It was a clear night, moonless, and they filled the sky. Diamonds. Lucy in the sky with diamonds. She sang the old song in her head.

Her phone beeped and she pulled it out of its home at the bottom of the box of fortune cookies.

ONCE UPON A TIME THERE WAS A SISTER

WHOSE BROTHER WISHED HE COULD TURN BACK TIME

The screen went dark after that. Charlie. She hugged the phone to her heart as if it were him.

Darkness

HIS LITTLE SISTER WAS HAPPY HE STILL LIVED AT HOME. SHE was nine years younger, a mistake — that's what his mother had said when they told him he was going to have a baby brother or sister, but mistake wasn't a good word for a baby, especially when there was no dad in the picture, so he called her a happy accident. She called him Big D. Which was funny, because he wasn't all that big. Big to a little kid, though.

She was almost thirteen now. But to him she was still a little kid He used to push her on the baby swings over at the playground. He used to take her there every day when he got home from school, give his mother a break so she could put her feet up or start supper or just be alone for a while. His mother's life hadn't been a piece of cake. She worked the night shift and then she came home and made breakfast for all of them. He had offered to do that, so she could go straight to bed, but she said she liked making their breakfast.

Even for him.

He said, "Mom, I'm twenty-two," and she said, "Once a mother, always a mother."

He still saw Mack and the others sometimes. Mostly by accident. Coming in and out of the grocery store, at the gas station, Friendly's ice cream. The last time he'd seen Mack was at the DMV. They were both getting their licenses renewed. Both born in July, within a week.

"Hey, man," he said.

"Mack. How are you?"

He hoped he would say *Good* or *Fine* or *Can't complain,* so he could just take his number and fill out the form by himself, without talking, but Mack shook his head.

"The question is how you're doing," he said.

He looked down at the little tab of paper in the red machine, waiting for him to take it: 078. Why did numbers from machines like that always begin with a zero? Made no sense.

"What happened to you?" he said. "I mean it, D. Why'd you quit us all?"

He shook his head, as if nothing had happened to him.

"Look, D. We all know it was bad for a while. I'm sorry you got into that shit and I'm sorry it was my brother who got you into it and I'm sorry it messed you up so bad. But it's done now, right? You're through it, right? You're clean?"

Yes, it was done. It was all done, the desperation and craving, the need for money to stop the desperation, the things he had done to get the money. It hadn't lasted more than a few months anyway. It was done with him and he was done with it and he wanted Mack just to go away because he, Big D, was not clean. There was nothing clean about him. But Mack kept standing there, until a lady came up and reached around him and said, "Excuse me, gentlemen," in that stupid-loud way that really meant *Get the hell out of my way.*

———

The place where it happened wasn't far from his house. He'd walked down it hundreds of times in his life. It was so close, you know? It was like no one could believe such a horrible thing had happened right there in their own neighborhood. His mother had been on the phone the next morning, talking to her best friend, Cindy, who used to live two blocks away but moved to South Carolina last year.

"That poor girl," his mother was saying. "That poor, poor girl."

He stood in the kitchen while she talked, trying to make another pot of coffee. He didn't know how much coffee to put in the filter thing. Making coffee was something his mother did, when she got home from work, before the rest of them woke up. He was shaky and trembling. It had been a bad night. Bad. He was blocking it out of his mind. He dumped in some grounds and filled the pot halfway with water and pressed the on button.

"I guess she was waiting for her brother to leave a party," his mother said. "In one of those big brick apartment buildings, you know the ones I mean over on Hawthorne? She was waiting to give him a ride home."

His head hurt. The coffeemaker started to make those burping sounds, and the first dark-brown drops appeared on the bottom of the glass coffeepot.

"No, Cindy, don't say that," his mother said. "That's not fair. It wasn't late but it wouldn't matter if it was."

She was drumming her fingers on the kitchen table. She was on the home phone, the old one with the twirly cord. No one had a landline anymore except them. Cindy was Ma's best friend but that didn't mean they agreed on everything.

"You're only saying those things because the idea of it terrifies you," his mother was saying now. "The police think he raped her on the lawn of the church and that she came after him down the sidewalk and that's when he bashed her head in. I mean, just imagine if it were one of our girls."

There was a knock on the back door just then. His little sister, wanting in. She saw him through the glass windowpane and smiled. Then she pressed her face into the glass so that her nose and mouth and cheeks were all smushed together. She looked horrible. She looked like she was suffering. The sight of her face like that made his stomach turn. It was all he could do to walk over to the door and let her in.

The story was on the front page next day. He came downstairs late; it was Sunday, and even though other crews worked on Sunday, Billy's Roofing didn't. Which was something he used to be grateful for, because it gave him one guaranteed day off a week. Now he wished they did work on Sundays.

"Would you look at this," his mother said. She was sitting at the table with a cup of coffee, reading the paper. "What a nightmare. That poor girl."

She pointed at the headline and shook her head. She was good with dramatics. She was that woman who, if one of their neighbors stalked into a school with an assault weapon and started spraying bullets, would talk to the reporters and say she never suspected a thing, he was always a quiet boy, she'd lived next to him his whole life, his parents were nice people. His mother liked to sit in the morning with the paper after she got home from work and shake her head at all the horrible things in the paper, all the horrible things that people did to one another. So he took it with a grain of salt, the daily newspaper drama, but she liked backup for her opinions, so he leaned over her and read the headline.

AREA WOMAN ASSAULTED, LEFT FOR DEAD

He looked at it and knew it was her. There was no name, no photo, but sometimes you instantly knew something, and there was no shaking it. His gut turned to ice.

"So terrible," his mother said. "Can you imagine?"

"What happened?"

He managed to keep his voice normal.

"This poor girl on Hawthorne," his mother said. "Raped and beaten."

"When?"

"Friday night."

Look at her, shaking her head like that. There was something about his mother that made him angry, as if she thought she could somehow keep them safe if she kept shaking her head and making sympathetic noises. Then she looked up at him and the anger instantly went away. Because it was real, that look in her eyes.

"What if it was Beth?" she said. She was whispering, as if Beth were in the next room, even though she was sound asleep upstairs. "Can you imagine, if that was your sister?"

"Is she going to be okay?"

"She's in the ICU. Her head was bashed in. They think whoever did it called 911 from the girl's own cell phone. I mean, what kind of a monster . . ."

"Maybe he felt bad and called 911?" he said. "Maybe it was drugs and he didn't mean to do something so awful? He must've been out of his mind. That's the only possible reason. Meth, maybe. Maybe he didn't even remember it when he woke up the next morning."

The words tumbled out and she looked up at him oddly but then there was a sound at the kitchen doorway. Beth, standing there in her pajamas. "What are you talking about?" she said. "What happened?"

"Nothing," his mother said. She turned the paper over and then rolled it up and reached out and tapped Beth on the shoulder with it. "Nothing."

"Something," Beth persisted. Her eyes went from their mother to him and back again. "Just tell me. Tell me what you guys are talking about."

"Something that happened a couple nights ago," their mother said. "Nothing to worry about."

"Mom's right," he said. "Some strung-out asshole. Out of his mind."

That night, when his mother and Beth were at church, he unrolled the paper and read the whole article. The ice came back and filled him. He couldn't breathe right and his head filled up with fuzz and blur. Dizzy. Like he was going to fall down, even though he was sitting in a kitchen chair at the kitchen table. Christ, could he possibly have done that?

William T.

T THE SOUND OF WILLIAM T.'S CELL PHONE RINGING, BURL
and Crystal looked up from their game. The three of them
were sitting in Burl's garden, at the table he had made from
two stumps and a long, curving flat rock he had prised out of Nine
Mile Creek. Burl and Crystal were playing Bananagrams, the speedy
Scrabble-like word game that William T. had no patience with but
they loved. The game that had helped get them through the early
weeks and months of the siege. The phone was a hot wafer in his
hand. It was Mallie.

"Mallo Cup! Finally. Where are you?"

"I'm here."

"Where's here?"

She ignored him. "I'm trying to figure things out, William T."

Burl and Crystal were leaning forward now, trying to overhear.
Mallie's voice was tinny and far away. William T. closed his eyes so
he could concentrate. *Let her lead the way*, he reminded himself, and he
forced himself to stay quiet and let her talk.

"Remember equations, William T.? Like in algebra?"

Strange question. Algebraic equations, yes, he remembered them.
Barely. Math had never been his strong suit. Why was she talking
about algebra?

"Sure, I remember equations," he said. "A and B and C and D, that
kind of thing?"

"Yeah. I made one up. D is the guy. Darkness. Him."

Him, as in the evil bastard who started all this? The one that he, William T., sometimes dreamed about killing? She was talking again. *Switzerland,* he told himself.

"I turned the whole thing into an equation," she said, "all of it. Me and Time and Pain and Darkness. D was the only variable I could change so I made him a meth-head and I named him Darkness and that's how I picture him now. I picture him as a roofer up high on a roof, looking around the city. But inside he thinks about what he did and he hates himself."

What kind of strange story this was he did not know. It sounded like a perverted version of the Once Upon a Time game she used to play with Charlie, and now the image was stuck in his own mind, a man on a roof, hunched over, nailing shingles into wood, eyes looking down over a dark city. Burl and Crystal were making faces, gesturing at him—put her on speakerphone? Is that what they wanted? He shook his head, the phone pressed to his ear.

"I'm trying to make it bearable," she said. "So I can figure out how to live with what happened."

"But it's not bearable. What happened isn't bearable."

"Stop, William T. It's my life, not yours. Remember?"

"I remember," he forced himself to say.

"You have to beat off the dark birds, William T. You can't let them live inside you. They will take you over, William T."

Dark birds. The words she had said on the first day she came back to the world. Her name for evil, maybe. For the terrible things that people did to one another.

"I don't want the things that happened to me to turn into dark birds. That's why I made him into a man with a mother and a sister. A man who did something horrible that he regrets."

"But you have no idea if that's true or even close to true, Mallie," he said, in a tone that he hoped was reasonable.

"That doesn't matter. The only thing I can change is the idea of him, so I made him into someone who hates himself for what he did. It's a way to solve something unsolvable."

"I'll tell you something, Mallie. If I knew the bastard who did it was a strung-out roofer I'd find him and throw him right off the god-damn roof myself."

At that, Burl and Crystal shook their heads at him, their faces as grim as the sound of his own voice in the phone. So much for being Switzerland. But Mallie's voice on the other end was calm.

"Then that means the dark birds have you," Mallie said. "You have to fight them off, William T."

"Not possible."

"You have to make it possible. Try something, William T. Tell me one hard thing about this situation. Just one."

At that, the anger left him and a lump rose in his throat. She was playing the One Hard Thing game again, the game he had heard Zach play with her when something troubled her. He swallowed hard. He pictured her there, wherever "there" was, holding the phone to her ear and being patient with him.

"Everything about this is hard."

"Narrow it down. One hard thing."

"That someone hurt you."

"Now one impossible thing."

It was on the tip of his tongue to say *Everything* again, because it was the truth and because the everything-ness of it crowded his mind and wouldn't let him go. But he held back. She was leading the way and he had to let her.

"That baby. The fact of its existence."

She was quiet for a little while and he worried that maybe she'd blocked the baby out of her mind and now he'd brought it back by mentioning it. He shouldn't have mentioned it. He should have kept the thoughts of the baby in his own dark mind. Maybe he *was* filled with dark birds.

"And now one good thing."

"Jesus, Mallie. You're asking the impossible."

"Decide there's something good and tell me what it is, William T. That's how this works."

But he couldn't. Nothing came to him. Patient girl, she waited on the other end of the line. Mallie was being Switzerland. One hard thing, one impossible thing, one—

"That you're alive," he said, and slumped with relief, because it was true.

"See? It works," she said, and he could hear the smile in her voice.

Then the phone went silent and still in his hand. He looked up at Burl and Crystal and pushed the phone down into his pocket.

"She brought up the baby?" Burl said.

"No. That was me."

"So she didn't talk about it at all?"

"No," William T. said. "All she said was—" but he stopped, because Burl's shoulders had slumped. Why did he look so downcast? Then it came to him in a sudden wave of knowledge. Burl wanted that baby in his life, that was why. He opened his mouth but Crystal was faster.

"Burl," she said. "Oh, Burl," and in her voice was the half of the equation that William T. would have missed, the part that had nothing to do with the baby and how he came to be in this world. The half that was about Burl, who had never had children. Burl, who would welcome that child, any child, maybe, no matter how that child had come into the world, into his life and show him how to make a table out of a stump and a flat rock. How to plant a garden, how to open a letter with a letter opener instead of ripping it, how to eat a stack of pancakes at Keye's Pancake House up in Old Forge. Jesus. Burl.

There was too much loneliness in this world, there was too much hurt, and his oldest friend should not have lived his life alone. *He has you*, he could hear Crystal saying in his head, *and he has me, and he has Charlie and Johnny. He has his garden and his mail route and his church choir. Now he has Mallie back. He has us all.* And yes, it was true, and no, it wasn't true, because Burl had missed out on something that all his life he had wanted. He had to turn away from the sight of Burl's face.

"I talked to Zach," Burl said. "The other day."

Both Crystal and William T. turned to him in surprise.

"He picked up the phone for you?" William T. said.

"I didn't call him. He called me."

"Why the hell would he call *you?*" William T. said, before he realized how rude it sounded.

"He wanted to know if I'd heard from Mallie. He's worried."

"He should be. She's making up stories now about the rapist being some kind of roofer, a meth-head or something. Why'd he call?"

"I think he's lonely, William T. I think he misses home. The way things used to be."

"Well, welcome to the world, Zach Miller."

Burl flicked his hand at William T. as if to shoo him away.

"Look, William T. You can be angry all you want, but it's not your business to judge Zach, or Mallie, for that matter. If she wants to make up a story about a strung-out roofer, if that's her way of getting through this and out the other side, then good for her."

"You can't just make up stories, Burl. You can't just decide something's good when it isn't. You can't just pretend your way into a whole new life."

"Sure you can. We all do."

"Yeah? What's my story, then?"

"Anger and bitterness. Too much of the time."

Burl sat there looking at him, eyes resolute. Quiet Burl. Hold-himself-in-the-background Burl. But not all the time, and especially not recently. Look at the way he'd collected all that money for Mallie and then urged her to go. William T. clenched his fist around the phone in his pocket. He had not done a good job. He had not stayed calm and steady. He was not Switzerland.

"Burl's right," Crystal said. "Mallie and only Mallie gets to choose how to frame what happened to her."

"And if she frames the rapist as a roofer who hates himself? Just makes it up out of thin air? That's crazy. That's called magical thinking."

"No. What it is, is her decision. If she wants to see the baby, then that's her decision. If she wants to see Zach, that's her decision. Nothing is cut and dried the way you want to believe it is, William T. Can't you see that?"

"No, I can't," William T. said. "I'm sorry, but I can't."

Crystal was silent, her eyes on him, unblinking. The image of Johnny rose up in his mind. Johnny, born with the cord wrapped around his neck. Johnny, who would not ever live independent of them or the caretakers at the group home. Johnny, whose life had been blunted in so many ways from the moment he was born. Johnny, whose existence had brought so much love and happiness to them all, his whole life long.

Mallie

—

F LY AWAY, DARK BIRD.
   She used to send the command silently into the hurt bodies of the women at the shelter. She sent it via her own body,
through her hands and fingers and sometimes her whole arms, and
into the bound-up ball of twisted pain lodged within the women. *Go
away. Rise into the sky. Do not come back.* Sometimes it was magical, like
the time she saw—literally saw—a huge black bird rise into the air
of the tiny dim room. *Go!* she told it, with the client silent and still
and closed-eyed on the table beneath her. The dark bird had vanished
through the ceiling, into the cold night sky above the shelter. And in
that moment, the client drew in a sharp breath and opened her eyes
in surprise.

   You don't want to get bound up in another's history, her teacher had
cautioned them. *You have to remain your own self. You have to be clear.*

   And she had learned how to be. But what about now? How could
you be clear when you had no memory of what your body had en-
dured, no memory of the people who had touched you without your
knowing? When, at the thought of that baby, alive and in the world
and living in Utica, you felt no connection?

   She and the Datsun had made it all the way to the eastern edge of
Montana. Zach lived in this state now. Nothing about his days was
familiar to her. Charlie hated him for leaving, and William T. tensed
up at the mention of his name, and Crystal went silent. But none of
them knew Zach the way she did. None of them had been there those

late nights on the couch after work, when she couldn't shake the dark birds from her own body. *One hard thing, one impossible thing, one good thing.* Each night, Zach had waited until she found one good thing. Even on the hardest and most impossible nights, she had been able to find one good thing.

"I don't know what I would do without you," she had said on one of those nights. "I wouldn't know how to be alive without you."

A cheesy-movie thing to say, but she had meant it. The thought of Zach disappearing had been her biggest fear. She wouldn't let herself think the word *died*. *Disappeared* was as close as she would let herself come to that. He knew what she was thinking, though. She was twenty years old, he was twenty-two, and they had been together four years already.

"You'd figure it out." His hands were on her shoulders, pressing and releasing. "One hard thing, one impossible thing, one good thing."

"There wouldn't be any good things if you were gone."

"There would have to be," he said.

Three years had passed since that night. A year and a half of them she had no memory of, but Zach did. How had he gotten through all the months after the night they found her lying on the street? Who had been there for Zach? Had he asked himself the series of questions? Had he been able to find one good thing?

Questions were all she had. She was driving west by instinct, into the sunset, like a migrating bird pulled toward an unknown home. A dozen miles west of Miles City, Montana, she parked the truck on the shoulder and laced her hands over her belly, over the place where a whole other life had begun. The sky outside the windows was crazy with stars, a fury of stars, dark canopy pricked everywhere with light. Stars that shimmered and glittered and shook with everything that was unknown. My God, my God, why hast thou forsaken me? Panic clawed its way up inside her and she sat up and cried his name over and over — *Zach, Zach, Zach* — picturing an invisible cloud of birds that rose into the sky and bore his name westward.

Next to her the box of possible futures rode shotgun. She had shoved William T.'s box of pain behind the seat so she wouldn't have to see it, but the fortune cookies had kept her company these thousands of miles. They rustled when the truck went over a bump. Their cellophane wrappers twinkled when the sun shone on them. Her little black phone lay hidden at the bottom of the box.

It used to bother William T. that she and Zach saved their fortune cookies.

"You're playing with fate," he used to tell them when he was at the cabin and caught sight of the white liquor store box. "Tear them open, toss the fortunes, and just eat the goddamn things."

It was the unopened-ness of the fortunes that made him uneasy, he said, like a curse they were inviting into their lives.

"I don't like fortune cookies to begin with," he had said. "Number one, they taste like crap. Number two, you can't let your destiny be ruled by superstition. Are you going to trust a crunchy cardboard cookie over your own heart and mind?"

Back then, she had laughed at him. But now she thought about it again. Wasn't William T. actually doing the opposite of what he claimed? Giving weight and substance to the idea of a fortune influencing one's fate seemed like the very definition of superstition. And whether or not he thought it was the right thing to do, of all the things William T. could have saved for her from their home, he had chosen to keep the box of fortunes.

And she had chosen to bring them with her. She had brought them both — documents detailing the past and cookies full of possible futures — with her on this migration to Montana. What if she opened all the cookies right now, read the fortunes, picked the ones she liked and tossed the rest out the window? *And don't you want to be the master of your own fate?* Zach had asked, way back at the Golden Dragon the night of their first date. But he was the one who had saved those first two cookies and then kept adding to the pile over the years. Wasn't choosing *not* to read the fortunes a way of saying that he too believed in their power?

If she had to figure out life without Zach, what would she do with their box of possible futures?

As if in response, the box buzzed. She plunged her hand down through the cookies and felt around for her phone. Charlie! Eight words glowed on the screen.

ONCE UPON A TIME THERE WAS A BROTHER
She thought and counted and tapped out the words.
WHOSE SISTER DROVE A THOUSAND MILES TO MONTANA
The response was immediate.
TO TALK TO THE ASSHOLE WHO ABANDONED HER?

Back when she and Charlie and Zach all lived together in the cabin in Forestport, Charlie had watched Zach play the One Hard Thing game with her. He had watched her walk in the door after a late night at the shelter and go straight to Zach. No words. No explanation. Just the three of them together in the small house surrounded by deep woods, three people who knew one another so well that when one was upset, the others sensed it and knew why. Charlie had known Zach a long time. He should know that no matter the reason Zach had left, Mallie would need to hear it from him.

STOP IT, she tapped back, breaking the eight-words-per-line rule of the game. I MEAN IT, CHARLIE. She tossed the phone back into the box of cookies. She was about to start the engine again when Charlie called, the jazzy ring tone she'd assigned to his number years ago shimmering up from the bottom of the box.

"Mal."

"Don't talk about him that way, Charlie."

"What if he deserves it? What if it's all hard when you see him? What if it's all impossible? What if there's nothing good?"

"I won't know that until I see him."

"Listen. You want me to come with you? I can look for a flight and you can pick me up somewhere out there."

"No. Thank you, but no."

"Jesus, Mallie, I hate the thought of you driving all that way by yourself."

"Now you sound like William T. I'm not defenseless. And I'm not by myself. I brought the fortune cookies."

"Toss the goddamn cookies. They're stale."

"You can't just throw out all your possible futures, Charlie."

"How can you sound so normal? I mean, you actually sound like yourself."

"I *am* myself," she said, and that seemed to shut him up.

"Mal, can I ask you something?" he said, after a while. "Am I, like, an uncle now? Are you a mother?"

"No. Yes. Maybe? Whatever we are, we didn't choose to be."

"I know we didn't. But are we, anyway? Even if we don't want to be? That's the hardest thing about this, to me. That we had no choice in anything that happened. It was like being on a train and knowing you wanted to get off, but the train just kept going."

"Was Mom part of the train?"

"Maybe. She was surrounded by everyone from her church. She let them do what they wanted. Unless she believed it was the right thing too. I don't really know."

At the end, what had gone through their mother's mind? Charlie had not been with her when she died, nor had William T. or Crystal. She had died at home, her fellow congregants around her. Had the baby been there too?

"You think she was lonely when she died, Charlie? Do you think she had regrets?"

"It's not something I can think about, Mal. If she did, it was too late. Too late to rethink things. Too late to stop the baby from happening."

Darkness

H OW IT HAPPENED BEGAN WITH MACK. NO. HOW IT HAPPENED
began with Mack's brother. No. How it happened was he, Darkness, was in trouble. He was in trouble and the things he did to
stay in trouble were worse and worse, were out of his control. How it
happened was he was walking down the street and she was at the end
of it in the mist, peering down at something on the street and then
he pushed her down and snatched her bag and ran, and as he ran he
felt for the wallet and he pulled out the cash and he threw the whole
thing, the whole of it—bag, little things spilling out of it—into the
yard of the church. On the ground behind the bush by the church. By
the side of the church.

How it happened was she came after him. He was out of his mind.
Wasn't he? Wasn't he out of his mind? She came after him shouting
and yelling and he had to make her stop and he was strung out. That
was the term, *strung out*. Otherwise he could not have done what the
paper had said he had done. It wasn't in him to do something like
that. He didn't remember doing it. Right?

He had been twenty. He was going to start at MVCC in January.
He still lived with his mother and his sister but that was about to
change because he was going to get an apartment with Mack and the
others.

In the photos they kept showing afterward she was pretty. Smiling.
Her in a blue dress, her in jeans and a T-shirt that said IMAGINE on
the front, like his mother's favorite John Lennon song. All the inter-

views with people who knew her, her mother, her brother, her boyfriend—Zach was his name—that older guy, William something,
William, who wouldn't shut up.

His DNA was on file now. It must be. It was the first thing they
checked for, on the crime shows, anyway. Samples. She must have
been unconscious when they took the samples. He hated imagining
it. But he couldn't stop imagining it either. How it was dark and raining and what she must have looked like when the first cop showed
up. What the EMTs must have thought when they saw her. How
they must have stabilized her head before they got her up onto the
stretcher and slid her in through the double doors, the way you slide
a package of hamburger into the refrigerator.

He thought about it all the time. If there was some way to erase
memories, like in that movie about the spotless mind, he would do it.
He would start all over again. It would be good if they could take
out everything but leave the memory of how to shingle a roof, so he
could still get a job. But if it was all or nothing, he'd go with nothing.
Then he wouldn't have to think about that night anymore.

It had been dark. The kind of rain that was more like heavy mist,
like the air itself was rain. She must really not remember a thing.
Otherwise wouldn't she have said something by now? And if they
found him, if somehow they found him, then they would take a cheek
swab and they would match it against the DNA that they had on file.
Wouldn't they?

If he couldn't remember it, all of it, he wasn't entirely responsi-
ble. Was he?

Did he remember more of it than he thought he did? Was it buried
inside him somewhere?

Up on the roof it was quiet. Sound was muted. Even this little bit
farther off the ground, the wind blew stronger. You could feel its
power. Once he had lain down on the roof — the others were off getting lunch but he told them he would work through—and looked up.
Way high up, the wind was blowing stronger than you could imagine. It circled the earth in an endless stream. It carried the dust and
the dirt and the gas and the filth that everyone gave off there on the
ground, the endless stream of filth, and it swirled it up and away. It

hauled up good things too, like songbirds that floated on its currents. Where the rest of it went, the filth, he didn't know.

Sometimes he played Possible Futures when he was up on the roof. In one possible future, he was there in Utica, walking down the street, thirsty because it was an all-day-long job on a roof with no shade. And spur of the moment, he spun around and detoured down the next block to Hassan's Superette because Hassan had a whole shelf of root beer from all around the country. Root beer was his favorite soda and Hassan knew it, because he used to go to Hassan's with his little sister, Beth, to buy her a frozen candy bar in the summer. He had quit going after that night. He quit most of his familiar places after it happened. They might know somehow. They might be able to look into his eyes and know what he had done. What they said he had done.

In this particular possible future, he decided that it was time to change the course of things and go back to Hassan's. Because he was thirsty, and Hassan had a whole shelf of root beer, and it wouldn't be so bad, seeing him again after all this time. In this future he pushed open the door and it made the same needs-to-be-planed scraping sound it always made. He was ready to say hi to Hassan, ready to tell him he was sorry he hadn't been back, that things had been rough. The words were on his tongue. It was like he'd practiced saying them so often that they were just ready to come tumbling out.

"Hi, Hassan," he said.

Hassan was behind the counter talking to a woman, who turned around and looked at him. It was her. It was the girl. She was wearing the blue sundress from that one photo. It was her. She was back.

"D—" Hassan said, and there was surprise in his voice. But the girl was looking right at him, she was looking right at him and, Jesus, maybe it would click in, maybe she would remember right that very minute, and Hassan was starting to come around from behind the counter, and that was when he ran back out the door and right back to the same future that he was already living in.

"D, tell me what's going on," his mother said. She kept saying that. Every week or so, she'd ask him again. She was worried about him. "You're not yourself. Tell me what's going on in that still-waters-run-deep head of yours."

But what could he tell her?

A sky full of silver needles slanting down and disappearing once they fell past the streetlight. One streetlight, at the far end. A girl looking at something on the pavement, her bag dangling at her side. *Go. Quick. Run.* It had happened fast. He wasn't himself when he did it. Had he done it? He must have. He needed money. He remembered some things. She fought back, and that pissed him off — it filled him with rage and he wanted to hurt her. Right? Was that how it happened? He remembered how hard it was to shove her when she came after him screaming, to shove her down and shut her up. When it was over she opened her mouth and she was going to start again, start screaming. She kept fighting him. She wouldn't stop. There was a big clay pot. She was going to keep on screaming and keep on fighting and he had to stop her. He had to stop her. He was strung out. That changed things. Didn't it?

It had been 543 days. He walked down that block sometimes. Not the first few weeks, when it was all still happening. When the news was everywhere, every newspaper and every news station, the internet, posters, even, stapled to poles and taped on store doors. Witnesses or anyone with any information, please call.

The first time he walked by, he made himself look at it. *Look at it. Goddammit, look at it.* This was where it had happened. He tried to make himself remember.

They had gone up and down the block, over onto the next one too, and they knocked on all the doors and questioned everyone, every single person, about what they had heard. No one remembered hearing anything.

Who made the call from her cell phone, then? Who was it who called 911? They hypothesized it was the attacker but they didn't know for sure. The voice was a male's. It was a little garbled, they said, but he sounded tense. Maybe distraught. The television people had played the tape so many times that he heard it in his head like a soundtrack. Sometimes when he was up on the roof it looped over and over like a song he hated but couldn't get out of his head.

911 operator. Please state the nature of your emergency.

There's a girl. She, I don't know, she's . . . maybe she's dead.

Where are you, sir?

Hawthorne, I think. Yeah, Hawthorne. Between Redmond and Forest.

Okay, stay there. Don't hang up. Is the woman moving or making any sounds?

I don't think so . . . no.

Help is on the way, sir. Do you know CPR?

She's not . . . fuck. Fuck!

Then there was a buzz and a clicking noise and the tape in his head went quiet. Sometimes he could nail down another square, measure the distance with his eyes from the ridgeline to the edge, gauge how far it would be from the edge to the ground if he dove headfirst before it started up again:

911 operator. Please state the nature of your emergency.

There's a girl. She, I don't know, she's . . . maybe she's dead.

No one knew who made the call. Nothing could be traced. You would think that now, the way the world was, where so many things were invisible but not really, that the voice on the call could be traced. That someone could figure out whose voice it was. That the person could be found.

No one had been found. She went to sleep for a long time and then she woke up but she didn't remember a thing.

There was no going back. That was the thing. In his mind, sure, he went back in his mind, over and over in his mind he went through the sequence of events, but nothing in real life was going to redo itself. Not the fine, fine drops of rain, autumn rain. Not the girl bent over the pavement at the end of the block. Not the streetlight shining down on her and the bag dangling from her shoulder. Not the way she fell forward when he grabbed the bag and ran. Not everything that happened afterward.

The tape played itself in his mind.

William T.

HEN MALLIE WAS LITTLE, A FIERCE AND UNSWERVING BE-
lief in reincarnation had sprung up in her after her father
died. William T. remembered her peering at babies at the
diner, or on the sidewalks down in Utica when he took her and Charlie there in the summer while Lucia was at work. She had a way of
staring at them, her whole body rigid with focus, that made him want
to laugh and cry. *The soul appears through the eyes*, she used to tell him
back then, and she would stare and stare at the eyes of a newborn
until it unnerved the parents and they removed the baby to a safe
distance.

"Remember how you used to stare at every new baby that came
your way?" he had asked her once, when she was in high school and
they were picking sweet corn. "Back when your dad died?"

She had shot him a look that he couldn't interpret.

"You tried to train Charlie into doing it too but he would have none
of it."

"I wanted my dad to still be in the world, William T.," she said.
"And thinking he might be reincarnated was one way to do that."

She had turned back to the sweet corn, dragging the burlap sack
to the next row. This was shortly after she and Zach began dating.
His parents were pulling up stakes for Alaska but Zach just shook his
head when they told him of course he was coming with them, they
were a family, it would be an adventure. *I'm eighteen,* he had said, *and
I'm not leaving Sterns or Mallie.* Young, and Mallie even younger, but

a future together was already a done deal between the two of them. Zach began building the cabin, and later, when Lucia gave herself over to the church, Mallie and Charlie moved into it with him.

Zach was a Miller, and Millers, with the single exception of Zach's father, stayed put in Sterns. They were upstate New York men of the woods and the fields. They made their livings with their hands. The Millers were thought to be wild—teachers and principals and coaches feared their presence—but to William T., they were wild in the way of animals. They knew what they wanted and there was no bullshit about them.

And what Zach wanted was Mallie.

William T. had long figured they would end up together. One night in particular, the annual Octoberfeast at the Twin Churches on the village green, he and Crystal had been waiting in line with everyone else to pay their $9.99 and be shown to a seat at one of the long tables. Mallie had been the ticket seller, sitting on a stool by a makeshift cash register, making change and tearing tickets off a heavy roll. He had watched as Zach Miller and his cousins Tom and Joe handed over their money and took their tickets. He had seen the way Zach's fingers touched Mallie's, the sideways smile he gave her.

"Mark my words," William T. said to Crystal, and nodded toward the head of the line. "Zach Miller and Mallie Williams are about to embark."

A strange way to put it. But Crystal had known what he meant, and he had been right. A few weeks later he had been in Utica getting his hair cut, walked out of the barbershop and saw the two of them standing outside the Golden Dragon restaurant. Mallie was holding a white waxy box of leftovers and a couple of fortune cookies and Zach was jingling the keys to his truck. She had looked up at Zach, laughing, and he reached out and brushed a lock of hair out of her eyes. And that was it. They had been together from then on. Nights she had class late at MVCC, Zach would sometimes drive down with her and read a book at the Roasted Bean next to campus until class let out. None of the books he read—complicated essays about human beings and the natural world by people like Wendell Berry and Aldo Leopold—were books William T. would touch with a ten-foot pole.

But William T. was not a reader. He wouldn't have pegged Zach as one either, but it just went to show that you could not predict.

Like Zach abandoning Mallie. In a thousand years, he would not have predicted that one. He could still see Mallie rising up from the pillow in the hospital, alive and alight for the first time, at the thought of Zach Miller. What sort of look had he himself had on his face, that she would shut down so completely? It must have been bad. Charlie had said Zach turned out to be an asshole, as if trying to convince himself it was true. But it was bewilderment, more than anger, that filled William T. now when he thought of Zach.

Zach was the one who had come up with the One Hard Thing game in the first place.

"Try," Zach used to say to Mallie. "One good thing. There has to be one tiny, good thing about this."

The trick with Zach was that he had chosen to believe that something good could be found in any situation, and that gave him the patience to search until he found it. It was a game that had always frustrated William T., and it still frustrated him. One hard thing about Zach moving to Montana? That he'd left Mallie behind. One impossible thing? That he'd left Mallie behind. One good thing? That was where William T. got stuck. Hard things, impossible things: they were easy to name. It was the good things that came hard or not at all.

Take the Stampernicks. William T. had wrestled with their presence in the whole unbearable story of Mallie's assault and the aftermath. But meeting Aaron Stampernick and talking with him, experiencing the young man's politeness, the quiet about him, had been unsettling. Aaron Stampernick struck him as less judgmental and more understanding than he had built him up in his mind to be. The conversation had been hard. But it had not been unbearable. If a situation was not unbearable, could there be something, even a tiny something, good about it?

On the spur of the moment, he got in his truck and headed south to the Stampernicks' house. There was something new in the yard: a water sprinkler in the shape of a daisy with a bendable stem writhed and twisted and danced on the grass, shooting sprays of water in un-predictable directions. Something that little kids would love.

At the far end of the block, adjacent to the playground, a team of roofers swarmed the high peaked roof of a two-story frame house. A hand-lettered sign, one of those temporary ones on wire legs, was stuck into the boulevard grass. BILLY'S ROOFING. 315–555–9723. NO JOB TOO SMALL. At the ridgeline, a young roofer was standing straight up, his arms stretched over his head as if he were about to do jumping jacks. William T. peered up at him and shook his head. Kid couldn't care less that he was thirty feet in the air with no support. Where did that kind of fearlessness come from? *Here's your strung-out roofer, Mallie,* he thought, and then wondered if it was a mirage: the roofer, the roof, the sun that turned him into a dark outline.

William T. killed the ignition and got out of the truck. Something good. He was trying to find something good. That was his goal here. He walked up the steps, his heart pounding, and he put his hand on his chest as if to comfort it. This was an unbearable situation and he was looking for one good thing.

Knock. Knock. Knock.

He kept up a steady, calm rhythm of knuckles on flimsy wood. He would keep knocking until someone answered. Knock, knock, who's there? William T. Eventually someone would have to come to the door and open it, if only to stop the nonstop knocking. But the door opened right away.

"Mr. Jones?"

Aaron Stampernick stood on the other side of the screen door. He did not seem upset or surprised at the fact of William T. stand-ing there. He opened the door and dipped his head, as if to say, *Come in,* and William T. stepped into the house. Melissa Stamper-nick was standing in the doorway of the kitchen, a bowl of chopped apple in her hand and a toddler pulling at her shirt. Another child, elementary-school-age from the look of her, was sitting at a table with a book. A third child was standing at the top of the stairs in his underwear, peering down. "Who's that?" the upstairs child shouted.

"Who's that? Who's that? Who's that?" and William T. remembered how exhausting small children could be.

"Please sit down," Aaron said, and Melissa smiled encouragingly and said, "Yes, please sit down. Sorry about the mess. Would you like something to drink?"

These people were so calm. William T. sat down at the table with the little girl and her book. He again put his hand over his heart, stampeding in his chest, and the gesture reminded him of pledging allegiance to the flag when he was in elementary school. Did they still do that sort of thing? Maybe he should ask this child next to him. He made an effort to collect his thoughts. *Focus, William T.* He cleared his throat.

"I'm trying to find something good," he said.

The child at the top of the stairs was now bumping his way down on his behind. He was too old to be the baby, and so was the toddler hanging on Melissa.

"Zach and Mallie used to play a kind of game," he said, by way of explanation. "When something felt impossible. One hard thing, one impossible thing, one good thing. I'm trying to play the game now."

Aaron and Melissa regarded him quizzically. They were patient people; that much was clear.

"I'm tormented," William T. said. "I keep thinking about that baby."

"Understandably," Aaron said. "Why wouldn't you think about him?"

"It feels unbearable to me. The fact of its existence, I mean, like a living reminder of everything awful that Mallie went through."

Aaron cleared his throat and nodded. "That's understandable too," he said. "I choose to believe that the child is innocent. That he should not bear the sins of his father."

"Where is it?" William T. said. "I know you know. Tell me."

Melissa regarded him strangely. She patted the clingy toddler on the head mechanically, without taking her eyes off him.

"The custody hearing was closed and confidential," Aaron said, after a minute. "As you know. And I am the attorney for the child who was born to Mallie, as you also know."

What a strange way to put it. "The child who was born to Mallie." It sounded like a term from a futuristic movie, in which the world had gone to hell and weird cults had taken over. Maybe that was how the Stampernicks kept their lives semi-sane. A social worker, an attorney for children, and also foster parents. It was too much.

"We are legally bound to confidentiality," Melissa added. "You must know that."

"Mallie may want to see it," he lied. Or maybe it wasn't a lie. How the hell would he know? "That's why I'm asking."

The Stampernicks both nodded. That Mallie wanted to see the baby seemed to make sense to them. But what if she wanted the baby back? Ever thought of that, Stampernicks?

"That makes sense, Mr. Jones," Aaron said, as if he were trying to choose the right words. "I mean, why wouldn't she? The fact that she has recovered and is now in possession of her faculties raises questions for her with regard to the child."

They were so cool and calm and collected and formal. Maybe their professions had trained them to be this way.

"So will you tell me?" William T. said. "Where it is?"

Aaron and Melissa looked at each other, communicating without words. William T. wanted to shout at them to stop it, but he didn't. Melissa lifted both shoulders and then dropped them, and Aaron turned back to William T. She must have given him some kind of go-ahead.

"We cannot, Mr. Jones," Aaron said. "With the best interests of the child in mind, the judge ordered the hearing closed and the records sealed. The child is safe and healthy. Beyond that, we can tell you nothing. Mallie's situation is, of course, different from yours. But this is an issue of personal and legal boundaries."

They both nodded, as if they'd cleared things up. Stampernick was so formal. His diction. His presence. William T. didn't trust overly formal people.

"We prayed about it," Melissa added. "We felt Lucia would have wanted that."

"Please," William T. said. "I'm trying to find one good thing. One small, good thing."

"The baby is safe and healthy," Melissa repeated. "That's a very good thing."

Her voice had turned smooth and professional. This must be her social-worker voice. Aaron stood behind his wife, his hands on her shoulders, and William T. could tell that no more information about the baby and his whereabouts would be forthcoming.

Mallie

B Y THE END OF A SESSION, IF IT WENT THE WAY IT WAS SUP-
posed to, an exchange of energy had taken place between her
and the client. Questions had been asked and answered. A story
had been told, and all of it without words. This was happening between her and Charlie, now that they were talking and texting again.
The gap between them was narrowing. When she thought of her
brother now, a picture formed itself in her head.

Charles, not Charlie. Tall and lean, wearing their father's old army
jacket and walking across a campus lined with birch and maple trees.
An orange backpack. The Converse she had noticed on his feet that
one time he had come to the hospital. Not the one time he had been
there, but the one time she had been awake for him. Mal and Charlie,
Charlie and Mal. They were filling in the empty spaces.

Zach was still a blank.

She stood on the rocks by a river in the wide-street town he lived
in, here in the wide-open state of Montana. William T.'s slip of paper, with the name of the restaurant where Zach worked, was in her
back pocket. The yellow-brown waters of the Yellowstone River
churned at her feet. Gravity had tugged that water down from the
mountains, and gravity was pulling it south. She held her hands up
in front of her face and watched the veins smooth themselves out and
hide behind her skin. The center of the earth pulled water toward itself and blood pulled itself earthward. The human body was mostly
water, she remembered from biology.

The West was the same as Sterns—no need for parallel parking. Parallel parking was a city thing, a thing done all the time in Manhattan, or Boston, even Utica, sometimes, places where people and cars were jammed up together. But not here. Here, you could pull right up to where you wanted to be.

Outside the restaurant where Zach worked, a long bench with wooden slats painted alternately green and yellow sat in front of a big picture window. Pots of geraniums stood at either end. A little girl sat on one end and Mallie sat on the other. The front door swung open and a girl with a clipboard stepped into the sunshine.

"Chang? Party of three?"

The little girl leapt off the bench. "That's us!" she yelled to a man and woman a few yards away. "That's us!"

The hostess glanced at Mallie, sitting on the bench. "Do you want to add your name to the list? It's about a half hour at this point."

She shook her head. The hostess looked at her curiously and smiled. White, white teeth, even and straight. She wore tight jeans, rolled at the cuff. Flip-flops. A white tank top. A shark tooth suspended on a brown leather string around her neck and clanking silver bracelets on her wrist. Her black hair was pulled back in a loose knot held in place with a single chopstick.

"Okay. Let me know if you change your mind."

The door swung shut behind her. Behind that door, somewhere in that restaurant, unless it was his day off, was Zach. This girl knew him. She worked with him. Were they friends? Did they work late together, close the place down, drink beer as one scraped down the grill and the other turned chairs up on tables and swept the floor? Did they blast music and sing along? Did they dance? Her mind pushed itself up against the edge of an imaginary cliff by an imaginary canyon, where Zach Miller stood on the other side, the bottom of the canyon yawning a thousand feet below.

One hard thing, one impossible thing, one good thing.

She was too nervous to sit. She stood up and walked down the sidewalk to the alley. The streets of this western town were wide the way the whole West was wide, and the alley was narrow and cool and out of the sun. She leaned against the brick wall at the entrance and breathed. Breathe. Breathe. Breathe. *Go back there, and this time walk in, Mallie.*

Then the scrape of a heavy door echoed toward her from down the alley and she peered down to see two figures walking in her direction. Too shadowy to make out their faces, but they were laughing, meandering along. Their words were indistinguishable but the sound of their talk was like music, low notes chasing higher notes, weaving together.

They were coming toward her, where she leaned against the rough brick of the building. Except that she wasn't leaning anymore. She was walking, backing away. Back toward the restaurant and the painted bench. Turning her head so that when they emerged into the sun from the alley they wouldn't see her. Because no matter how shadowy an alley, no matter how indistinct the outline of a man, if that man was someone you knew in your bones, you would know him. You would know him by the sound of his voice and by the way he walked. You would know the woman with him because you had just spoken with her, just seen her. You would know that Zach Miller and the girl with the flip-flops and the chopsticked hair were walking together down the alley, and you would also know, from the sound of their voices and their laughter, that there was ease between them, a longstanding kind of ease. They were talking.

"Want me to take Sir and Mister out after work?" the girl said. "Give you a break?"

"Nah. Let's both go. Let them play for a while and wear them out."

Sir! The image of her dog floated before her, her dog Sir, their dog Sir, Sir, who had slept at the foot of their bed, ridden behind the front seat of the truck, Sir, who had once chased down and killed a squirrel and then stood there looking at it as if he didn't know what he had done, or why. And now there was a Mister. Sir and Mister. What kind of dog was Mister? Her mind scrabbled. Mister and Sir both had a lot of energy to burn. Did Mister and Sir sleep at the foot of the bed?

Zach and the girl, Sir and Mister, a bed they all slept on.

You could hold your breath for a long, long time—days, weeks—

without knowing that you were holding it. You only realized you'd been holding it when it was punched out of you.

"She blacked out, I think."

"Get her some water."

"It's hot. Maybe she's dehydrated."

She opened her eyes to a forest of legs. One pair was tanned and hairy, with big calf muscles and strong feet. Splayed toes in the kind of sandals you could climb mountains in, the expensive kind with multiple straps and cinches. Another pair was thin and white, black ballet flats on narrow feet. Another pair she couldn't see, because the ruffles and folds of a long yellow and blue granny dress covered them. She closed her eyes again.

"Hey. Are you okay?"

This was a deep, quiet voice coming from directly in front of her face. Someone attached to one of the pairs of legs had crouched down. She opened her eyes. Calm brown eyes under a thatch of sun-bleached hair. She nodded, because in order to make them go away, a nod was necessary. Brown-Eyes looked up at the heads attached to the legs.

"She's okay," he said. "Too much sun, not enough water. Maybe a little altitude thrown into the mix."

He looked down for confirmation and she nodded again. Just keep nodding. That was the way to make them all go away. One after another, the legs slipped quietly out of vision. Brown-Eyes helped her up onto the bench. He held out a paper cup filled with water.

"Drink."

She drank.

"I figured you probably didn't want a crowd staring at you. But are you okay?"

Nod.

"You from around here?"

"No."

"So it actually might be the altitude, then."

When the water was gone he held his hand out for the cup and disappeared into the restaurant — wait, she was still at the restaurant! — but he returned just as she lurched up in panic. The cup, filled.

"Sit back down and drink this, okay? Just sit for a bit until you're sure you're okay."

The end of the sidewalk was so far. The sun was so hot. She closed her eyes and saw Zach Miller and the girl coming down an alley over and over, a looping three seconds of video. They were about to see her so she turned and ran. Then they were there again, coming down the alley toward her, and again she ran. She sat back down and drank the water. Dizzy.

"Better?"

"Yes, thanks."

The door of the restaurant opened and she was there again: the girl. Chopstick-hair girl. Flip-flops girl. Clipboard-in-one-hand girl. "Brian"—she nodded at Brown-Eyes—"said you fainted. You okay?"

Mallie nodded. Then she pushed herself up from the bench and started down the sidewalk.

———

The wig was under the driver's seat in the Datsun. If she had worn the wig when she walked up to the café, when she sat on the bench next to the flowers, when the girl with the chopstick hair and the clipboard came out and asked did she want her name on the list, then maybe none of this would have happened. She would not have walked down the street to the alley. She would not have heard the employee door down the alley open and then clang shut, and she would not have seen Zach and the girl. She would not have overheard them talking about Sir and Mister.

She went back to the truck, scrunched up her hair with one hand and pulled the wig on with the other. It was probably crooked. Her own hair was probably sticking out a little. She leaned forward and looked at her unclear reflection in the window. It was too late anyway. She had messed up. She should have worn the wig.

"You sound crazy," she said out loud. "Start walking." She started walking. She focused on her feet and her arms, the way she had when they helped her learn how to walk right again, during the long weeks of recovery. Wasn't walking how she had always managed to calm herself? Wasn't walking what had brought her to William T.'s house, that very first time she had gone without an adult to his house? She had loaded up her wagon with a blanket and her little brother and off to William T.'s house they had gone.

"Keep walking, Mallie," she said, and down the sidewalk she went. "There you go. There you are."

There she was. There was Mallie, reflected in every shop window, every plate-glass picture window of every restaurant she passed. Keep walking, Mallie. Her feet knew what to do. It had been a long time since she had walked her way out of something. She had lived with Zach Miller for three years before that dark night in Utica, and in those years, she had walked her way out of the pain of her clients' lives. When the sorrow ebbed, there had been Zach to put his arm around her, Zach to dance with her, Zach to laugh with and make plans with, Zach who would wake from a deep sleep if he sensed she was awake and thinking.

Was all that gone now? *That's the hardest thing about this, to me,* Charlie had said. *That we had no choice in anything that happened. It was like being on a train and knowing you wanted to get off, but the train just kept going.*

"Keep walking, Mallie. Keep walking."

She kept walking. Ten blocks this way, take a left. Ten blocks that way, take a left. Ten blocks that way, take a left. Ten blocks, back to the beginning. Ten + ten + ten + ten for how long? The sun was going down, going down, going down, and then the sun was down. Where was the Datsun? Three blocks out of the ten-by-ten square. What would she do now? It was almost dark and her body hurt from the walking.

Then she saw them. They were across the street. Sitting at a table, eating. Talking. Lamplight pooled on their faces. The girl was on one side of the table, Zach on the other, a baby in a wooden high chair at the head of the table. Without thinking, she crossed the street in the middle of the block. A car blared its horn at her, the ugly loudness of the sound. Night had descended, and if she stood to the side of the window, she could look in at Zach Miller and the girl and their baby. *Of course,* she thought. *This explains it.* She heard herself say it out loud. "Of course, this explains it," as if she were a rational person who had just discovered a small thing that explained other, larger things. Of course, if Zach Miller had a new girlfriend, and they had a baby, then that would explain why he had abandoned her. *Abandoned.* Now she herself was using the word. She heard herself say that one out loud too: "Abandoned." Of course, the abandonment made sense now. Of course, it made sense that Zach would keep this from William T. and Charlie. Of course, they would be even angrier once they found out.

Zach's hair was longer. Something was curling up out of the neck of his T-shirt. A tattoo. She peered and peered but she could not tell what the tattoo was. He was eating spaghetti with a fork. He lifted his head to look at the girl and his eyes—his eyes, his eyes—

"Something hard, Mallie." She said this out loud, even though this wasn't hard, it was impossible. She was standing outside a restaurant looking in at Zach and the girl and their baby and it was impossible.

She didn't know much about babies and toddlers. She had never been a babysitting type. This one wore overalls, and a yellow bib was tied under his chin. He was stirring spaghetti noodles around on the high-chair tray. He held a clump of them up to his mouth and sucked at it. He might not be a boy, come to think of it. He might be a girl. Or gender-nonconforming. No need to box the baby in. Right? She watched her thoughts scrabble around, tumbling and contradicting themselves, inside her head.

The girl talked and talked and laughed and laughed. Zach and the child were quiet as the girl spread her arms out and brought her hands together in a praying motion as she leaned back and laughed. What was she saying? What was she talking about? Suddenly, Zach put his fork down and leaned back and laughed too.

A family, a happy young family, eating together and laughing together.

The server brought the bill, folded and propped up in an empty glass. Zach reached in his back pocket for a wallet—the back pocket of Zach's jeans had always had a faint outline of a wallet—and that was when she started to cry. It was the wallet that did it. The faint outline of a wallet on old worn jeans and the memory of Zach walking away from her and her watching him, the way his T-shirt rode his hips, his angular, swift walk.

Zach.

Now Zach was scooping up the child while the girl dipped a napkin in her water glass and scrubbed at the child's cheeks. The child kicked and flailed and opened his mouth in a sound that she could tell from here was a *No no no no*. She felt that way too. No. No no no no no.

She huddled back in the darkness at the edge of the building, her face turned in the opposite direction, as they walked right by her. Zach held the child in his arms and the girl chattered on, something about did Daddy know that Mister had tried mango this morning and what had he thought of it, Mister? Did you like it? Tell us what you thought of that mango. Tell. Come on, tell us. Can you say yummy? Say yummy. *Shut up. Shut up shut up shut up.* The baby burrowed into Zach's arms and hooted. He was like a prairie dog, burrowing into the tunnel of Zach's arms. Zach laughed, and the girl laughed, and the three of them kept walking on down the sidewalk.

William T.

WILLIAM T. HAD MADE IT THROUGH MOST OF THE WALTZ Boss's instructional videos. One thing he liked about the man was that he kept his videos short, no longer than three minutes. And he got straight to the point. The music was already playing when the video opened; the Waltz Boss was already standing on the little stage with the floor clearly marked with tape.

"Let's fire her up, Jonathan," William T. said.

It had become their weekend routine. Crystal at the diner, Johnny in his red pajamas, sitting at the table eating breakfast, and William T. practicing his dance moves with the couch cushion as his partner. The Waltz Boss's dance partner never said a word. She appeared just as he was finishing his Waltz Fact of the Day, took her place, with one hand on his shoulder and the other aloft in his hand, and moved smoothly and silently in rhythm with his steps. She smiled throughout, the sort of professional smile that Olympic figure skaters always produced the minute their own music began.

"Today's music is Waltz Number 2, by Dmitri Shostakovich," the Waltz Boss said. "I chose it because Shostakovich is someone I admire greatly. He composed his Fifth Symphony under conditions of great deprivation, fear and ongoing threats to his life during the siege of Leningrad."

"And what does this have to do with the waltz, Jonathan?" William T. said, which made Johnny laugh. "Let's get to the point, Boss."

"This historical fact doesn't have anything to do with the waltz," the Waltz Boss said, as if he had heard William T., "but it's important to me. It might have been easier for Shostakovich to go into hiding and stop composing at that time, but he didn't. He forged on and left the world with one of its greatest symphonies."

The Boss's dance partner emerged from behind the curtain and walked to her place. But the Boss was not quite done.

"Shostakovich is one of my heroes," he said, and nodded.

A lump rose in William T.'s throat, and he did not know why. Maybe because the pudgy Waltz Boss, whose YouTube channel had only three subscribers, had a hero and was unashamed to say so? Maybe because he himself, who had barely heard anyone utter the name Dmitri Shostakovich before the Waltz Boss did this morning, had just been shown again that there were worlds within worlds about which he knew nothing? Maybe because in the face of Stalin and his henchmen, and their ongoing campaign of terror, Shostakovich had kept going?

That was what it boiled down to, didn't it? You just kept going. Whatever slings and arrows came your way in life, you had to keep going. Crystal had once told him, late at night when they were sitting on the porch, about the early months of Johnny's life, after her sister had abandoned him to her. How he cried and cried, shook with his crying, and she had not known what to do or how to soothe him. How she had narrowed life down to fifteen-minute segments of time in which she told herself that was all she had to get through. Fifteen minutes at a time. And when those fifteen minutes were up, all she had to get through was another fifteen minutes. She would sit with him all night long, in the trailer where she used to live, where the closest neighbors were too far away to hear Johnny's screams.

"Which was a good thing," she had told him. "Because it probably sounded as if I were trying to kill him."

"Did you ever think of leaving?" he said. "Giving him to the state, maybe?"

She had looked up at him, eyes unfathomable in the moonlight. "I didn't let myself," she said. "It felt like a door I could never open."

Now he looked across the table at Johnny, still finishing his cereal.

The red spoon dipped in and out of the bowl, carefully conveyed to his mouth. Johnny concentrated on the job of feeding himself the way he concentrated on everything. He looked up and flashed a grin at William T. and held up the red spoon. A small, triumphant gesture.

Johnny was a pivot point, the steady center around which Crystal and William T. moved when he was home with them. Johnny was the only one of all of them who could not have said what had happened to Mallie, or where she had been during the long passage of time he hadn't seen her. Maybe it hadn't seemed long to Johnny. Maybe it felt to him as if Mallie had been there one day and then the next had walked into the diner, seen him coming out of the restroom, given him a hug and told him she liked his red owl T-shirt. William T. did not know and he would never know what it was like to be inside Johnny's mind.

"I guess this is how we do it, Johnny," he said. "Fifteen minutes at a time, over and over."

Johnny was refolding his napkin. Soon he would rise from the table and carry his bowl and spoon to the sink.

"You ever heard of AA, Jonathan?"

Johnny looked up at William T. and laughed the way he always did at the sound of "Jonathan" instead of "Johnny."

"It's a twelve-step program for people who are addicted to alcohol," he said. "You work your way through the steps, one at a time."

William T. barely drank. A beer a few times a year, maybe. But he had friends who drank, and some of those friends were devoted to AA the way Lucia and her friends had been devoted to the Faith Love Congregation.

"Step Nine is the one where you make amends," he said. "It doesn't apply to you, of course, Jonathan. You've never done anything you need to make amends for."

Years ago, William T.'s friend and coworker at the farmer's co-operative, Harwin, had made amends to him. William T. had come to work one morning and, on his desk—on top of the spread-out trucking charts and weather reports that he never put away at the end of each day—was a note.

Dear William T.,

My addiction has meant that I have not worked to full capacity most days of the week for years now. You have done more than your share of our work as a result. This unfairness was my fault entirely, and while I don't have money to pay you back, I vow to work to full capacity from now on.

Sincerely,
Harwin Jacobs

It's "sincerely," had been William T.'s first thought, *not "sincerly."* Then he read through the note again. It was puzzling. What addiction? Harwin was an ordinary man in an ordinary job, even if he did have the best desk in the best location on the entire floor. He picked up the note and went straight to Harwin's large desk, in the corner, by the large window where light streamed through. Harwin's head had been bent over his own mess of spreadsheets and trucker schedules—he and William T. were in charge of getting the milk from the farms to the processing facilities within the required number of hours, and routes and drivers could change any day, depending on the weather—and he was fumbling with a pen, flipping it end over end on the desk. Avoiding William T.'s presence.

"What the hell's this, Harwin?"

"Step Nine," Harwin had mumbled, then cleared his throat and looked up from the pen. His face was pale but resolute. "I'm an alcoholic, William T. I've been an alcoholic since I was twenty-three, and I've been sober for nine months and three days."

"How old are you now?"

"Forty-nine."

"Jesus, Harwin. That's a long time. What a hard thing. I had no idea."

"I'm on Step Nine," Harwin said. "Making amends. Which is different from apologizing, because an apology is not action. Although I feel terrible about taking advantage of your generosity all these years."

Harwin was not a man who spoke like this: stilted and formal. He had picked up the pen again and was now tossing it from hand to hand. If the man had been hiding the booze all these years, William T. thought, wasn't that suffering enough? But now here he was, clearly miserable but determined to do what he could.

"I tell you what, Harwin. You want to make it up to me, why don't we switch desks? You can sit in my dark corner and I'll bask in the sunlight."

Harwin had jerked his head up, surprise and confusion on his face. William T. laughed and shook his head to make it clear he was joking, just trying to lighten the amends-making mood. But next day, when William T. came to work, Harwin had swapped their desks. No matter how William T. protested, insisted that he had not meant it, please go back to the way it was, Harwin refused. For the last three years he worked at the cooperative, William T. had sat in the sun. It had turned out to be an unenviable location. Too hot too much of the time, and the glare reflected off the papers and hurt his eyes.

Click. Click. Slide. Click slide slide.

"Peel."

"Peel."

"Peel."

Crystal and Burl were playing Bananagrams, and from the sound of it, they were both closing in on a win. William T. could feel it. They were cool customers, Crystal more so than Burl, but they gave off an invisible, silent thrill of excitement and competition when they had only one or two letter tiles left. Burl's fingers hovered over his letter grid as if he were playing Ouija, the way they had back in high school. Crystal's head was bent and her hands were placed carefully on either side of her own grid. Only her eyes moved, but she, like Burl, was taking in the entirety of the words she had formed.

These nights, these dozens of nights spent playing this game at this table in this kitchen in this old house north of Sterns, were part of what had gotten Crystal and Burl through. They were all of them changed people from that first night, only days after the assault, when Burl had burst through the kitchen door, the little yellow Bananagrams bag in his hands. There had been a kind of suppressed desperation in his eyes, a panicky determination for something to hold on to, something to occupy them, something to get them through the crisis. William T. could see that now.

"Bananas!" Burl and Crystal said simultaneously.

"Jinx," William T. said.

Look at their grids, the two of them. Burl had built his vertically. It climbed the table like a small, starved skyscraper. Crystal's was compact and dense, a warren of two- and three-letter words that crawled into and around one another. Burl's was the tower that the migrating birds soared up and over, and Crystal's was the nest they built in their new land. The next time they played, their grids would be entirely different. They would always be making and remaking themselves, the same way that Mallie, back in the world, must now remake herself. The same way he was trying to remake himself.

Maybe that was why Zach and Mallie had kept all those unopened fortune cookies over all these years. It had been a joke between them —their box of possible futures—but when he thought about it now, maybe it wasn't a joke. Maybe it was a way of keeping possibility alive.

When you came back from the world between, the way they all had, you didn't come back all the way. Part of you was still there, living in a world before and also beyond this one. The Mallie who had come trundling up the long road with Charlie in her wagon, when she was a little girl who had just lost her father, was still on that road, walking in that same determined way. The Mallie who had lived with Zach Miller in the cabin in Forestport was still there. Someone walking by the cabin now might feel a shadow pass over, or a breath of wind that felt like a whisper, and that would be Mallie. She had left behind the air she had breathed there, the things that had changed because of her when she was alive in that place.

Maybe it was like that for everyone. The pebble that you stepped on shifted position, the apple tree altered when you picked its fruit. Every minute, everyone was changing, and because of that, so was the world.

If Mallie was still in all the places she'd ever lived, then everyone else was too: Zach and Charlie and Crystal and Johnny and Burl and William T. himself. And Darkness, her word for the anonymous man he had nightmares of finding and killing. If Mallie's unsolvable proof was to be solved—and solve it, they all must, if they were all to keep on living—then there was no way out of the fact that Darkness was also in the world. He would always be there, waiting.

Burl swept the letter tiles into a big pile in the middle of the table. "Another?" he said.

"Another," Crystal agreed.

Click. Click. Click. The quiet clicking of the tiles and Crystal's and Burl's hushed tones as they murmured, *Peel, peel, peel,* calmed him as William T. thought about making amends.

Across the room, Johnny stood up from his big cushiony recliner. He looked directly at William T. and smiled. Crystal, always alert to Johnny's movements, looked up from the Bananagrams game.

"What is it, Johnny?" Crystal said.

But he was bent over the couch, working at something. Trying to pry up one of the couch cushions, William T. saw, but it was too big and cumbersome.

"You need some help?" Crystal said, and started to get up, but William T. held out his hand and she sat back down. Johnny looked back up at William T., that same grin on his face.

"Jonathan, you want to dance?" William T. said. "Is that what you're trying to do?"

At the "Jonathan," Johnny, as always, began to laugh. He bent down to the couch again, tugging, but William T. reached him and held out his hands.

"Come on," he said. "Let's the two of us give it a try."

He placed Johnny's crabbed left hand on his own right shoulder and then closed his big paw around Johnny's right hand. He started to sing. *Moon river, wider than a mile, I'm crossing you in style . . .* He tried to ease Johnny backward, inch by inch, but Johnny was not used to moving backward, and his body tensed. All right, then, he would try it a different way. He wrapped his arms around Johnny in a hug, and then he himself began to move backward, singing all the while. *You don't know how to follow,* he told himself. *You only know how to lead.* But he was following, wasn't he? He was leading and he was following, all in the same motion. Johnny was like an extension of his own body. They swayed and box-stepped and moon-rivered their way around the living room.

When they had made it around the couch once, then twice, he looked over at Burl and Crystal. The look on Crystal's face, caught in surprise and fascination, the same way he had probably looked when he'd glimpsed her through the window of the diner's back door, dancing alone in the kitchen. He raised his eyebrows at her and tried to shrug — *I learned to waltz for you; this is for you, Crystal* — but she got up and came around the table to the two of them in their awkward box-step shuffle and put her arms around them both. She was crying, he realized.

But Johnny, Johnny was smiling.

Darkness

W HEN SHE STARTED TO GET BETTER, THE FIRST AND ONLY thing he felt was scared. His mother was watching the news and suddenly she screamed. He went running out and there she was on the couch, with Beth next to her, and they were both screaming and hugging. He looked at the TV and there was the girl, that same photo, the one of her in some driveway with her arms up like she was dancing.

"She's alive!" his mother said. "She's going to be okay!"

And all he felt was scared. He still felt scared.

More than that, though. Sick. That was how he felt most of the time. All the time. Like the outside skin of him was moving and talking and eating and sleeping, smiling at Beth and his mother. But inside, he was nothing. Worse than nothing.

The only time he could get out of himself was when he was on the roof. When the nail gun was in his hand and the air was thin and invisible over his head. The nail gun was heavy and solid. It had to be, to put those nails through the shingles. He would take a nail gun over a staple gun any day. Staple guns were easier—light, and the staples were light too—but it was easy to mess up. The staples had to be put in straight, not at a slant. Slanted staples were the problem. Better do the job right with a nail gun, even though it was harder.

He hated finishing for the day. Hated climbing back down. Because on the ground was when he couldn't get away from himself. It all came back to him and it went around and around in his head. He imagined her there in the dark, like an animal that was so scared it couldn't move. Like the rabbit in the garage, when he was a kid. They had come home at night and there it was, a rabbit in the corner next to the lawn mower. How it got in there, he didn't know. But the lights of the car shone on it and it was like a cement rabbit. Frozen with fear.

If you could go back in time and do one thing over again, what would it be? That was a question he'd heard his mother ask Cindy once on the phone. He was a kid then, so he didn't think about it. There wasn't that much further back in time he could go. It was different now. Now it felt like time stretched back forever, to thousands of years before he was born. Before he was thought of. Now there was only one thing he would do over again if he could.

They'd found tiny bits of that flowerpot embedded in her scalp. Pieces so tiny they were like sand. He thought about that sometimes, up on the roof. He thought about telling, sometimes. If he told, if he went to the cops, they would know.

His mother. Beth. They would know.

There was nothing he could do about any of it. It didn't make sense to tell now. What would be gained? That was what he told himself. But the truth was that the reason he didn't tell was he kept picturing the look in Beth's eyes if she knew what he had done. How it had ended up the way it had, he didn't know. He didn't know. He didn't know, didn't know. How something that had begun so simply, with a few pills and a little money, then a few more and a little more money, then a few more, then a few more, then a lot more, and a lot more money, ended up with her on the pavement with her head dented in — it was like he had had nothing to do with it.

He had made a mistake. A bad one.

If he could tell her he was sorry, he would. If he could somehow transport his sorry into her, through the air, through the ether, by telepathy, in a dream, any possible or impossible way to let her know how sorry he was that what happened that night had begun with him, he would.

The video played out in his head — beer, rain, church, dented head — when he was up on the roof, in the rhythm of the nail gun. When the sun beat down and he was moving steadily and slowly at a crouch, square to square. There were cliffs on the side of every roof. The gravity that held the house down, that held the shingles down, that held him down on the squares? That same gravity would pull him straight down to the ground if he misstepped.

Guys fell when they were shingling. It was something that happened. A hazard of the trade.

In another of the possible futures he imagined for himself, he looked down from the roof and saw a cop talking to Billy. Relaxed, no urgency, just a conversation. But Billy glanced up at him, there on the roof, and the cop did too. As if he were sizing him up, somehow. That was when he knew the jig was up. That somehow they had tracked him down. Then the cop started walking—ambling, you could call it; that was the kind of walk it was—across the scruffy grass where they dropped the old shingles and the rusted nails onto the tarp, toward where he was standing on the roof. And he pictured Beth's face and his mother's face and the questions they would have to answer and everything they would have to go through, and that was when he put his backup plan into action. Because the look on Beth's face, that was the one thing he would not ever be able to bear. He got up and stretched the way roofers stretch, a half-crouch, and then he stood up straight and walked straight up to the ridgeline and then he ran down the slope and dove. Headfirst.

He had played it out many times. There was one good thing about that possible future, which was that, cops or not, it could happen anytime he wanted it to.

Mallie

S HE SAT ON THE STEPS OF THE COBURN MEMORIAL LIBRARY, AN
apple and a bag of chips from the gas station next to the Sleepy
Inn — forty-five dollars a night for a single — next to her. She
was tired. Tired. Tired.

A crow in the oak tree next to the library cried its harsh cry and
she looked up as it spread its wings and flew off. Was it true, as William T. claimed, that she had always loved birds? Or had his own love
of birds traveled into her and never left? It was his flock of lame
birds, back when she was a child, that had opened her eyes to the fact
that birds were everywhere, silent or loud, swooping down or soaring up, wings beating frantically or still and calm. From his flock
she had learned about birds that were threatened, birds with broken wings and broken legs and broken spirits, which had to be approached with caution, so filled with fear were they.

A shadow fell across the grass and the cool marble steps of the library. A hand was on her shoulder, and she knew that hand.

"Mallie."

His voice. His hand. She should have gotten the wig out of the
truck. She should have put it on. He lowered himself and sat next to
her on the step. A white bandage was wound around the deep cleft
between his thumb and index finger, and she stared at it because she
couldn't look at his face.

"William T. told me you'd left and then when I heard about the girl who fainted at the restaurant, I just knew it was you," he said. "I've been out looking. You didn't answer your phone. I've been looking all night."

"I turned it off," she said, and, "You hurt your thumb," and then everything turned blurry and she leaned forward and rested her head on her knees.

The words sounded polite and calm to her ear. They didn't sound as if they came from the mouth of a suffocating person, a person with a torment of unspoken words churning and bubbling within.

"I'm glad you have Sir," she said in the same polite voice.

"Mallie." His voice was his but not his. Too quiet for him. Too, what? Unsure? Was that the word? She couldn't look at him.

"Did you know that my mother died? But Charlie and William T. and Crystal and Johnny are still alive. So that's good."

She watched his hand, the one with the hurt thumb. The hand was draped over his knee now. It curled and flexed, curled and flexed. There were Band-Aids on two other fingers.

"Like Burl," she said, pointing. Paper cuts and Band-Aids. "Like a mailman."

"Like a cook. Cuts and burns."

"Burl's alive too. He's good. He said to say hi."

Burl had not said to say hi. There was no limit to the stupid things that kept coming out of her mouth. She didn't know how to talk to him anymore. She reached out and pressed her thumb against the white bandage.

"I'm sorry you hurt yourself," she said. With every word, she hated herself more. But then he reached out and took both her hands in his and she fell against him, crying, and then his arms were around her and he was crying too. The steps of the library were cold beneath her. In her head, she kept hearing Zach's and the girl's footsteps approaching down the alley. She opened her eyes against his shoulder to see the curl of dark ink rising out of the hem of his T-shirt. The tattoo she had glimpsed last night. Zach had not had a tattoo when she knew him. *Knew.* Past tense. She turned her head so she couldn't see the ink.

"It happened so fast, didn't it? You and her. The baby."

He didn't say anything for a while. Maybe she hadn't spoken out loud. But then he answered.

"Is that how it feels to you? Fast?"

There was something careful in his voice. Careful was not something she had ever heard from Zach Miller. She was sitting right next to him but he couldn't see the huge black bird beating inside her chest, trying to spread its enormous and powerful wings against the cage of ribs. Fly away, dark bird. Swoop and wheel over this sun-bleached town. She willed the bird to stop. Stop trying to open its beak inside her chest and send that wild caw clamoring out. Zach was talking again.

"I can't imagine what it's like," he said, "to be you now."

There it was again. That careful tone, as if he were looking for words that wouldn't hurt, wouldn't upset. She lifted her eyes to his shadowed face. It was him but not quite him, in the same way that Charlie and William T. and Crystal were themselves but not quite. The same way she herself must not be quite the same.

"I'm trying to figure out how it feels to be me now," she said. "Everyone looks older, somehow. William T., especially. It's been hard on him."

"It was hard on all of us, Mallie. On everyone who loved you."

"Loved?"

The past tense of *love*. His face stiffened but his eyes didn't budge from hers. Now he was Zach again, Zach who never looked away.

"Mallie, I have to talk to you. I should have talked to you before, but when I called the rehab unit they said it might mess you up, it might set your recovery back. That I should let you lead the way."

"How would talking to you mess me up any more?"

"It might hurt you more."

"More than everything else already has?"

"Shhh. Please, Mal. Look, I have to ask you something. If you had known you were pregnant, would you have wanted the baby?"

"The rape baby?"

He winced. The word *rape*, probably. It was a hard word. A bad word. A harsh crow caw of a word.

"The Darkness baby," she said. That sounded better. "'Darkness' is what I call him. The rapist. Remember Ms. Bailey? In math? I made an equation: A and B and C and D. The problem has to be solved so that the dark birds can't get me. So that I can keep on living."

"Mal, I don't really know what you're talking about. You made up a math problem about someone named Darkness?"

His voice was patient, as if he were talking to a child, or to a girl he used to know who wasn't the same person anymore. Who maybe had not come all the way back from wherever she had been. Who was still recovering. She plowed on.

"It was the only thing I could change. I gave him a name and a job and a sister and a mother. I made him a roofer. I made him an addict. I picture him standing on roofs. I made him hate himself."

"He should hate himself. He tried to kill you, Mallie."

"He didn't kill me, though."

He held her against him and pushed his hands through her hair. Behind her ears, back from her face, over and over. A brush made of fingers.

"I gave them that photo," he said, "the one from the party, and then it was everywhere. And they thought you would never recover. That's one reason I came out here. Because that life we had, Mallie? It was gone."

She sat still and waited for words to catch up inside her. *That life we had.* Zach was looking away. He was thinking. He was trying to figure something out. She could tell.

"You didn't answer me," he said. "Would you have wanted to keep that baby?"

"No."

Her answer was flat and hard. It came out of her without her thinking, and she was glad, because that flat, hard no meant that somewhere inside of her, she was fundamentally clear about something.

"No," she said again. It was a good word. It felt good, coming out of her mouth. "No. *No.*"

"Okay," he said, and then he was quiet for a time. She kept her head down on her knees, her eyes on the step below the one they were sitting on. An ant was crawling past her foot. She could shift her heel half an inch and crush it to death, and no one would ever know.

"So you would have had an abortion?"

"Yes."

"Would it have been a hard decision?" Zach said. That careful tone in his voice. "Would you have had to think about it at all?"

She shook her head. The ant was still trundling along. Where was it going? *You're shit out of luck, ant,* she thought. *No anthill anywhere near.* The ant had lost its way. It was depending on migratory ant instincts, if there were such a thing.

"Why are you asking me about this?"

"Because it's important," he said. "And I didn't have a chance to before. I spent a lot of time trying to figure out what you would have wanted. You and I never talked about things like that."

"We never had to."

"But what if, Mallie? What if you and I had gotten pregnant?"

"That would be different. We would have a baby."

Something low and flickering jumped in his eyes then, a small flame that he turned off instantly.

"As simple as that?" he said.

She nodded. "Yes. As simple as that. If you knew—" But she stopped talking, because that moment, those few seconds, when William T. and Crystal had told her what the silver scar on her belly was from, and her heart had leapt with a wild excitement, was flooding through her. She didn't trust herself to speak. Because look at the way it was now. Look at Zach, living here with Sir and a chopstick-hair girl and their baby.

She sat on the steps and saw Zach and the girl and the baby's life as a braid, three strands together, stretching out in a straight line here in this small Montana town. She saw them laughing and talking and cooking and eating and walking and hiking and working and sleeping. She saw their possible futures: A house and a car and closets filled with jeans and shirts and fleeces and boots. A kitchen with a dog bowl. A child's school photos magneted to the refrigerator. School conferences and school performances and school basketball games and cross-country meets. The three of them at the top of a Montana mountain in winter, goggles and helmets and skis and poles. Christmas trees and Fourth of July fireworks. Birthday cakes. She saw it all, images and sound clips whirling through her mind as she sat there on the steps of the library. They were ants on the surface of the earth, a planet spinning. Away, away, away. Toward what, toward what, toward what.

"That's what we all wanted too, Mal—an abortion—but no one listened to us. We had no legal rights. But is it true that you wanted to see the baby? That's what William T. said. Is it true?"

She nodded. "I'm trying to fill in the blanks. Because I don't feel anything when I think of him."

"Does that mean you don't hate him?"

"I don't know what I feel." Panic clawed up inside her again and her heart beat wildly. He had left her. He had taken off. He was sitting here but he had left her alone in the hospital all those months. "Zach, you took off! You left!"

"I know."

"And now you have this new life. A girlfriend. A baby. I saw you!"

A fire blazed inside her. She was a girl they figured would die, and then she was a pregnant girl they thought would never come back. And somewhere in there, Zach had taken off.

"You *saw us?*" he said. "When?"

"Last night. In the restaurant. You and her and your baby."

"No, Mallie. No. It's not what you think. I don't have a girlfriend. The girl you saw is Caroly. She works in the restaurant."

"Don't lie to me."

"Mallie, listen. Please listen. I don't have a girlfriend. But the baby is mine. They all help with him, Caroly and the cooks and the servers. They help me take care of him. His nickname is Mister. It takes a village, you know that saying? Well, they're the village."

There was a wild undertone in his voice, climbing and falling under words that made no sense. What the hell kind of name was Mister? A dumb name. A stupid name. *Mister.*

"They're the goddamn village," he said again, and his voice was clogged with something he wasn't telling her, but what? She put her head on her knees and prepared to wait as long as it took for Zach to calm down, to un-confuse himself, to tell her what was going on in a way that made sense, so that the pieces would fit together and she would understand what he was talking about.

"The baby is *him*, Mallie. *The* baby."

The shock of it, when she finally understood what he was saying.

William T.

Dear Charlie,

I am not an alcoholic but I am doing Step Nine anyway.

My focus on Mallie caused me to lose sight of you and what you needed during that time. You were just a boy who was traumatized by what happened to your sister, and I forgot that. I did not do right by you in your time of need. I will reach out to you, Charlie, and I will listen to what you have to say. I will even learn to call you Charles if that is truly what you prefer.

Sincerely,
William T.

Dear Burl,

I am not an alcoholic but I am doing Step Nine anyway.

I did not see how hard you were trying. I was sometimes mean to you, and I ignored the jars you made and worked to get inside all those stores because I thought they were a bad idea. The truth is that it hurt to look at the jars, but they were not a bad idea. You have worked hard, Burl, and I stood in your way. I thought I knew better than anyone else. I thought I loved her more than anyone else. From now on I will give you the credit you deserve, Burl.

Sincerely,
William T.

Dear Zach,

I am not an alcoholic but I am doing Step Nine anyway.

I thought it was my way or the highway. I thought everyone should handle what happened the way I handled it. I was so angry when you took off for Montana that I let my anger blind me to what was happening with you. The truth is that you know her better than anyone. The truth is that I should have trusted you were doing the only thing you could. From now on I will listen to you, Zach.

Sincerely,
William T.

Dear Mallie,

I am not an alcoholic but I am doing Step Nine anyway.

I was so undone by what happened to you that I did not see my anger wasn't helping you. I wanted to take care of you and keep you safe, which meant that I did not respect that you are in charge of your own life and must do what is right for you. I forgot that you have the right to choose your own path. I am still not doing a good job at this. I promise that I will try harder.

Sincerely,
William T.

Dear Johnny,

I am not an alcoholic but I am doing Step Nine anyway.

I am sorry that I have not seen you fully for what you are in the world, and how you have influenced the lives of those who love you. I promise that I will not take you for granted anymore.

Sincerely,
William T.

Dear Crystal,

I am not an alcoholic but I am doing Step Nine anyway.

I am sorry that I let my fear and worry about Mallie turn into an obsession. I am sorry I neglected you. I am sorry that I have not shown you that you are the most important person in the world to me. I am sorry that it took me so long to learn how to waltz.

I love you, Crystal.

William T.

He stacked the notes one on top of another and placed the pen next to them. A personal pile of amendments to his personal William T. Jones constitution. Deep in his pocket, his phone buzzed.

"William T., she took off. Have you heard from her? Do you know where she is? I told her about the baby and she took off. She said she had to go to the bathroom and she went into the library and I waited but she never came back out and I went in and they said she went out the back door and I don't know where she is and has she called you?"

Library. Bathroom. Out the back door. Baby. Zach's words made no sense.

"Slow down," William T. said. He would cultivate patience if it killed him. He had promised Zach in his making-amends note that he would listen to him. "Mallie was there with you? You told her about the baby? She already knows about the baby, Zach."

"Not that he's with me. She didn't know that. So I told her."

Zach's voice was a controlled panic. William T. took the phone away from his ear and looked at it. The boy's voice was a tinny rasp drifting up from the screen. *And then she went into the library and I don't know where she is now—*

"What did you just say, Zach?"

He himself had asked Aaron Stampernick, attorney for the child, about the baby. He had listened as both Stampernicks told him that the second custody hearing, in the wake of Lucia's death, had been closed and confidential. That no one wanted the child to grow up in a cloud of publicity, and that the judge had agreed. He deserved a private life, they had said in interviews. The sins of the father are not visited upon the child, they had said. Leave the church stuff out of it and what you had was a foster child and foster parents who wanted a life for him. A life away from the madding crowd.

Zach was making no sense. He himself, William T. Jones, had been in the Stampernick house. The Stampernicks had regarded him with concern, as if he were losing his mind. As if he had finally gone off the deep end.

"He's mine," Zach said again. "I have custody. His nickname is Mister."

"You *tried* to get custody," William T. said. "That's what you told me. You *tried* to get custody after he was born but they gave it to Lucia."

"That's right. But Lucia died, and in her will she stated that she wanted me to have custody."

"What the hell are you talking about?"

"And both Aaron and Melissa advocated on my behalf."

"Advocated on your behalf? What the hell kind of language is that?"

"Their language, William T. They stepped in during the whole mess, after Lucia died. Lucia wanted me to have the baby. She thought I would do a good job, I guess. That he belonged with me. And Aaron and the judge agreed."

William T.'s head was crazy with confusion, thoughts flying around like birds caught around the Empire State Building. Zach was still talking, rattling on about foster-parent training and foster-parent licensing and the custody hearing and Lucia's will, and finally William T. could not listen anymore—amends be damned—and interrupted.

"His father was a goddamn rapist, Zach!"

"Wrong, William T. His father is me. I am his father."

William T. had never heard Zach sound like that. Stern. Angry but in that icy, calm way that some people got angry, the kind of anger that comes from protectiveness.

"That baby doesn't belong with you. He should be with another family. People who aren't afraid of his history."

"I'm not afraid of his history."

"You *should* be afraid. You know nothing about his father."

"His biological father. And I know everything about his mother."

William T.'s life was changing again before him, the patterns laid out shifting like letter tiles in a game of make-a-new-pattern Bananagrams. The baby he had been driving down to Utica to try to catch glimpses of was living in Montana with Zach Miller. Against his will, that image of Zach's truck with a car seat, and a baby strapped into it, came back into his mind.

"'Mister'?" he said. "What the hell kind of name is that?"

"It's a nickname. His name is Thaddeus."

"Thaddeus is *my* name. *T* for *Thaddeus.*"

"I know that."

Say her name, you goddamn chickenshits! William T. had tossed commands at the vultures, back in the thick of the chaos, back when they were calling Mallie "the young woman." *Don't call her the young woman and don't call me the neighbor or the man who has been a father figure. Call her Mallie. Call me William T.*

"*Thaddeus* means 'gift from God,'" Zach was saying. "Which is what you are. You're the one who watches out for everyone. You're the best person I know, William T. And Lucia was the one who named him after you."

Names were power. Names were gravitas. A name stitched a baby to the planet, gave him a place on this earth. *Thaddeus.* Against his will, William T. felt the name pulling him toward itself. He resisted. He had to keep his focus clear.

"What about Mallie, Zach? Whose side are you on here?"

"Not a fair question, William T."

"Have you forgotten that you used to love her? Have you forgotten what that man did to her? Have you forgotten all the months when we thought she wouldn't make it?"

"I haven't forgotten any of it. She told me she would've aborted the baby, William T. She said it would've been a cut-and-dried decision."

"And that would have been her choice. Mine too."

"Mine three," Zach said. "But he's here. He's alive and he's here and he's not going anywhere and he deserves a shot, William T. He deserves a fair shot."

Darkness

CRISIS CONNECTION, MY NAME IS ANDREA. MAY I HAVE YOUR first name?"

"... No. Sorry."

"That's okay. Are you somewhere you can't talk freely?"

"No. I can talk."

"I'm glad to hear that. Is there something going on, something that's upsetting you right now?"

"... It upsets me all the time."

"That must be awfully hard, to have something that's always upsetting you."

"Yes."

"Is there someone in your life who knows about this upsetting thing?"

"No."

"Maybe that makes it even harder, then. To hold something painful inside like that."

"Yes."

"Is there a name that I could call you just for this phone call? A nickname, maybe?"

"D. You can call me D."

"Thank you, D. Everything you tell me here is confidential, if that helps. I am listening and if you want to tell me about this upsetting thing, you can, and I will listen."

"It happened a long time ago. It was my fault."

"I see. Why do you feel it was your fault, D?"

"Because I did something bad."

"And you feel upset about that."

"I feel guilty. When I wake up it's the first thing I think about. And when I try to go to sleep, it comes back. And when I'm up on a roof I think about it."

"So the guilt and pain are always on your mind."

"Yes."

"I see, D. I'm sorry. That must be a hard burden to bear."

"It never goes away."

"How so?"

"Like the other day. This kid on the playground bounced his ball over the fence and I threw it back to him but he started screaming. It's like I'm poison. It's like maybe he knew something about me, like maybe he could tell I was a bad person."

"Do you believe that, D?"

"Yeah. Kind of. Like what if it's always like that, for the rest of my life? What if everything is dark and I'm dark and everyone runs away from me because I can never, never undo what I did?"

"What's the hardest thing about this feeling, D?"

"That it will never go away."

"Is there anything that would make it go away?"

"If I went away. That would do it, I guess."

"Is there any other way to make it go away?"

"No. Maybe. Like maybe if I went to the cops and told them what I did. That I was the one. I think about that sometimes."

"Does that feel like a possibility?"

"No. Kind of. Maybe. My sister, though. My sister and my mom. Everyone would know. Then not just my future but *their* futures would be wrecked."

"Is that how it feels to you?"

"Yes. Like there's no way out."

"The fact is, though, that it might still be a way out, D. Keep in mind that sometimes there is no way out that doesn't cause pain. Sometimes it's a choice between something hard and something harder."

Mallie

HE SAT IN THE CAB OF THE DATSUN. THE MAN AT THE CHECK-
out desk at the library had given her a strange look when she
burst in and ran past him, but he hadn't said anything. Neither
had the woman returning books to the fiction shelves when Mallie
said, "Is there a back exit?" She had just pointed in the direction of
the restrooms and then turned back to the cart of books. Out the
back door the sun was blinding, unlike on the cool front steps, where
Zach had just told her about the baby.

The constants were colliding. Time and Pain and Mallie and Darkness had come together in a dot on the map: the front steps of Coburn Memorial Library in Coburn, Montana. The math problem she
had come up with had been missing essential information, like the existence of a baby, and the reappearance of Zach. It was back to being
unsolvable. Who could she talk to? Who else was out there? A faceless couple rose up in her mind.

She spoke their names into her phone — *Please find Aaron and Melissa Stampernick in Utica, New York* — and their number shimmered
up on the screen. She touched the call button and waited. Hers was
an unknown number. It was doubtful anyone would pick up. But the
phone rang only once.

"Hello?"

"Is this Aaron Stampernick?"

"It is. With whom am I speaking, please?"

She almost laughed. So formal. Who spoke like that anymore? She tried to picture the man attached to this formal voice, and an old-fashioned stereotype of a fussy professor came to mind. Tweed jacket with elbow patches. Button-down shirt. Rumpled. Eyeglasses.

"This is Mallie Williams."

Silence. Had he hung up?

"Are you there?"

"I'm here. Hello, Mallie. How are you?"

This time she did laugh, at first silently and then out loud. Through the thousands of miles that separated them, she could feel him relax.

"I don't know why I'm laughing," she finally managed, but that made her laugh harder. In the background she heard a child calling, the kind of insistent shout of a child who wanted a parent's attention. "I really don't."

"Because the situation is so absurd?" he offered.

Yes! That was it. The situation was so absurd. And the word *absurd* was so absurd.

"Absurd," she managed, and they both laughed.

"It's an English-major thing," he said. "Absurd instead of messed-up."

"Instead of fucked-up."

"That too. But not in front of the kids."

The child's background shout was suddenly cut short, as if someone had picked them up mid-wail and spirited them away. Or closed a door. Or drawn a cone of silence down around Aaron Stampernick.

"There," he said. "Now we can talk."

"Are you free to say 'fucked-up' now?"

"I'm free to say that this is an entirely fucked-up situation, yes."

She could hear in his voice that the f-word was hard for him. Maybe he was religious. Or maybe his personal code of ethics forbade cursing.

"What can I tell you, Mallie?" His voice was serious now. He was a serious man. A man of gravity. She could sense that too. "What do you want to know?"

"What happened, Aaron? From your point of view?"

"I don't know what my legal obligation is here, Mallie. I am first and foremost the Attorney for the Child, and everything I did—everything we all did—was in the child's best interests. Whether it is right for me to be talking to you at this moment, I don't know."

"Please," she said. "Just . . . please."

She sensed his hesitation, and she felt him decide to override it.

"I don't know as there's legal precedent for this sort of conversation, Mallie, but I will tell you the basics. What happened was that your mother had legal guardianship of you, and she felt that it was best to let your pregnancy proceed. She was then awarded custody of your child. Then she was stricken with cancer, and the whole chain of events began thusly to unspool."

Had she ever heard anyone use the word *thusly* in real life? The man's language was ever more formal, spiraling upward the chain of grammar command. Maybe this was what he did in times of stress. She could almost feel the knots in his body, the tension held within. He kept going.

"As attorney for the child, I developed a friendship with your mother, and she confided in me her wishes, which she then relayed in her will."

"Do you think my mother's church was the reason she made me have the baby?"

He hesitated. "Made you have the baby? Is that how it feels?"

"I would've had an abortion."

"I see. Then Zach and Charlie and William T. were correct. But Lucia was your guardian and she did as she felt best for you."

"'Best'? My mother abandoned us for her church."

"I am sorry it felt that way, Mallie. But in the eyes of the law, it is not a crime to be religious. Religion, no matter where or followed by whom, forms the underpinnings of many moral philosophies."

So many commas, small pauses, in his speech. Hesitation cloaked in stilted grammar. She decided to bypass his formality.

"You sound sad, Aaron," she said.

There was another pause, and then, "I *am* sad. Sad for you and sad for Mr. Jones and your brother. Sad for your mother and Zach too, maybe most of all for the two of them."

"How did Zach end up with him?"

"Ah. So you know."

"Yes. I know."

"Your mother talked to us frequently in the last month of her life, when Melissa and I were alone with her. She told us she wanted the baby with Zach. To please make sure he raised the baby, because she knew that he had already tried for custody. 'He knows my daughter best,' she said. 'He knows her better than I do.' We helped her with her will, and we promised that we would do everything we could to advocate for Zach. We felt that she deserved at least that."

"Thank you for that. Was that all she said?"

"No. The last thing she said to us was strange. We couldn't make sense of it, maybe because she was fading in and out at that point. It was something about fortune cookies."

"Do you remember it?"

His voice hushed and slowed, as if he were trying to remember exactly what Lucia had said. "She said, 'Tell her Zach was right about the fortune cookies.'"

———

She put the key in the ignition but didn't turn it. The bag of fortunes sat silently on the passenger seat, different, somehow, as if it were judging her. She picked it up and slid it behind the seat. Every Chinese restaurant she and Zach had ever been to, beginning with their first date at the Golden Dragon. What had her mother meant? Sun beat down through the windshield. She wanted to be back on the road, to drive and drive, to put the miles behind her, but where would she go and how would she put any of it behind her? Wherever she went, Zach would be alive and in the world and so would her wanting to be with him, the way it used to be, the way it used to be, the way it used to be. But the baby was alive too, and with Zach, and nothing could ever be the same. *The way it used to be* repeated itself in her mind, a lyric-less song that was only refrain.

She pulled the key out of the ignition and put it back in. Pulled it out. Put it back in. Where could she go? What could she do? *Tell her Zach was right about the fortune cookies.* Right how, though? What did being right mean? The sun beat down. The sky was high. Big Sky country. Then the passenger door clanked open. Zach. She reached out to block him but he climbed inside anyway.

"Just listen to me, Mal. Hear me out, okay? Just hear me out. Maybe you hate him, I don't know, maybe you hate the fact that he's in the world, but he's a good kid, Mallie. He's a good, good" — he turned his head away and his voice got softer — "boy. His name is Thaddeus but I call him Mister. I've always called him Mister. He's almost a year old. He's about to start walking. He likes mango. He likes birds, Mallie. He likes birds. He follows them with his eyes. A bird will stop him in the middle of anything. He almost fell off the slide once because he turned around at the top to watch one but I grabbed him in time."

Zach rushed on. She had never heard him talk like this. Zach had always been calm.

"*Thaddeus?* That's William T.'s name," she said. "*T* for *Thaddeus.*"

"I know. Your mother named him after William T."

Lucia had named the baby after William T.? But she and William T. had stopped talking long before the baby was born. *Tell her Zach was right about the fortune cookies.* But Zach was still talking.

"He's the restaurant's kid, like he belongs to everyone. Sometimes I bring him to work and he crawls around the office until someone goes off shift and takes care of him. I bring Sir too. Sir watches out for him. Sir's like a dog babysitter."

In her mind a restaurant began to grow around Zach and the boy and Sir, the hustle and bustle and clanging of a restaurant kitchen, servers winding their way through crowded tables, the smell of fry cooks and simmering sauces and the liquid sound of beer being pulled from the tap and in the middle of it all a baby, learning his way in a world crowded with sounds and smells and people.

"I swear to God he's a good kid. He's half you, Mallie. How could he not be?"

He was half her. Half her and half Darkness. She could never get away. Her body had grown a creature from darkness and there was no getting around it, no going back.

"It's one more thing I had no say in, Zach. One more huge, enormous thing. Are you asking me just to accept this too, on top of everything else?"

"Not accept. Fight," Zach said. His voice was soft now. "You have to fight the forces of darkness, Mallie. Right?"

"But he's still out there. That man is still out there. What he did is never going away. He's still standing on the roof. He's Darkness."

"Thaddeus isn't."

"Put yourself in my place, Zach. Time and Pain and Darkness and me and now a baby? It's not a solvable problem."

"Expand it. Make it bigger. That's one way to fight them off."

"Why didn't you tell me before now?"

"I was afraid to," he said, and she could see in his eyes that it was true. "I was afraid that if you knew, you'd hate me. Hate him. Reject both of us."

He reached over and took her hand.

"Try to put yourself in my place, will you, Mal? William T. and Charlie, it was like they all wanted the baby gone. Like they hated him because of how he came to be. They were consumed by it. But they saw only half of him. Like the half that was you didn't exist. Like *you* didn't exist."

The air in the cab was close and hot and suffocating. She rolled down the window and let the cool air rush in.

"It felt like if I had Thaddeus, I still had you," he said. "It was the only way I could still be with you, Mallie."

She pulled her hand out of Zach's and placed it on her belly, above the hidden silvery scar.

"How could it possibly feel like you were with me?"

"Because it felt like something of you was alive and would still be in the world, no matter what happened to you. Like the future was still open, in a way. Still an unwrapped fortune cookie."

The box of cookies was right there, hidden in the darkness behind his seat, but he didn't know that.

"Zach, do you think we cursed ourselves by not opening any of those fortunes?"

"Hell no!"

He sounded like himself just then, like the Zach who had decreed on their very first date that they would not allow themselves to be influenced, or persuaded, into one direction over another. That their futures were theirs alone to decide. She reached out and touched the dark curl of ink rising up from his shirt.

"You got a tattoo," she said. "What is it?"

For answer, he pulled up his T-shirt. A bird, dark wings spread, talons extended, rising up from his heart in a spiral of feathery wind, heading skyward.

"Fight," he said. "You have to fight."

———

KNOCK, KNOCK.

WHO'S THERE?

DUNCAN.

DUNCAN WHO?

DUNCAN COOKIES IN YOUR MILK MAKES THEM SOGGY.

DAMN, M.W. THAT'S A GOOD ONE.

I'VE GOT MORE. KNOCK, KNOCK.

WHO'S THERE?

IMUS.

IMUS WHO?

IMUS GET OUT OF THIS PLACE.

WHAT PLACE ARE YOU AT?

MONTANA.

YOU TALK TO HIM?

YES.

AND?

I'M COMING HOME.

———

After she told Zach she had to stop talking, that it was too much right now, that she would call him, she drove to the Sleepy Inn motel and sat in the parking lot. She thought about his tattoo. She thought about the dark birds hidden in the women's bodies at the shelter. She thought about the birds that waited for nightfall so they could spiral up into the sky and float on the wind to a future home. She thought about the day when she was a child and darkness flew from the sky and huddled into a dense and moving mass on the tree by William T.'s garage. A small black cloud on the surface of the earth, shimmering and quivering with power, small flutters and sighs and low *chirrups* erupting from deep in the throats of the birds. She had looked at it and seen something strange, something mysterious, something that made no sense.

A tree eaten alive by darkness. A tree, *her* tree. She tore toward it. *Get away from there!* she had howled, and, *Don't you dare hurt them!* The tree was swarmed and crawling and she would not let them hurt her hummingbirds. Full-speed and shrieking, she had run at them, and at the last second they had lifted off, a swarm of them, fled into the sky above the broken-down barn.

You had to fight. You had to fight the darkness with what you had in you to fight.

"I did it!" she had said to William T., that day of the dark and quivering tree. "I scared them off!"

She had turned in triumph to the porch, where he was standing, watching her.

"You did, Mallo Cup," he had said, and shook his head in admiration. "You sure as hell did, kid."

To this day the tree was still there, green and living. The hummingbird nest had been unharmed. The only way to stop the darkness from growing and growing and growing inside you, from taking over your heart and your soul, was to run toward it. Shout and wave your arms and run. She had turned Darkness into a man on a roof, and she could either keep him up there or, if she couldn't stand it any longer, make him jump. She was doing what she had to, so that she could go on living and not be eaten up from the inside. She would push out darkness and pull in light.

In the single math class she took at Mohawk Valley Community College, the professor told them that given the size of the universe —a vastness so vast that it was beyond the comprehension of human brains—it was a certainty that the world as they knew it, all its inhabitants and events, everything that had ever happened to anyone throughout the millennia, would eventually be replicated elsewhere, in another world that was the mirror image of theirs. To people who were the mirror images of them. Who spoke like them, lived like them, loved like them. Could they even begin to comprehend such a thing? It almost hurt his brain to think about, he had added.

She could still see the look on that professor's face when he was talking about those other worlds. His eyes were far away and his voice was soft. Was this what had brought him to math in the first place, the giant ideas that numbers could express? The idea of an unseen world existing in an unknown realm, the idea of maybe finding that world someday? That professor was a formal, reserved man, but on that day, she had learned something about him, which was that he could turn soft and full of wonder. On that day, he had reminded her of William T. the day he took her to New York City, showed her the Empire State Building and told her about the birds that rose high in the sky above it on their migratory paths.

Maybe the universe held universes within itself. Look up, and the stars shimmering down could turn, instantly, into pinpricks in the dark fabric of the ceiling. The floor of another world, a world that looked like this one. Another world where a girl sat on the cement steps of a library in a faraway town, watching a lost ant crawl determinedly toward nothing, or toward something invisible. A world where a baby who had grown inside her was alive and in this world, forever a part of her and Zach Miller and an unknown other.

Like it or not. Want it or not. Choose it or not.

She had had no choice in anything that had happened to her. She had been fought over by pro-choicers and anti-abortioners, by people who loved her and people who didn't, people who knew her and people who didn't, and this was who she was now: the living embodiment of opposing forces. The child was a child borne of opposing forces. You had to expand the problem, Zach said. You had to make it bigger. That was a way to fight. That was a way to keep going.

"Mallie?" he had said, before he got out of the truck. "One hard thing?"

Not the One Hard Thing game. Too much time had passed. The One Hard Thing game had been created to help her shake out the pain of other people, release it from her fingers and hands. And now it was the people she loved, like William T. and Zach, who had to release the pain of her and everything she had been through from their own bodies. There was no way to un-connect yourself from the ones you loved or had once loved.

"One hard thing?" he said. "Just one?"

His voice was low and soft. He was willing her to play the game again. He was trying to fill in the long gap between them. Okay, Zach. All right.

"Seeing William T.'s face when I first woke up," she said. "Seeing how worried he was, how much older he looked. That was a hard thing."

He nodded. "One impossible thing?"

"The thought that you were gone. That I had lost you."

"One good thing?"

She shook her head. It was too soon to talk about good things. There were hard things and impossible things, but good? No. He sat there, waiting. She thought. Zach making pancakes on Sunday for her and Charlie—that came to mind. Zach pouring her a beer from the tap on the wall at The Tied Fly in Alder Creek. She and Zach dancing late at night in the living room to Smokey Robinson while Charlie played DJ. Zach floating next to her at the water park in Old Forge. These were good things. There were endless good things, but they were all from the past. *You*, she thought, *you and me and our life. That was a good thing.*

Mister

SKY, POLE, SKY, POLE, SKY, POLE, SKY, POLE. HUM OF TIRES, ROAR of wind. Away, away, away, away, toward what, toward what, toward what, toward what. *What are you crying about, Mister? Too windy for you? Hang on.* The window slid up and up, shut out the roar. Sky, pole, sky, pole, sky, pole. *What are you staring at back there, Mister? You see some birds?* Sky, pole, sky, pole . . . *That's right, Mister. Go to sleep. You too, Sir. Go to sleep. We have a long, long drive ahead of us.*

There was only the truck roof above him, not the ceiling in his room, the ceiling high above, dull white with the almost-invisible outlines of stars and planets, meteors and moons that glowed yellow at night. *These are the constellations of you, Thaddeus. Sparrow and Hawk and Gull and Hummingbird. You're not going to find them in any night sky. I made them all up for you.* There were constellations of him here in the truck. He opened his eyes to a black night. Dark window dark sky dark blanket dark shape of his father in front of him. Pinpricks of light in the dark sky out the window.

William T.

E AND CRYSTAL STOOD UNDER THE MULBERRY TREE AT THE
far side of the playground. They had parked the truck directly
under the tree, so that Johnny, who had fallen asleep stretched
out on the backseat of the truck with both seat belts strapped around
him, could sleep on. The windows were rolled all the way down, and
it was cool. Johnny would be safe.

It could be hours still before one of the others arrived. It was a
long, long drive for them, all coming from different directions. William T. had thought they should all come to Sterns, meet at the house,
but no. Neutral territory, Zach had said when he called to tell William T. that he and Mallie had talked, that he had told her everything,
and that both Beanie and Charlie, who was driving up from Pennsylvania, were going to meet them there. William T. had not argued. He
had listened and agreed. *Switzerland*, he told himself. *Be Switzerland.*
This was part of what making amends was about.

Crystal lowered herself to the base of the tree and pulled her
knees up to her chest. William T. occupied himself by watching the
roof of the house across the street from the playground, a sloping
two-story, crawling with men shutting down the job for the day. Pallets of shingles lined up on the cement walkway, extension ladders
leaning on both sides and braces nailed onto the roof. Three men
crouched near the roofline. The one nearest the edge stood straight
up and stretched, just like the one he'd seen before. What was with
these young men? Did they not know they could fall? Did this one

not know how close to the edge he stood, how dangerous it was? Maybe he was too young yet to know how short life was, how fragile. How you had to protect it. The roofer was a heedless man, dark against the sky, and then he moved down the roof, down the ladder, lowering himself to the ground.

A child was making his way across the grass, staggering in that toddler way, with his parents close behind. They headed toward the baby swings, the kind with the bucket to lower a child into so they would be safe. Saf*er.* The baby's father picked him up and lowered him in and the boy looked down to angle his feet into the holes at the right angle, like he knew exactly what to do. The father grabbed the back of the bucket seat and walked backward holding it until his arms were extended and the boy was above his head.

"Ready?"

"Ready!"

The man let go. The little boy sailed through the air, laughing. He threw his head back and his hair blew back.

"Push!" he cried, and his father pushed and his mother watched and smiled.

At the base of the tree, next to William T., Crystal slipped her hand around his calf. He looked down and saw that she was smiling too. Another child was perched at the top of a slide, frozen, unable to launch himself down the long silver river. Another played with a bucket and crane that dipped into the sand and out again, into the sand and out again. He rubbed his eye with a sandy hand and then started to shriek. Children.

Sun filtered through the leaves of the big mulberry as William T. watched. Voices floated toward him. Parents curved into the shape of the benches they sat on, legs crossed, heads tilted back to the warmth of the sun or turned lazily to one another. If you could see words coming out of mouths at a playground, then the words between parents sitting on benches would spiral up into the air like slow circles puffed from a cigar. Nothing was hurried at a playground, except for the once-in-a-while screech that propelled a parent into action. Like the sandy-handed boy, still yelling about his eye, his eye, his eye.

Shhh. Shhh, it's okay.

William T. leaned against the mulberry tree and watched. The great heart of the truck was still ticking even though he had turned off the engine minutes ago. What would the baby look like? He was nearly a year old now. Beginning to walk? Beginning to talk? A sentient being.

William T. waited. He adjusted the brim of his Jim Beam hipster cap, whatever a hipster was. He was a man in his sixties, an almost-father to fatherless Johnny, an almost-father to fatherless Mallie. He thought of the way Crystal had looked at him the night he told her that he kept driving down to Utica, bent on catching a glimpse of the Stampernicks, maybe even a glimpse of the child, rumored to be living with a foster family nearby. And she had said she never wanted to see that baby, never behold his face, because she was afraid that if she ever saw that child, she would see Mallie in him and want to take him and keep him and never let him go.

But William T. didn't know anymore if blood mattered, in the end, when it came to love. Look at Crystal, the woman he loved but was not related to. Nor was he related to Zach, or Johnny, or lonely Burl, or even his girl Mallie. None of them shared his blood or his DNA or a single human being related to him, and did it matter? It did not. Did he have it in him to be an almost-grandfather? Could he somehow learn to love this small boy?

You had to fight the darkness with everything you had. Fight the dark birds with other birds.

Bring it on, he thought then. Which was something Mallie used to say to Zach, laughing, goading him, teasing him: *Bring it on.* He, William T., would bring it on. He would fight the darkness and he would keep on fighting.

———

Maybe there was traffic on the thruway. Maybe they were each exhausted and had stopped to rest before continuing. Maybe Charlie had turned around and gone back to Pennsylvania. Maybe Beanie had been called in to work. Maybe the baby needed a diaper change. Johnny was still asleep and Crystal was still sitting at the base of the tree, her eyes closed. She was patient in a way that William T. was not. He looked around, checking the perimeter, and that was when he saw Charlie's little Civic pull up and stop on the far side of the baseball diamond. He watched as Charlie and a girl—who the hell was she? He squinted until the girl's dark cloud of hair gave her away as Amanda, stretching her long arms skyward. Charlie must have detoured to pick her up on the way. He bent low and examined his front tire. Stood up and kicked it, experimentally. Was the tire going flat? Did he have a spare? William T. was the one who had taught him how to change a tire; did he need help? He was ready to help, if need be. He had not taken good care of Charlie—Charles—in his time of need. He would make amends now.

Charlie and Amanda stood up and sauntered—that was the word for it, William T. thought, *sauntered*—along the sidewalk toward the swings. Charlie was grown now, William T. realized. Filled out the way boys often did in their twenties, even though he was only seventeen. He had had to grow up fast and hard. William T. resisted the urge to follow the boy, catch up with him, because it seemed right to hang back.

Now a small bright spot of yellow appeared by the slide. Beanie was here. William T. tried to remember if he'd ever seen Beanie without that hat. Was he hiding something beneath it? Did he have a terribly scarred skull or something? Probably not. Maybe Beanie didn't feel dressed without his hat. Or maybe someone had given it to him, someone he loved. William T. watched as Charlie sat down on a bench by the swings and Beanie lowered himself onto the little sidewalk curb by the sand pit.

William T. scanned the perimeter of the playground. It was second nature now. When you had been on guard for a long time you tended to stay vigilant. It seeped into your bones. Sweep your eyes around a parking lot, around an auditorium, around a store. Stay on the lookout.

Some people would do anything for publicity. They were the ones who had gotten a boy to hand over the hidden photo of his girl, gotten the old guy in the Jim Beam cap to spill his guts on video. Even though she had come back to life, even though she was Mallie, and back in this world, William T.'s guard was still up. After you'd had a microphone stuck in your face a few times, you learned to put a wall up. And once up, walls were hard to take down. Maybe he would never quite be able to relax again.

Mallie had returned from the world between with no conscious memory of where she had been. She had worked and worked to come back. But as he himself would never be the William T. Jones he had been before that dark night of the broken girl, she too would never be the self she used to be. The truth was that no one could be who they used to be. Minute by minute, everyone was becoming the person they would be. Minute by minute, all the possible fates were being decided.

Mallie

S HE WAS TWO HOURS FROM HOME NOW, CRUISING ALONG THE thruway in the Finger Lakes region of upstate New York, hungry and low on gas. On impulse she took the Geneva exit. When she had turned twenty-one, Zach had brought her here to celebrate. They had driven up and down the shore of Seneca Lake, stopping at each winery for a wine tasting. The tiny cups, the sips, the swirling in her mouth. The listening to what each wine was like and the grapes it was made from and how upstate New York wine was its own wine, not like any other wine made anywhere, because that was what all wine was—particular to its region, specific and unique.

By the end of that day she, a beer girl, had drunk a lot of wine, and all of it legal. She had crawled into the truck, laughing. She made up a song called "Legal at Last," a meandering song with many verses, and sang it to Zach while he drove. She had laughed the whole way home. They had stayed up late that night, dancing.

Geneva, New York, was a college town. A pretty town. A tired town. An old town. And a poor town, like most of upstate New York. This was day three of the drive home. The first two days, the box of pain and the box of fortune cookies had ridden hidden behind the seat. Neither box was heavy but they were a psychic weight in the truck. She hated to picture William T. reading all those newspapers, taking scissors to them, laboriously printing out the articles he'd found online, paper after paper wafting one after another into that slumping cardboard box. The fortune cookies weighed her down in a different way. But she couldn't just throw them all out. Could she?

She pulled into a Sunoco and bought a carton of yogurt and ten gallons of gas and paid with Burl's cash. While the gas was pumping, she hauled the boxes out of the cab and hoisted them into the bed of the truck. No rain was predicted, no high winds. The old clippings and the old cookies could stay out in the elements, where she wouldn't have to feel them right behind her. She drove down to the lakeshore, parked at the edge of a motel parking lot, got out of the truck and wandered, glancing up at the college that spread itself along a bluff overlooking the lake, the beautiful brick administrative buildings, the large houses.

What would it be like to go to a college like that? What would it be like to pick up and move to a town like this and begin life all over again? You could be a massage therapist anywhere. There was no end of need. What if she just parked herself here, in Geneva, and set up shop? She pictured herself walking around the town, getting a studio apartment, living sparsely on Burl's money until she was established. She would give herself a new name. She would wear her wig all the time. No one would know who she was.

At first she had wanted to claw the wig off her head, the constriction of it, the unnaturalness. But you could get used to things that at first seemed impossible. Now it fit her skull like a snug winter cap. When she wore it, she could almost forget she was wearing it. But walk by a store window or lift off the seat even an inch to check the rearview mirror, and the glowing blue-green of her fake hair was a shock. The wig was like armor. Maybe people who carried handguns or knives or cans of mace felt the way she did when she had her wig on. Protected.

A new life on her own in Geneva. A new life on her own anywhere. It was an option. Let everything from the past go—the people, the events, the unsolvable equation. Begin again anew.

She sat down on a bench with her yogurt. Gulls wheeled and cried in the sky above the lake. Were they looking for food? Were they

lonely? Had something upset them? Maybe they just liked the sound
of their own voices. There were two more hours of thruway to go
before Utica. She called Charlie, who picked up immediately. In the
background she heard wind.

"Charlie? Are you driving? You shouldn't drive and talk at the
same time. It's distracting."

"You have no idea what I'm actually doing," he said. "I could be
waiting in line at McDonald's for all you know."

"You hate McDonald's."

"Or maybe someone else is driving. Maybe I made a detour and
picked a friend up. Ever think of that?"

"*Is* someone else driving? Are you not alone?"

"Maybe."

"Amanda's not with you, is she?"

"Mal! Jesus. No witchy stuff!"

"Don't think you can hide from me, little brother."

"Damn, Mal." She heard the happiness in his voice and pictured
Amanda, lovely, shy, fierce Amanda, behind the wheel. "Where are
you?"

"I'm in Geneva. Considering just staying here. What would you
think of that plan? If I scratched all the other possibilities and just
started over on my own and didn't tell a soul?"

"Too late. You've already told a soul. Me. And Amanda too, by
proximity."

"Oh. Damn. You're right."

"You'll have to go with Plan B now," he said.

"Which is?"

"Plan B is like Plan A, with a slight variation. You still get to start
over, just not on your own. Now get back in the truck. Hurry up!
Drive! Bye!"

There was a commotion in the parking lot when she got back,
a great squawking and flurry of wings. Gulls dive-bombing a car,
from the looks of it. No, a truck. *Her* truck. A group of people stood
watching in fascination and mild horror, arms crossed. She picked up
her pace, even though there was something fearsome about the gulls.

They were intent on the Datsun, lifting and settling en masse. Then she saw why. The box of fortune cookies was decimated, cookies crushed, torn cellophane wrappers floating to the ground. It was the futuristic version of that trip that she and Charlie and their mother had taken to the Jersey shore in childhood, when she had watched the enormous gull haul their block of cheese into the sky, indifferent to her shouts.

Now she stood with the other onlookers and watched the gulls gulp down the cookies, fortunes and all.

"Quite a sight, isn't it?" one of the men in the watching group said His arms were crossed and his little girl leaned against his legs as if they were trees. Their roller bags, his large and hers small and purple, stood sentry beside them. "Kind of like a Hitchcock movie."

"All the possible futures," Mallie said. "Gone."

The man looked at her questioningly. Strange girl with the blue-green hair and the strange statement. There were only a few cookies left now in the bottom of the box and they watched together as three gulls fought for them and, finally, gave up and flew away into the sky. Mallie walked over to the truck and peered into the bed, littered now with smashed bits of cookie and torn cellophane. William T.'s clippings were in disarray, as if the gulls had clawed through the paper looking for more fortunes. She leaned over and hauled the boxes up out of the truck, walked them over to the motel garbage can and shoved them inside.

———

Utica, New York. Foothills Park. She parked beneath a young sugar maple, the playground and playing field spread out before her, stretched her arms up to the lowest branch of the tree and hooked her hands over it. Rough, cool bark. Green leaves brushing her skin in the breeze. She hung her head and the muscles of her neck pulled and stretched under the weight of her skull, and she thought again of her massage clients. *Relax the muscles of your neck and let me support your head.* People were not used to letting their heads be supported by another's hands. Not used to letting go.

When she looked back up, there was a small commotion by the playing field fence—a child had kicked his soccer ball over it and was crying. A young man picked it up and tried to hand it back to the boy. But the child shook his head and ran away, crying, and the man visibly drooped. Over the yards that separated them, Mallie could feel his sadness and how he was consumed by it. There was a story there.

She turned away to see Zach's truck pulling up to the curb behind the Datsun. Zach was shadowy behind the wheel, half turned around to the car seat visible in the truck, a car seat that held the baby who must still be sleeping, because Zach was getting out of the truck. As he stepped down, Sir bounded past him, tail pluming, straight to Mallie, and bowled her over onto the grass. He didn't even bark, so desperate was he to see her, to push his snout against her hand, to leap and snuffle and crawl on top of her. Then Zach was there too. She stayed on the ground, her arms around Sir.

Yes, she would have had Zach's baby. No, she would not have thought twice.

Yes, she would have aborted Darkness's baby. No, she would not have thought twice.

That time was past, though, and those choices were not choices anymore. The baby was alive and in the world. He had a name: Thaddeus. He had a life stretching out ahead of him, and what Zach had really been asking, back in Montana, was did she want to be part of it? But she already was. The baby was the result of a dark night and a girl left for dead. Like it or not, want it or not, she and the baby were part of each other.

Zach looked once at the truck, making sure the child was still asleep, then covered the ground between her and him in a few long strides. Sir was pressing her against the trunk of the sugar maple, as if he didn't trust that she would stay put if he didn't guard her, but Zach pulled her up and put his hands on either side of her face. They curved together, silent, against the slender trunk of the tree.

Woof. Woof. Woof. That huge deep bark that ended with a choked-up little yip. Mallie didn't know until she heard it how much she had missed Sir's bark. She reached down to stroke his head but he was intent on something else, his whole body rigid. It was William T., across the playing field. Big man in the Jim Beam cap.

"Sir!"

William T.'s hands were around his mouth and he was calling to the dog he too loved. Zach raised a hand in permission and Sir took off, arrowing across the playing field toward William T. and the woman who rose from the ground to stand next to him. A woman whose light way of movement Mallie would know anywhere. William T. and Crystal. Sir was an arrow across the yards of patchy grass, tail flying as he tore across the tired playground to William T.

"Mal!"

In the other direction, her brother, Charlie—*Charles*—was cupping his hands around his mouth and calling her name. Slender Amanda with her gorgeous hair, rings glinting in the sun, stood on one side, and a lean man in a yellow cap—Beanie—on the other. *Knock, knock. Who's there? Everyone.* Beanie and Charlie and Amanda and William T. and Crystal and Sir and Zach, together in this tired park in this old, tired city. All of them so familiar to her, bodies and smells and voices and touch. Their lives were laced throughout her own, inseparable. She could start all over again in a new town, a new life, but even if she did, she would be connected to these people forever.

Mallie leaned back into Zach's arms, this man she had touched thousands of times, the person closest to her in all her life. She had touched him as a friend and touched him as a lover but she had not touched him as the father of a child and she could feel the difference in him. Familiar and different, at the same time. She would once have said there was nothing she did not know about this man, but she knew now that was not true. Not about Zach, not about anyone.

Both the baby and Johnny were still asleep in the shade, a breeze drifting over them through the open doors. Somewhere out there was Darkness. Darkness would always be out there, his presence weaving its way through her life and the lives of everyone close to her. When the dark birds closed in, she would have to fight them off. The equation of Time and Mallie and Pain and Darkness was unsolvable, and she would forever be solving it anyway.

Mallie stood with her arms around Zach as the people they loved, Crystal and William T. and Charlie and Beanie, closed ranks around them. *Maybe there could be good things to come*, she thought. *Maybe there could be beautiful things.*

ACKNOWLEDGMENTS

This book was a long time coming, and it went through countless re-visions and permutations. My thanks to those who helped midwife it into being: Julie Schumacher, lifelong *compadre*, brilliant writer, unshakable support. Kathi Appelt, my Texas soul sister, and Aria Dominguez, poet and reader extraordinaire, whose reactions to an early draft buoyed me through multiple revisions. John Zdrazil, legendary English teacher, whose love for my first novel, *Rainlight*, helped keep the memories of Mallie and William T. alive in me. Mark Garry, the Painter, who listened with typical patience and insight through many conversations over the years it took me to puzzle my way through this book. And my children, those born to me and those not—where would I be without you? My people. My thanks and love and eternal devotion to you all.

For their great kindness, generosity, professional expertise and whole-hearted interest in the themes of this book, I thank Megan Hunt, Laurel Ann O'Rourke, Rebecca Zadroga, Kathy Insley and Sharon McCartney.

My gratitude and respect to Helen Atsma, editor of my dreams, whose stellar editorial eye divined the possibilities of this book and whose wicked wit and big heart sustained me during multiple revisions. Thanks to Amy Edelman, whose sharp eyes always manage to see what I missed. Thanks to Pilar Garcia-Brown, organizational whiz, Jenny Xu, Liz Anderson, Martha Kennedy, Jenny Freilach, and the entire wonderful team at HMH. And finally, Doug Stewart, agent and beloved friend, who believed in my writing long before anyone else did, you are a prince among men.

READING GROUP GUIDE

1. Local towns, and by extension the nation, are divided after Mallie's rape. In Mallie's family, William T. leads one side and Mallie's mother, Lucia, leads the other. What do you think about their arguments? Is there a right or wrong answer?

2. "Burl was mild-mannered but stubborn to the core. It was people like him who would eventually rule the earth someday, millennia from now when everyone else less obstinate had just given up." What other instances of obstinacy and stubbornness occur in the book? Do they define any of the other characters, and if so, how do these traits affect their own lives, and the lives of others around them?

3. Birds appear frequently as imagery, or as literal presences —in your opinion, what do these birds represent? Do they hold different meanings for different people? How are they related to themes of magic and transformation?

4. There are many examples of parent-child relationships— how do emotional ties compare and contrast with biologi-

cal ties? What does family look like for each person, and
what does chosen family look like for each person?

5. Mallie is a trained massage therapist. What is the role of
    physical touch throughout the book?

6. There are many descriptions of games that the characters
    play with each other, from Zach's "Something hard, some-
    thing impossible, something good," to Mallie's "Once upon
    a time there was a sister," to knock-knock jokes, to Banan-
    agrams, Candyland, Chutes and Ladders. Who instigates
    these games, and why?

7. Are the sections from the perspective of Darkness real, or
    all Mallie's imagination? Discuss.

8. Mallie and Zach have their box of fortune cookies, and in
    many instances, Mallie thinks about the symbolism of the
    cookies and imagines multiple different futures and possi-
    bilities. How does the author play with the concept and lit-
    erary device of fate? Why do you think the author decided
    to title the book *The Opposite of Fate?*

9. Why is Mallie so fixated on math, like algebraic equations
    and fixed and unknown variables? What do these thought
    processes reveal about coping in the face of trauma?

10. Why does Zach run away without telling anyone about
    Mister and Sir? If you were in Zach's place, what would
    you have done?

11. Throughout the novel, characters give each other nick-
    names: *Mallo Cup, William T., Charlie, Darkness, Mister.*

When do characters embrace these nicknames, and when do they reject them—and why?

12. By the end of the novel, secrets come out that change the way we see characters, and the way characters see each other. Whose character changed the most from the beginning? Do any of the revelations change your mind about a character? Does more information about individual actions draw out any forgiveness from the other characters, or from you?

ABOUT THE AUTHOR

Alison McGhee's best-selling novel *Shadow Baby* was a *Today* Show Book Club pick, and her picture book for adults, *Someday*, was a number one *New York Times* bestseller. She is the recipient of many fellowships and awards, has three grown children and lives a semi-nomadic life in Minnesota, Vermont and California.

alisonmcghee.com